# Praise for *A Reckoning Up Black Cat Hollow*

"This tense, gut-wrenching, and ruminative novel is highly entertaining from start to finish."

—*Booklist*

"A blistering tale of the human condition filtered through a rural lens and sealed with the kind of gut punch that only Jones can deliver. A novel both thought provoking and smart, yet brutally tense and paced faster than a bullet. For everyone that didn't already know, Matthew F. Jones is the true heir apparent to the kingdom of Cormac McCarthy. Yeah, he's that fucking good."

—Brian Panowich, author of *Bull Mountain* and *Nothing But The Bones*

"*A Reckoning Up Black Cat Hollow* is as fast-paced and unrelenting as any thriller you will find, but what makes Jones's book so compelling is its psychological, at times metaphysical, journey into one man's tormented soul. Reading the novel is like entering a clear mountain stream. You take a few steps and suddenly plunge into depths you'd not imagined. Matt Jones is an immensely talented writer, and this harrowing novel deserves a wide and appreciative audience."

—Ron Rash, author of *Serena* and *The World Made Straight*

"A psychological thriller cut on the steepest grade with more switchbacks than a mountain haul road. *A Reckoning Up Black Cat Hollow* roars downhill with the brakes on fire. Jones sets a masterful pace."

—David Joy, author of *Those We Thought We Knew* and *When These Mountains Burn*

"Haunted hills and dead ends and deep nights fill the pages of *A Reckoning Up Black Cat Hollow*, the latest from Matthew F. Jones, who is not afraid to go dark and dare you to look. Black Cat Hollow Road winds through a treacherous landscape, for a cast of characters who are caught somewhere between the real and the imagined, the truth and lies, and ultimately between what is right and wrong. A gripping, hardnosed tale told with balance, beauty, bleakness."

—Michael Farris Smith, author of *Salvage This World* and *Desperation Road*

"Beginning with a chance encounter on a dark country road, and taking place over the course of a single brutal night, *A Reckoning Up Black Cat Hollow* is one of the most gripping, fast-paced crime novels you're ever going to read. Jack Spinks is a fantastically complex character and *A Reckoning Up Black Cat Hollow* is a stunning read. I could easily see a sequel. Matthew Jones has proven once again that he's one of the best and most original storytellers around."

—Donald Ray Pollock, author of *The Heavenly Table* and *The Devil All The Time*

"Matthew F. Jones is a hard, wonderful and very powerful writer you might not know yet, but ought to soon. He will not spare your sensibilities should you be among those poor souls afflicted with such. He rakes you over the coals at a measured pace, unfurls rath from six angles and the amen he delivers will keep even twisted m...f's… awake at night. Jones is major, he's got the piss and vinegar and moral rigor that make books matter."

—Daniel Woodrell, author of *Winter's Bone*

"*A Reckoning Up Black Cat Hollow* is a brilliant and searing novel that reminds us that Matthew Jones isn't just one of our best writers of rural noir. He is one of our best writers. Period."

—Mark Powell author of *The Late Rebellion*

"*A Reckoning Up Black Cat Hollow* is deeper, richer, better-written, and far more nuanced than the standard TV-inspired dross that passes for rural noir. Matthew F. Jones' novel unfolds with the hallucinatory quality of meth and mescaline, immersing us in a world as searing as a fist in the face, as complex and beautiful and fast as life itself. Read it and hold tight. It's like nothing you know."

—Paul Cody, author of *Walk the Dark*, *The Stolen Child*, *Love is Both Wave and Particle*

"An epigraph from a Tom Waits song and an allusion to *Paris, Texas* on page one clued me in immediately that Matthew F. Jones's *A Reckoning Up Black Cat Hollow* would be very far up my alley. The prose crackles, the pace is unrelenting, and Jones's characters make an indelible impression. This is extraordinary work—thrilling, ambitious, and sharp-eyed. I can't recommend it enough."

—William Boyle, author of *Saint of the Narrows Street*

## Praise for Matthew F. Jones' previous novels

## *A Single Shot*

"A harrowing literary thriller…a powerful blend of love and violence, of the grotesque and the tender."

—Christopher Lehman-Haupt, *The New York Times*

"A backwoods drama that is part *Crime And Punishment*, part *Deliverance* and all white-knuckled suspense…A Single Shot packs a helluva punch."

—Pam Lambert, *People*

"[A] high-voltage thriller, a gritty, claustrophobic blend of Jim Thompson and James Dickey."

—*Publishers Weekly* *Starred Review

"*A Single Shot* {is} the finest portrait of guilt since *Crime and Punishment*."

—Susan Salter Reynolds, *The Los Angeles Times Book Review*

"Jones owns a fine writer's eye for the kind of details that matter… it is Jones' skillful straight-from-the-shoulder depiction of [Moon] and his pinched world that resonates…the author draws his disoriented thoughts with dark and excellent detail."

—Daniel Woodrell, *The Washington Post*

**Book Tracks**

"Superlatives have been sapped of their meaning by overzealous critics, and somehow it sounds fake to say that a book is one of the 'best things' you've 'read.' It's just that, sometimes (as in the case of Matthew F. Jones's *Boot Tracks*) that happens to be true. I haven't read something that made me empathize with a bad guy this intensely since I read *In Cold Blood* in high school."

—Katy Haegele, *The Philadelphia Inquirer*

"More than just a very good crime thriller, this dark but illuminating novel shows us the psychopathology of the criminal mind. Brilliantly chilling in its step-by-step examination of the mechanics of committing a criminal act—the novel's true terror is an interior one: an extreme close-up vision of the drive toward homicide. A nightmare thriller with the power to haunt."

—*Kirkus Reviews* *Starred Review

"*Boot Tracks* is a strange but artful novel enlivened by some of the best low-life dialogue this side of Elmore Leonard….and Jones, who has written other well-regarded novels, is a writer worth meeting."

—Patrick Andersen, *The Washington Post*

"*Boot Tracks* has the grace of a Japanese Noh poem and the violence of two lives burning out in front of our eyes."

—Dick Adler, *Chicago Tribune*

"A swiftly paced thriller about a hit gone wrong, Matthew F. Jones's *Boot Tracks* is also a brooding character study of a man who's morally compromised though not entirely soulless."

—Hannah Tucker, *Entertainment Weekly*

### *Blind Pursuit*

Jones is unpredictable and, therefore, terrifying. His characters are knowable, if changeable and complicated. If you say yes to his use of language (like deciding to read poetry) you will not be able to shake him. Jones is a surgeon throughout the novel, extracting the kernels of relationships, the black holes in the characters' characters and giving even the smallest cameo roles unforgettable, essential quirks (reminiscent of Hitchcock)."

—Susan Salter Reynolds, *The Los Angeles Times Book Review*

"*Blind Pursuit* is the kind of novel the phrase 'a page-turner' might have been invented for, an extremely well constructed (and sometimes quite moving) mystery."

—David Pitt, *Booklist*

"*Blind Pursuit* stoops to little of the crude button-pushing typical of child-kidnapping thrillers. As in *A Single Shot*, Jones's 1996 novel about a hunter who accidentally shoots a teenage runaway, the interior story is as gripping as the exterior plot, both unfolding with an awful inexorability."

—Gary Krist, *Salon*

### *Deepwater*

"Matthew F. Jones's *Deepwater* is one of the best novels to cross my desk. Full of darkness and rage and nightmares its premise evokes James M. Cain's *The Postman Always Rings Twice.* Brilliantly written, sweatily erotic, and unbearably suspenseful, *Deepwater* should go directly to the top of your reading list."

—Les Roberts, *The Cleveland Plain Dealer*

"*Deepwater* is a harrowing and unsettling piece of fiction. It accomplishes the neat trick of fulfilling its literary aspirations without belying its affinity for genre fiction…it dissolves the boundaries between present and past, memory and prediction, doing and dreaming…inescapably chilling, it is the dark shadowy figure that lives on the other side of magical realism."

—*Austin Chronicle*

"It's a grim story, and one told exceedingly well...[Jones] creates tension with remarkable economy and intricacy in a sinister narrative that ultimately reveals itself as a powerful expression of loneliness, dangerous passions, and the quest for identity."

—*Publishers Weekly*

"Jones and Daniel Woodrell are the leading contemporary authors of country noir, a subgenre whose roots trace back to James M. Cain's *The Postman Always Rings Twice.* Jones builds tension from two seemingly contradictory sources: the noirist's stock-in-trade, the disaster waiting to happen, and the crackling unpredictability that comes from the expert melding of genres: noir thriller crossed with psychological horror."

—Bill Ott, *Booklist* *Starred Review

## *The Cooter Farm*

"*The Cooter Farm* will remind readers of John Irving one minute, Joyce Carol Oates the next. An altogether remarkable debut."

—Gene Lyons, *Entertainment Weekly*

"Dickens and Irving are high standards against which to measure any novel, let alone a debut. It's a tribute to *The Cooter Farm* that those are exactly the comparisons it invokes."

—Steven Kane, *Los Angeles Daily News*

"Jones's blackly humorous first novel, set on the Cooter family's failing dairy farm in New York State arouse(s) childhood angst and terror in (an) alternately amusing and tragic coming-of-age tale."

—*Publishers Weekly*

## *The Elements of Hitting*

"*The Elements of Hitting* approaches issues more important than keeping one's eye on the ball and taking a level swing: the nature of forgiveness, the importance of self-respect, the many faces of love. At its core...[it] is an often haunting and occasionally beautiful story of man's attempt to rebuild his life with two strikes against him."

—Chris Bohjalian, *Washington Post Book World*

# A Reckoning Up Black Cat Hollow

Matthew F. Jones

Regal House Publishing

Published by
Regal House Publishing, LLC
Raleigh, NC 27605


ISBN -13 (paperback): 9781646036967
ISBN -13 (epub): 9781646036974
Library of Congress Control Number: 2025937268

Cover images and design by © studiochi.art



Printed in the United States of America

Regal House Publishing, LLC
https://regalhousepublishing.com

For KSJ,
Then, now and forever

Your spirit don't leave knowing
Your face or your name
The wind through your bones as all that remains

—Tom Waits, *Dirt In The Ground*

# 1

Spinks had the Durango's windows down, traveling slow in the warm night, half-an-eye out for deer, what he first thought she was when his headlights picked her up stepping out of the woods in front of him.

His second thought watching her walking away from him was that he'd created her out of desolate lonely thoughts.

She moved her eyes at him as he pulled up alongside her trudging up the road's shoulder with the blindered look of Harry Dean Stanton in that movie *Paris, Texas*. From what Spinks could tell she had on only a small pink backpack over a long sleeve button-down shirt that ended a foot below her crotch and black high-tops. Her short auburn hair was tucked behind her ears.

Spinks stubbed out in the ashtray a half-gone joint he'd been smoking. He reached across the seat and rolled down the Durango's passenger window, imagining the girl's footfalls echoing off a concave roof that had closed over that part of the world and the girl a visible spirit moving through it. She said into the cab toward Spinks, "What road is this?"

Her bluntness caught Spinks off guard. As it did that she seemingly didn't know what road she was walking on well past dark miles from the nearest town or highway.

He said, "It's Black Cat Hollow Road."

The girl turned her eyes from the cab back to the dark road. Spinks had the uneasy feeling she was peering at something up the road he couldn't see. At something only she could see. She said without slowing her stride or moving her eyes from whatever she was peering at, "I don't want to be on this road."

"What?"

"I must have walked in the wrong direction."

Spinks wasn't sure if the edge in her voice was a manifestation of anger, fear, shock or lunacy.

"Where are you walking from?" he said, watching a faint yellow glow appear at the top of the hill in front of them.

The girl didn't answer him. Spinks wondering if she hadn't heard him inclined his head at the window and said in a louder voice, "Where are you looking to get to?"

The girl taking a lunging step at the cab grabbed the passenger door handle.

Spinks slammed on the Durango's brakes so not to drag her.

The girl started jerking the handle up and down.

Spinks said, "The hell you doing?"

"It won't open!" said the girl.

"It's locked," said Spinks.

"Fucking unlock it!" screamed the girl, her eyes moving from him to a set of yellow lights between smaller orange lights coming steadily toward them from just past the top of the hill.

Spinks, with an unsettling feeling that he'd stepped onto an enclosed path he was powerless to get off of before its end, put the Durango in park, reached across the seat and opened the door. The girl trying to jump into the cab stumbled. Spinks lunged at her and to keep her from falling into the road grabbed her by the arms. He pulled her forcefully into the cab the girl, half-coming out of her shirt, at once fighting with him and hollering at him as if he were the getaway driver in a bank heist they'd just pulled off, "Go! Go! Go!"

Spinks seeing her looking at him in the distorted dull glow of the yellow lights coming at them wondered if she was seeing him; if in her eyes he was only another of the trees making dark shapes in the woods out the driver window behind him. He said to her in the tone he had used with Iris as a child throwing a hissy fit, "Now slow down, take a deep breath and—"

The girl grabbed the Durango's shifter and jerked it down into second gear and Spinks, his left foot still engaging the clutch, yanked her arm away. The girl started swinging her free arm and spitting at him. Spinks with his free hand pushed her away from him. The girl fell back against the seat, her shirt falling off her shoulders, panting and snarling like a feral cat nabbed in a snare.

Spinks seized her in one hand by the neck trying to control her, her animal toughness belying the fragile look of her and said, "I'm not driving you anywhere until you calm down and we've talked some!"

The girl said, "I'll fuck you!"

Spinks, struck by the thought that fear, anger and insanity were a single emotion more powerful than any one of the three alone, tilted his head at her. "You'll do what?"

"Any way you want—you can fuck me in the ass even!"

"I don't want that," said Spinks.

Spinks looking at the girl's eyes, frozen like the eyes in a stuffed deer head on a spot out the windshield behind him, imagined sporadic drops from a block of ice melting in a ray of sunlight dripping into his brain. "Why would you think I want that?"

The girl hissing saliva at him said, "They're looking at me right now! They know it's me in here—fucking drive!"

Spinks turned around and saw out the windshield a dark colored vehicle halted fifty-odd feet from them, its headlights between orange running lights all but blinding him. He looked back at where he'd seen the girl's face and saw a hardened woman's face. He gasped and closed his eyes. He opened them and again saw the girl's somewhat familiar face. The button-down shirt had slipped down around her waist. Only a sleeveless undershirt covered her hungry-looking upper body marred by the sort of shallow scratches marring her face. "What do they want?"

"…me dead…" the girl answered Spinks in a strangled whisper.

Spinks realized he was gripping her neck too hard. He loosened his grip and the girl gasped in a huge mouthful of air, then resumed fighting with him, surprising him again with strength Spinks figured had to be adrenaline induced.

Struggling to hold her against the seat he looked out the windshield and saw the vehicle's front doors open. Masked in the glare of the headlights two large upright shapes stepped out of the vehicle. The shapes started moving at the Durango, a looming shadow on either side of the corridor of light the vehicle was throwing out. Spinks' heart raced. He told himself if the girl wasn't all out nuts she was exaggerating whatever jeopardy she was in. But if she was exaggerating it he guessed she was exaggerating it out of fear because something, even if it was in her mind, had her scared shitless. Chances were though the vehicle's occupants had nothing to do with whatever was scaring her. They were her family or concerned friends looking for her or passersby who'd stopped on the desolate road to offer assistance to the driver of a stopped truck and half naked girl—Jesus! Spinks suddenly had a vision of himself hauling the girl squirming and screaming into the Durango in a way that even to Spinks happening onto it would have looked like an abduction in progress. Spinks, darkly speculating on the mindsets of the two people on their way toward him, told the girl, "I need you to calm down, sit here quiet! I'm going to talk to them. See what's what."

He turned forward again and couldn't find the two shapes.

He leaned out his window searching in the dark for them and the girl taking advantage of his diverted attention lunged out of his grip and into the well beneath his feet. Spinks reached down to grab her and his foot came off the clutch. The girl with her hands jammed the gas pedal to the floor and the Durango shot forward into the road. Spinks glimpsed one of the shapes from the vehicle diving to get out of its way. He frantically probed with his foot for the brake but was blocked by the girl's body where she was flooring the accelerator. He jerked the Durango to the right, away from the drop off past the left shoulder, then, seeing the second shape from the vehicle mere feet in front of him, jerked it back the other way and half-a-second later the Durango smashed into a side of the vehicle and caromed off it toward the drop-off again. The

Durango's driver side wheels dropped into the dirt at the top of the drop-off. Spinks jerked the wheel back hard to the right barely managing to keep its passenger wheels clinging to the gravel road as the Durango, teetering at a near ninety-degree angle, barreled along the shoulder straight at a huge red oak tree in its path. Five feet before it would have collided head-on with the oak tree Spinks gave up trying to get it back onto the road and jerked the wheel hard to the left sending them plunging down the sheer fifty-foot bank.

He felt the truck rise up over the back of a large rounded boulder embedded in the bank then go airborne. He heard the girl scream and instinctively pushed with his feet against her shoulders in an effort to keep her head from banging against the top of the well when they landed. The Durango slammed nose-first into the side of the bank, the girl screaming more, bounced up several feet into the air, then came down hard parallel to the road and slid sideways down the last twenty feet of bank through thick brush and over small rocks before coming to a jarring stop.

In the next second the cab was filling up with water and Spinks realized they'd crashed into a massive maple tree felled mid-stream in a brook running hard with late spring run-off from the mountain at the hollow's top.

He pushed against his door but couldn't open it against the tree or current or both. He lunged across the seat, yanked up on the passenger door handle then pushed against the door until he had it open a couple feet. "Go on," he yelled down at the girl, "I'll hold it open for you!"

The girl didn't move. Nor did she answer him.

Spinks having no idea if she was dead, unconscious or in shock reached down, grabbed her by the armpits and dragged her across the seat to him. Pushing with his back against the door, he held it open and thrust the girl out of the cab into the stream and followed her out. The water reached only to the tops of his thighs but the current was an inexorable force set on casting him into it and the rocks lining the bed were slick with algae. Holding the girl under her shoulders with just her head above the water Spinks started carefully backing up, dragging her through the cold, churning stream for the far bank afraid if he lost his footing he'd lose his grip on the girl and in a heartbeat the current would take her downstream out of his reach. Halfway to the bank he felt her shoulders twitch and saw her legs kick a couple of times and knew at least she wasn't dead. Nor paralyzed—not totally anyway—though not knowing the extent of her injuries he knew he oughtn't to be moving her but to have a hope of keeping her alive in any state he had no choice but to.

He struggled, exhausted, onto the far shore and, gasping for air, collapsed into a sitting position with the girl's head in his lap, her legs and torso stretched out in the thick blue stem and sweet flag grasses lining the bank. He heard over the boiling stream indistinct noises on the road above him and wondered if he'd been hearing them all the while he'd been fighting his way with the girl through the stream and only now had become aware of them. Then a beam of white light hit the water and danced over it until it found the Durango. Spinks seeing the condition of his truck lodged against the maple's massive trunk woke up to what he and the girl had just been through. The cab's entire driver side looked like an empty tin can slammed by a giant hand against the tree trunk; its rear end, extruding out into the stream past the boulder, was fishtailing in the current like a kite's tail in a high wind.

Spinks looked down at the girl; soaking wet, pale, not much of her left hidden past whatever cache of jumbled thoughts she'd tried spouting to him up on the road. The shirt and backpack she'd been wearing had been lost to the stream. She had on only a drenched pair of blue and white bikini briefs with her drenched black hightops and drenched undershirt now sagging to expose most of her front side to her belly button. Maybe a hundred-ten pounds she had a waist Spinks could have circled with his thumbs and middle fingers, a wisp of pubic hair showing beneath her soaked briefs, thin legs marred by the same sorts of scratches that were on her face and forearms. Each of her breasts could have fit into the palm of a small hand. A fresh, dark bruise on her forehead was the only injury Spinks could see on her though he knew she might be dying from ones inside her he couldn't see. Her eyelids fluttered sporadically like she was having a bad dream or was too tired to open them.

Spinks looked up at the white light now moving lazily over the water around the Durango. He considered yelling out to let the light holder know where he and the girl were or, once he caught his breath, standing up and waving while he yelled. He was troubled though by what the girl had told him about the vehicle's occupants. They'd wanted her dead, is what she'd said. And she'd sure acted in the Durango's cab as if she'd believed it. But her believing they wanted her dead didn't mean they in fact wanted her dead. Not if the girl was touched in the head. Or out of her mind on some hallucinogenic drug. Or wanted so bad to get away from the people—her family possibly—trying to find her she had convinced herself they wanted her dead.

But where had she been walking from? And why in only a shirt too big for her and high-top sneakers? And with her legs and face scratched to hell? Spinks looked back down at her. In the shape she was in he had no hope on foot of getting her out of the hollow and to a hospital. And the only vehicle in possible working order anywhere nearby belonged to the two men (he assumed from the sizes of their shadows they were men and not women or a man and woman) working a light beam with the precision of a hound's nose slowly down the far bank toward the water. The two people the girl had said wanted her dead.

If she'd been telling the truth, Spinks, in asking for the men's help, would be as good as killing the girl. Himself too possibly.

And if she hadn't been telling the truth—if the girl was a stone liar or delusional—and she died out here because Spinks hadn't sought the two men's help? If the two men were two good Samaritans who'd stopped on the desolate road to help a half-naked girl being dragged into a pickup truck by a man who seconds later nearly ran them down speeding off with the girl?

"They're too close…!"

Spinks looked down at the girl's eyes circling in their sockets, doing laps around the moon past the treetops. "The cars…"

Spinks said, "There are no cars. Only a stream." He placed a hand on the girl's leg. "You're lying next to a stream."

The girl's eyes stayed circling the moon, Spinks' voice seemingly registering to her only as part of the rushing noise she'd woken to.

Spinks told her, "You ran my truck off the road into it."

The girl closed her eyes, her shallow breathing and hard set of her mouth making it clear she was suffering. Spinks told himself addressing whatever her physical ailments were would have to wait.

He said to her, "We need to talk about this situation we're in."

"Take it out of my head," said the girl.

"Take what out of your head?" said Spinks, but the girl's attention was light-years from Spinks. Spinks looked across the water to the light beam poking its way down the bank as carefully as a blind cripple down a cobblestone walk. He could hear branches snapping, dislodged rocks rolling down the acclivity into the water, but couldn't make out anyone behind the light. He looked back at the girl and she was mumbling words he couldn't make out up at the sky. He touched her shoulder and she opened her eyes and looked at his hand as if it were an ugly but harmless fly alighted there. Spinks said to her, "Tell me about the two people who got out of that vehicle up on the road. The two people making their way down to the water over there."

The girl looked back at the sky.

Spinks said, "What's your name? Can you tell me your name?"

The girl mumbled more gibberish at the moon, Spinks anticipating the moments that lay ahead of him how a man caught in a tornado anticipates a death of a thousand pieces while clinging to the hope he'll be spit back out into the world in one piece, even if forever altered.

"Do you remember where you were coming from?"

"Is it winter?" The girl rolled her eyes toward Spinks.

"It's summer. Did those men hurt you?"

"I'm shivering."

"You were in the water is why."

"You took off my clothes."

Spinks, suddenly feeling in a compromising position, removed his hand from the girl's bare leg. "What you have on is what you had on when I met you, except for a long-sleeve shirt and backpack that were lost to the stream."

The girl moved her eyes more directly at Spinks. Spinks had the idea she wasn't seeing him anymore than she'd been seeing him when she'd been looking up at the sky. "What have you done to me?"

"I haven't done anything to you. You did it to yourself driving my truck off the road."

"I don't know how to drive."

"That's pretty damn clear from where we're at."

"Did you fuck me?"

"I haven't laid a hand on you but to drag you out of the water!"

"I feel things I can't see. Something's happened. Something bad."

"You maybe have a concussion."

"People lie," said the girl.

"Some people do. Are you one of them that does?"

The girl's eyes came down from the moon. They dipped and swayed like fledgling birds through the dark air over the stream. "They're eating the mosquitoes so the mosquitoes won't eat us," she said.

"What?" said Spinks.

"Can't you see them?"

Spinks looked out over the stream at small, dark shapes darting through the air.

"Bats you mean?"

"The bats know."

"What do the bats know? Hell you talking about?"

"The bats know what happened. The bats were with me," said the girl.

The light beam across the way suddenly vanished.

Spinks said to the girl, "Two people in a vehicle with orange running lights." He grabbed her by an arm. "The ones up on the road you told me wanted you dead? You remember them?"

The girl's eyes found Spinks' face but wouldn't hold. They drifted off toward the water like two lovers slipping away together from a gathering.

"What's the truth?" said Spinks.

"The opposite of a lie," the girl said at the rushing water.

Spinks glanced across the water at two dark shapes emerging out of the jack pines at the base of the drop-off. He exhaled deeply trying to steady his nerves. He looked back at the girl. "I know what the goddamn truth is," he said. He gripped the girl's shoulder harder to make her look at him. "I need to know if you do. I need to know about the two people who were in that vehicle. The vehicle with the orange running lights. I need to make a decision here real soon."

The girl moved her eyes at Spinks' hand on her shoulder, then up at Spinks. Her look suggested the look of a TV game show contestant who's just seen the curtain she's selected opened to reveal a donkey cart instead of the Mercedes she'd hoped was behind it; Spinks had the feeling he'd somehow let her down in a big way. Her eyes slid sideways again. She said, "It's all smoke and pain in my head."

Spinks took his hand from her shoulder. He tried to stay connected to her eyes, but they wandered down into the water—or slid off its surface into the pine trees bordering it. "What else?"

"I don't know why people are afraid of bats. It's a lot of lies about them," she said, her voice sinking like tossed fish bait into the water she was facing.

"I'm not asking you about goddamn bats. I'm asking you what besides your head hurts! I'm trying to assess the situation we're in. I'm no mind reader."

The girl made no indication she'd heard him.

Spinks watched the light beam reappear and move out from the far shore to alight again on the Durango. He had a vision of his silver-plated Enfield 308 in the cab's gun rack soon to be underwater, another loss he could chalk up with the truck. He said to the girl, "I'm going to yell out to them, tell them you're injured, and need help then. Right?"

The girl looked out at the light as if seeing it for the first time. "Who? Who will you yell out to?"

"To those men. The two people from the vehicle with the orange running lights on it. That's them moving around over there. It has to be."

The girl said, "You don't know."

"They saw us crash. They must be looking for us."

The girl began shaking her head. Spinks couldn't tell if in pain, befuddlement, dismay or a mixture of all three. He thought it odd the men hadn't once called out, over the water or toward the Durango, seeking to contact any survivors of the crash. Then the light went off again. Spinks had the eerie feeling the two men's eyes were moving across the water toward him and the girl like two invisible light beams. The girl looked across the water as if feeling the same thing Spinks was feeling and said in a petrified whisper, "I'm scared I won't be able to run fast enough to stay ahead of them!"

Spinks envisioned Iris waking in the middle of the night imagining horrible things in the dark. In the water behind the girl a fish jumped, a silvery flash in the moonlight. Spinks said to her, "All right I carry you?"

The girl again looked at Spinks in a way that gave him an unsettling feeling he'd let her down asking her what had seemed to him a reasonable question. He reached down, carefully scooped her up in his arms and started walking with her through the high grass away from the stream, feeling from the far shore two sets of eyes seeking out the source of the sound of snapping twigs and rustling underbrush coming from across the water.

# 2

She felt to Spinks not much heavier than a full bag of groceries. With each of his steps her sneaker-clad feet banged his thighs, her damp hair slapped like a fresh hard rain the back of his right hand. Whenever he looked down at her he saw the same thing—her small, delicate hands folded on her stomach, her eyes opened in the purposeless look of a pasture gate standing ajar, the moon through the pines painting her pale flesh an even ghostlier shade while casting in shadow on the forest floor the image of a distorted giant making off through the woods with a child in its arms.

Spinks after several minutes stopped walking and lay her down softly on the needled floor, the girl moaning like a comatose patient gently nudged in her sleep, her blankly staring eyes the only evidence she was conscious. Cocking an ear at the woods they'd just walked through Spinks heard along with his own raggedy breathing, an owl hooting, a bird or light-footed mammal rustling the piney canopy, frogs croaking in wetlands somewhere left of them. Nothing resembling footfalls on the forest floor. He stared into the trailing dark trees for a light and after several seconds couldn't find one. He looked down at the girl. "They've given up and turned back. If they ever came after us at all."

"They're coming," the girl whispered to the trees.

Spinks said, "I don't hear footsteps."

The girl said, "Listen harder."

Spinks said, "I don't see a light."

The girl said, "Demons don't need lights."

Spinks looked down at the girl with the sensation he'd dropped through an invisible door into a world as far gone from the one he'd been driving down the hollow in not an hour ago as the girl's thoughts were from his ability to fathom them. "Demons?"

"Demons that can see in the dark."

"That something you read in some fantasy book?"

"I can't see through the smoke you put in my head. You did this to me, you fucker! You stole my pictures." She as well might have been talking to the moon as to Spinks and Spinks suddenly understood he was digging himself into a deeper and deeper hole; a hole even a man who didn't have a rap sheet and stash of illegal drugs in his truck would have trouble digging out of. He told the girl, "We're going back to the road. There's no one coming for you."

Fear boiled up in the creases of the girl's face like groundwater in the cracks of a dirt cellar. She said, "I can hear them. Sniffing where we've been—!"

She tried to stand and Spinks, wanting to keep her from hurting herself worse than she already was, pressed a hand to her shoulder, keeping her on the ground. Endeavoring to connect with a rational part of her, if such a part existed, he said to her, "How can you hear them and I can't?"

The girl hissed into his face, "You don't listen!" and Spinks understood that, even if every word she'd told him was a delusion or lie, her fear was as real as her flesh beneath his hand touching her.

He sat down by her in the pine needles, the girl's goosebump-laden arms and legs trembling like a cheap tin pot on low boil. Spinks took off his denim jacket, only its bottom couple inches damp from the stream, and gently covered the girl from her neck to her knees with it. The girl, staring fixedly into the treetops, took no apparent notice he'd laid it over her. Spinks said to her, "It would go a long way toward me accepting two people back there want you dead if I knew why they did."

The girl, appearing lost in a world up in the trees only she could see, didn't even move her eyes toward him.

Spinks said, "They have a reason you must know what it is right?"

The girl, more to the trees than to Spinks, said, "I'm alive?"

"By the grace of God you are," said Spinks. "That stunt you pulled up on the road could have killed us both. What is it that led you to it—to chance nearly killing us just to get away from the people in that vehicle? That's what I'm asking you."

The girl's eyes rolled sluggishly away from the trees, to Spinks. "It's in the smoke," she said, her small voice suggesting a miscreant child being made to recount the act she was being punished for.

"Smoke? What smoke?"

The girl, as if afraid of being heard by creatures concealed in the trees, whispered up at Spinks, "Because my eyes and ears work just fine."

"Right then," said Spinks. "You lay there a minute, catch your breath. Then we're going back to the road and with luck those men will still be at it and we'll get you to a doctor can diagnosis your ailments. 'Cause I sure can't."

The girl grabbed him by a sleeve and said, "Don't your ears work?"

Spinks, at a loss, just looked at her.

"Listen," the girl hissed at him. "Fucking listen!"

Adrenaline surged through Spinks' brain as faint crunching sounds from the woods they'd just walked through reached his ears. The crunching grew steadily louder. Spinks looked at the girl, her face frozen in stark fear. Spinks, his pulse suddenly pounding in his ears, stood, lifted her into his arms and took off walking with her again having no idea to where.

# 3

Spinks for near nineteen months had survived in mountains steeper and rockier than the ones he was in now with less vegetation to camouflage himself in from the people trying to kill him and with the added fear of blowing himself up on a concealed IED how two soldiers in his unit had done seconds after they'd sprinted past him to dive into the stream he'd been leading them along a wooded trail to. On the other hand, his standard dress in the Hindu Kush mountains had been combat boots, fire-retardant fatigues, a helmet, flak jacket and interceptor body armor; as opposed to a soaked pair of low-cut Rockport's, blue jeans and a T-shirt.

And he'd been outfitted with an M-4 Carbine, fragmentation grenades, a bayonet, lensatic compass, flashlight, and first aid kit. Not just a three-bladed pocketknife.

And he hadn't had to carry a hundred-pound girl.

His unit often went out late at night on some higher up's assumption, as often as not proved incorrect, that everyone but them in the area, including the insurgents, would be asleep. Spinks on those night patrols, same as on the day ones, and even just wandering out from camp to snap a few photographs, search for the source of an unusual bird call or take a leak, channeled a whitetail buck in upstate New York woods rife with armed-to-the-teeth hunters looking to make his head a trophy. Soldiering in those mountains he never didn't have his eyes moving, his ears open for out of context sounds, his nose alert for scents not indigenous to the terrain.

Trot-walking three-quarters-blind and too loudly through the pines he found getting in touch again with his internal buck four years from when he'd last needed to wasn't as easy as he'd heard riding a bicycle was after years of not doing so. He experienced a disconnected sensation of watching himself, more than of being himself, being pursued through these dark woods with this injured girl in his arms by what he wasn't sure weren't just the girl's hallucinations.

His footfalls on the needle-covered floor to his ears were like crashing waves he felt as powerless to muffle as a beach was to stop the waves from pounding it. He ploughed through overhanging branches and brush, doing his best to keep the girl's head and limbs from banging into them. Like some giant Phoenix a great horned owl flew screeching through the treetops overhead and the girl, half-raising her head from Spinks' arms toward it, opened her mouth and weakly screamed back at it scaring Spinks more than the owl had. A minute later he was slogging through thick mud where groundwater had bubbled up like froth squeezed from a soap-saturated sponge into a low spot in the forest floor. The mud gave way to water deep enough to house a few croaking frogs one of which died beneath one of Spinks' Rockports with a sharp pop suggesting, amid his splashing footsteps, a shouted curse on a busy street.

The terrain started angling gently upward in waves like an undulating tree-lined desert. Then the pines gave way to hardwoods—red oak, sugar maple, ash, white and yellow birch, a few hickory.

Laboring up a treed hillside undergrown with nannyberry, speckled alder, sumac, bramble thickets and various species of thorn berries Spinks stumbled on a root and nearly dropped the girl, her shoulders banging against the ground, the girl exclaiming, "Oh," with as little emotion as if Spinks had just reiterated to her the obvious fact he was carrying her deep into dark, unfamiliar woods on her word alone they were being closely pursued by two demons who wanted her dead. Atop the hill he lay her down on a patch of moss near the base of a giant oak tree then, trying to catch his breath, leaned back against the oak's trunk. A hundred feet below them the only visible parts of the pines they'd just run through were their uneven tops sticking up at the sky like jagged spires in the front gate to a black hell. A touch on his right calf led Spinks to look down at the girl, pulling with one hand from his jeans a clump of briars. She stared into her hand at the prickly mass as if it were a magic 8-ball she was hoping would reveal to her the contents of her jumbled mind. Spinks still breathing hard said to her, "You got any idea where we are?"

The girl cast her eyes slowly about the woods, halting them five or six times on the outlines of large trees as if, incredibly thought Spinks, she hoped to recognize something in one of them that would recall to her this very spot. Then she put her eyes on Spinks in the same way she'd put them on the outlines of those few trees and they said to Spinks she was as clueless to their whereabouts as he was. Spinks recalled how desperate she'd been to get away from the vehicle with orange running lights, offered to fuck Spinks to drive her away from it as if she'd surmised just from looking at him Spinks was a man would go for a deal like that. Spinks now guessed the girl's offer had been less a reflection of what she'd been seeing in Spinks than it had been a reflection of her own desperation. He guessed when she'd made the offer she hadn't been seeing Spinks at all. He wasn't certain she was seeing him yet. Recalling she hadn't said where she'd wanted him to drive her to, only that she'd wanted him to drive her away from where she was Spinks said, "Do you remember where you were walking to on that road I picked you up on?"

The girl's look at Spinks said she had no more memory of where she'd been walking to than she apparently did of anything else, past her fear of whoever had gotten out of the vehicle with orange running lights.

"They can see us in the dark," said the girl.

"What?" said Spinks.

"Yes," said the girl.

Spinks couldn't see anything past the welt on her head wrong with her, but as certain as he was sitting soaking wet next to her in the middle of the woods at whatever hour it was past dark he was certain something was; in her head, in her body, probably in more than one part of her. He again glanced down at the darkness blanketing the pines, again wondering how anyone trailing them could be doing so without a light. He looked back at the girl and said, "Where are they from?"

The girl gave him a blank stare.

"The ones following us? The people from the vehicle with orange running lights. Are they from where you're from?"

The girl said, "They're from hell."

A shiver went through Spinks. He remembered the girl back in the pines calling the two upright shapes who'd gotten out of the vehicle demons. Demons that could see in the dark. He said to her, "Is that around here somewhere—hell?"

The girl pressed her lips together, appearing to be studying hard on what Spinks had asked her, but didn't answer him.

"What makes you say they're from hell? Did they tell you that?"

The girl shook her head, confused.

"How do you know they want you dead?"

The girl looked as lost as a little kid who'd wandered away from her mother at a crowded beach whispering to Spinks, "I'm alive."

"I see you are," Spinks said, recalling it was the second time she'd told him so in response to the same question.

"That's why."

Spinks looked at her. "Because you're alive? That's why they want you dead?"

The girl looked up into Spinks' face and Spinks thought, no—she for sure wasn't seeing him. Her eyes were on him but she wasn't seeing him. Whatever she was seeing—an hallucination, a memory, a vision by way of some clairvoyant power she possessed—wasn't in Spinks' face; and it wasn't here, in this dark place they were sitting in. Spinks with a greater sense of urgency again wondered who was this girl he'd carried off into the woods? A girl in such terrible fear she'd been ready to fuck a stranger willing to drive her away from whatever it was—real or imagined—scaring her. A girl only fifteen years old. "You're the same age as my daughter," he told her, the certainty of it popping into his head like a name he'd been struggling for a while to remember.

He felt at least a little less in the dark knowing one piece of her puzzle.

The girl reached up and stuck the briars she was still holding onto the same spot on Spinks' jeans she'd pulled them from. She whispered something so softly Spinks wasn't able to make it out. "What was that you said?" he asked her.

The girl in the way a child years younger than her might speak to an imaginary friend said to the briars she was pressing to Spinks' leg, "How old?"

Maybe to do with the hit she'd taken in the head or maybe to do with whatever before that had caused her to be walking scratched, disoriented and half-dressed down the hollow road the girl, understood Spinks, didn't recall—or didn't know—her age any more than she knew her name or where'd she'd been before she'd stepped out in front of the Durango's headlights. Spinks told her, "You're fifteen."

The girl's look at Spinks didn't tell him if her hearing how old she was had enlivened any of her deadened memories. She took her hand from the briars on Spinks' jeans and said, "Hell isn't far away."

Spinks fought an impulse to shake her, to see if he could physically force her out of the place in her head she was stuck in but feared his doing so would only put her deeper into the place. He said, "You must have a family. In the smoke do you see faces that might belong to a mother or father?"

"And it's getting closer—real close," said the girl her eyes growing huge, her face taking on the exaggeratedly spooked look of a Halloween mask.

Spinks had a strong urge to leave the girl and run, she wasn't his responsibility or problem, he had his own responsibilities and problems, his own life to worry about. Then he heard them. An even more petrified look on the girl's face than had been on it a moment ago told him she'd heard them too. Rustling noises.

Spinks looked down the hill at the dark shapes of a few shrubs or bushes moving steadily back and forth in the still as death night. He looked back at the girl looking at him in the innocent way Iris looked at him when she knew she'd done something wrong and had no defense to it. The girl in a frightened whisper said, "I can maybe walk—we could go faster."

"We'll see if you can," whispered Spinks. He reached down, put one arm under her legs, the other under her shoulders; he lifted her up as quietly as he could. "When we're safely away from here."

# 4

Bobo Callender was from some piss-stop town off Route 95 in South Carolina. He chewed Red Man tobacco, was a huge Gamecock fan and listened to the twangiest sort of country music—Kenny Chesney, Glen Campbell, Toby Keith, Loretta Lynn. At the age of twenty-six he still believed Jesus fed five thousand people with five loaves of bread and two fish, all earthly pursuits were in reach of the average human being and lighting farts was hilarious. He would read to Spinks long rhyming poems he wrote containing his thoughts on the afterlife and extraterrestrial beings and invisible planes of existence in which extinct life forms such as Tyrannosaurus Rexes, saber-toothed tigers and Marilyn Monroe yet roamed the earth all subjects, from what Spinks could tell, Callender's muse viewed as intricately intertwined.

Spinks didn't talk all that much and Callender in Spinks' view talked too much. When awake he hardly stopped talking except to eat or when out on patrol. He and Spinks had next to nothing in common other than they were both soldiers with the goal of returning home from their Afghanistan deployments in as close as humanly possible—given the normal rigors of combat—to the physical and mental states they'd undertaken them in. Spinks never figured out if he actually liked Callender—or if he just liked being around him. Or if there was a difference.

Nearly as much as he loved composing and reciting poetry Callender loved showing around pictures of his two sons, a five-year-old mothered by a woman Spinks only ever heard Callender call SnackPack and a three-year-old mothered by Callender's then fiancé who, evidently to make clear her place in his heart next to SnackPack's place in it, Callender mostly referred to as his Five Course Meal By Candlelight. From their photos Matthew and Mark Callender were mini versions of their father, gangly, lantern-jawed, buzz-cut blonds with heads a couple sizes too large for the shoulders they sat on, eyes soft as applesauce and slack mouths that appeared incapable of holding for more than a few seconds a hard expression.

Spinks in his turn would show off to Callender pictures of the two females in his life—Rebecca and Iris. Callender called them Spinks' two angels—his Little Angel and his Boss Angel.

Spinks didn't often consciously think about those nineteen months he'd spent in the Hindu Kush Mountains fighting alongside Afghan anti-Taliban forces against Taliban militia forces they looked just like. Like every former fighting soldier he had his share of memories of what he'd seen and experienced in combat—scant good things, a lot of bad things and a few things utterly unspeakable. Though he wasn't one to dwell on past events all those memories had merged together in his subconscious and solidified into knowledge, in the way that different liquids blended together in a lab are solidified into a crystal, to forever change him in ways Spinks hardly realized. The human body, brain and psyche were more fragile than most things in nature. He'd seen all three blown apart in mere seconds by things that wouldn't even shake a tree. Like most soldiers in a war zone and emergency room doctors and nurses he'd been made more acutely aware than most people of mankind's fragility.

Bobo Callender was sent with Spinks and two other soldiers on a goodwill mission to a farming village ten miles from their base camp. Their chief objective was simply to reassure the local populace of the U.S. military's strong but friendly presence in the area in the hope it would persuade some of those living in fear of the insurgents to be less fearful of them and more forthcoming with information about their habits and whereabouts. Unable to locate any villagers who spoke even a few words of English—or any at any rate willing to admit they did—the unit mostly wandered the streets smiling and nodding and passing out free food. They handed out bubblegum and root beer balls to several kids in a dirt-packed field playing a game that had them chasing each other around on one foot while holding their other foot behind their backs. Callender handed Spinks his carbine and enthusiastically tried to join the game bringing it to an abrupt halt for everyone but Callender who continued hopping solo in a circle of kids appearing highly embarrassed for him. When Callender lost his balance and fell into a thorn bush the kids laughed uncertainly in the way of people watching a Tourette's sufferer loudly cursing in the town square. Callender pulled himself from the bush and wearing his loose, sloppy grin bowed deeply to the kids making it clear he was certain he was in on the joke rather than the butt of it. Then, after taking his carbine back from Spinks, he wandered across the street and made to engage a man leading a pack mule in a wordless, hand-flapping conversation that ended with the man hurrying away as if Callender were a bad-smelling outhouse he'd just exited after doing quick business in it. Callender made a disappointed shrug toward Spinks and Spinks could see Callender's failure to connect with the mule-leading man had hurt Callender in a way that a stranger's rejection should never hurt anyone.

Hiking back to base camp twenty minutes later Callender disappeared into the earth.

Darkness like a recurring memory was creeping into the day's last light.

It looked to Spinks walking just behind him like a giant hand had grabbed Callender's feet and jerked him into the ground.

The Afghans called what he had vanished into a kariz, an open, unmarked well that connected to underground waterways for irrigation in the arid landscape. The one Callender went into was sixty-plus feet deep and funneled into the earth like a mole hole. Spinks peering down into it was a few seconds realizing the shape resembling the back of a large turtle he was looking at was the top of Callender's combat helmet at the bottom of the kariz. The helmet tipped back and Spinks imagined, as much as he saw in the shadowy light, Callender's face, appearing at that distance no bigger than a moon pie. "Oh, Jesus! Oh, Jesus! Oh, Jesus!" Callender weakly cried out to Spinks, God or both of them.

"There water down there?" Spinks hollered down to him.

Callender maybe not hearing him hollered disjointedly up the shaft, "I broke some things—a few at least!"

Spinks going through a mental checklist of priorities and remembering Callender couldn't swim asked him about water again.

"Water ain't my biggest concern! I'm cracked open like a bag of nuts dropped onto concrete!" hollered Callender.

The two other soldiers, Carl Barlow and Sydney Dombrowski, arrived. They dropped to their knees and peered with Spinks into the hole. Dombrowski hollered, "Can you move?"

"Like a turd in a tight asshole I can move!"

"You think you might be paralyzed?"

"Don't it mean probably not if I hurt like hell?"

"In the places you hurt like hell I believe that's right," hollered Barlow.

"I hurt like hell everywhere's far as I can tell," called up Callender.

"That's a big thing we don't have to worry about then," said Dombrowski.

"Still," hollered Callender, and the pain in his voice said the rest.

"We're going to get you out of there, Callender," said Dombrowski. "Just hold on."

"How we going to do that?" Spinks said softly.

Dombrowski and Barlow looked at him. Spinks said, "How we going to get him out of there? One of you got a rope on you sixty feet long?"

Barlow said softly, "Four of us got smarts enough to figure out how."

"We're four trained soldiers got good heads on our shoulders," Dombrowski whispered in agreement.

"What you all whispering about up there?" Callender demanded feebly.

"Figuring on how to get you out," Spinks called down to him.

"What did you all come up with?"

"Nothing just yet," Dombrowski answered him.

"Night'll be filling this hole up soon," Callender called back, Spinks thinking of the four of them Callender, likely as a result of being in shock, sounded the least panicked. The three men at the top of the hole looked at each other and didn't say anything.

# 5

Spinks estimated they'd walked a big loop out from the stream they'd crashed in and were headed back now in the general direction of the hollow road. It was more a guess though, based on his occasional glimpses of the moon through the clouds and trees, than a calculation based on actual knowledge of astronomy or the night sky. His arms and shoulders burned. He worried under the girl's weight his back would give out rendering him more helpless than she was. He felt her shaking in his arms even as, in the warm night, he sweated buckets down onto her, the two of them both near as drenched now as they had been fresh from the stream.

Periodically he stopped and cocked an ear at the trailing woods. Each time along with chirps, hoots, screeches, trees cracking and his own labored breathing he heard rustling noises made or not made by two beings—human or otherwise—blindly tracking him and the girl through the woods. In a towering stand of box elder trees the thought struck him he'd somewhere lost perspective on the situation; he'd allowed the girl to poison him with her fantasies and paranoia and blind him to the passage of time. He stopped walking and looked at his watch. The hands were frozen at 8:54 p.m. Spinks, haunted by thoughts of some mystical force having cast him into a time warp, told himself the stream they'd plunged into must have fouled the watch's mechanism.

He lay the girl down at the base of a lichen-and-vine-shrouded boulder sitting in isolation like a meditating Buddha beneath the genuflecting box elders. The girl duck-walked a few feet away from him, reached a hand down to her crotch, pulled aside her soaked briefs and loudly peed onto the forest floor her eyes rolling over the night-shrouded woods like swells over an ocean's surface a thousand miles from shore. "I know it's just one of you out there," the girl said, sounding worn out, tired of having the same argument with whoever she was having it with.

Spinks hoping again to connect with her somehow if only to make more sense of what he was doing out here with her asked her, "Who are you talking to?"

The girl, peeing still, waved a hand at the woods. "The thing hiding out there making all that noise."

Spinks thinking maybe this was her first time in the woods at night said, "It's trees, animals, birds and reptiles making all that noise. When the sun comes up you'll see it is."

The girl shook her head, no. "When the sun comes up the thing out there will turn into trees, animals, birds and reptiles, until it gets dark again," she said, "and then they'll all disappear and the thing will come out again."

Spinks said, "And the two demons you say are following us? Have they disappeared too? Until the sun comes up?"

The girl eyed Spinks as if he were a coiled snake she'd nearly avoided stepping on. She said, "They are the thing."

She got to her feet trembling like she'd just walked in mid-February out of the North-Atlantic Ocean. Spinks said, "I'd like to know what I've put myself on the line for. It's only fair you tell me the truth about whoever—or whatever—was in that vehicle with the orange running lights. And the truth about yourself the best you can recollect it."

"I'm going to walk now," she said.

"To where?"

The girl, not answering Spinks, tightly hugged herself, her teeth chattering.

"I'm willing to keep carrying you," said Spinks.

"Where is it you're hoping to take me?" said the girl.

Spinks cocked his head at her. "Back to the road. From there we can get our bearings."

"They'll be waiting for us there."

Spinks looked off toward the rustling noises. "How can they be on the road waiting for us, if they're behind us?"

The girl raked her fingers through her soaked hair. Spinks suddenly had an unsettling view of her as a sorcerer of some sort who'd drawn him into this time-stopped world inside the real world for purposes she'd yet to reveal to him. He said, "Are you saying there's more than two of them?"

The girl dropping her eyes to her feet said in a near whisper that made Spinks think that even in lowering his estimate of her age to fifteen he may have guessed too high by three or four years, "You might be one of them."

Spinks said, "I'm an insurance salesman. When I saw you on the road I was on my way down the hollow from seeing a farmer client of mine lives at its top."

"You could turn into one of them," whispered the girl.

"How would I do that?" said Spinks.

"Men can turn into whatever they want to. Some of them can."

"Which men in particular can do that? Do they have names?"

"Men who act like they want to help you. Men like you."

Spinks read mental exhaustion in the girl's face. He imagined her using every ounce of her energy hunting in her muddled thoughts for a few she could express sensibly. He said, "It was you who asked me for help, then you nearly killed us. And yet I'm still here. Even though you haven't told me close to what I ought to know for trying to help you."

"Why do you want to help me?"

Spinks wasn't sure why. Though he suspected it wasn't the real reason, or at least not all of the reason, he said, "I had no choice after the situation you put me in not to help you. What I can't figure out is if, in all your craziness, you knew before you put me in the situation I wouldn't have a choice."

The girl turned her back to Spinks and started walking in a slightly different direction than he'd been carrying her in, her unlaced high-tops laces dragging on the ground by her feet. Spinks watched her a couple seconds noting she was still walking in the general direction of where he'd calculated the road to be. Then he walked after her.

# 6

They went up a long rise, through more box elders mingling with redbuds and hornbeams and under grown with witch hazel, Juneberry and sheep laurel. Spinks kept an eye out for signs of wavering in the girl's legs, ready to run up and catch her if she started to fall. Looking nearly lost in Spinks' size large jacket and naked below it to her high-tops she gave the impression walking in front of him of a young fawn still unsteady on its feet and several days removed from its last meal. She made no effort pushing through the foliage to avoid branches or brush nor did she cry out or react in any way to its raking of her bare flesh. Spinks, picturing as he watched her how she might have gotten the scratches he'd noticed on her face and legs when he'd first encountered her, wondered from who, what and where she'd been walking—or running—before she came to be walking three-fourths naked on the hollow road.

He wondered too if she had any idea to where she was leading him. She seemed to him to be wandering in the way of a lost in the wilds housedog guided only by its unhoned instincts and a vague memory of where its home was. The thought struck Spinks he was lucky to have no one in his life to worry over him not showing up where or when he was supposed to; then the thought struck him—if he did have someone in his life worrying over him, would he be out here at all? Would he have pulled up next to the girl and offered her assistance? And if he had offered her assistance, would he have gone out of his way to help her after she'd acted so insanely toward him, after she'd offered to fuck him for a ride and crashed his truck into a stream? Would he have taken her—a clearly mixed-up, disturbed girl—into these woods on her word alone that two demons were trying to kill her? Spinks pictured law enforcement officials tasked with finding him and the girl asking Jack Spinks' friends and acquaintances hordes of probing questions about him; dissecting every detail in the life of the insurance salesman/Marine Special Forces veteran and convicted felon last seen running off into the woods carrying like a rolled-up carpet in his arms the near-naked body of an alive or dead girl he'd physically forced into his truck before, in recklessly attempting to speed away from passersby happening onto the apparent abduction, he'd plunged the truck over an embankment into a raging stream.

And if they weren't fantastical, the girl's fears? If the two occupants of that vehicle with the orange running lights weren't mere passersby or the girl's concerned family members? If they were two people, demons or earthly equivalents of demons intent on killing her? In that case the only witnesses to the girl's and Spinks' accident on Black Cat Hollow Road damn sure hadn't alerted the law to it; and given the obscured view from Black Cat Hollow Road of the stream they'd crashed into the only people searching for Spinks and the girl were two worldly or otherworldly demons—maybe more than two given the girl's fear of returning to the hollow road—with the sole aim of seeing that the girl, and Spinks for being with her, didn't make it out of these woods alive.

Spinks nearing the top of the incline heard a branch snap in the trailing woods. He stopped walking. He heard another snap. Then he heard only the wind whistling softly through the trees and his heart pounding from his knowing a presence of some kind had muted the wildlife near the base of the hill as minutes earlier he and the girl had done. Spinks pictured two indistinct forms—human or inhuman—peering up the dark hillside at Spinks peering blindly down it toward them. He had a sudden urge to be invisible. He cursed himself for not wading back out to the Durango after he'd pulled the girl to shore and retrieving from the rack holding it his Enfield .308 and a carton of shells for it. Being hunted—by men or demons—didn't sit well with him. Unfocused anger simmered in his guts like warm water in a resting geyser's mouth. The mammals and birds beneath him resumed moving about and communicating. Spinks looked back to his front and the girl was gone. He darted his eyes into the darkness left and right of where she'd been walking and couldn't find her.

He started on a fast walk up the incline at where he'd last seen her, in his haste crashing into a Juneberry thicket. He glanced back down the incline, concerned the noise he'd made had alerted whatever had silenced the woods down there, and saw at the base of the hill, two hundred yards away, an upright shape disappearing into a stand of trees. He wasn't sure a second later if he'd imagined it. Then he was at the top of the incline, a brushy plateau of tightly spaced hardwoods forty-odd feet wide. He spotted in profile the girl standing back to him, peering down the far side of the incline. Spinks walked to her. The girl not moving her eyes from what they were aimed at didn't acknowledge him. Spinks visually followed her eyes down the incline into an area of widely spaced jack pines and firs where the terrain once more leveled out. The trees had the look of having been thinned out more by men's hands than God's hand. In a small clearing amid them stood a square-shaped structure with a peaked roof.

The girl looked at Spinks. Her face was a mask of studied confusion.

"What?" said Spinks

"The bear," the girl half-whispered.

Spinks fought an urge to snatch her up in his arms and start running with her again from whatever mythical force he was more and more concerned was on their trail. "What bear?" he said. "I don't see a bear."

The girl looked back to the cabin. She gritted her teeth like a child puzzling over a test question.

"Do you know that cabin?" said Spinks.

The girl slowly shook her head, more as if trying to clear it after she'd been punched in it than in response to Spinks.

"Have you walked to it? From a place on one of these roads nearby?"

The girl's look at Spinks begged him to answer for her his questions to her. Spinks glancing nervously behind them said, "Come on—maybe there's someone down there who can help us."

He seized her by an arm and the girl, jerking back from him like a horse shying from a snake, gave him a look that caused him to flash on Iris's face after she'd waken as a child screaming from a nightmare she couldn't remember past that it had terrified her. "You're going to be all right," said Spinks not at all sure either of them were going to be all right. "This is all just a bad dream we'll both wake up from."

The girl looking back at the cabin said, "It's not a dream."

Spinks suddenly felt as confused and helpless as everything about the girl told him she was. He said, "These demons you say want you dead—do they have guns? Are they armed do you know?"

The girl, not answering Spinks, took his arm and started pulling him with her down the hill toward the structure half-hidden in the trees.

# 7

Spinks as the team's leader radioed base camp and requested a rescue team be deployed to the well site; and he ordered Dombrowski and Barlow to hike the five miles back to the village they'd been at hoping they could locate in it some rescue equipment and return to the site with it sooner than the base camp team could get there walking ten miles through the mountainous terrain.

Spinks dragged to the hole's edge a fallen conifer limb and in the dusky, late afternoon light sat down on it, resting his carbine across his thighs, intent in the several hours it would be before Dombrowski and Barlow returned or the base camp unit arrived on keeping Callender from getting too down on his straits. Near seventy degrees Fahrenheit when Callender went into the well at midday the temperature four hours later had dropped thirty degrees. An hour later the sun had set and it had fallen ten more degrees. Spinks told Callender he was dropping his coat down to him.

"Keep it," Callender hollered up to him, freezing to death in the hole evidently as low on his list of concerns as drowning in it was.

Spinks figuring Callender to be far colder than Spinks was shivering on a log sixty feet above him said, "I'm dropping it, Callender. It'll only get colder after dark."

"Not in my world," said Callender, Spinks fearing this was Callender announcing he'd thrown the towel in on getting out of the hole alive and cared nothing for being a little more comfortable in the process of dying.

"Come on now, Callender"—Spinks inclined his head into the hole, Callender's indistinct shape in the dark shadows at its bottom implying an amoeba moving beneath a microscope—"don't make me get reamed out later by some higher ups for letting you get frostbit on my watch."

"It's fifty degrees in this hole and will be for as long as I'm here and for eternity after that," Callender's pained voice came back to him.

"I make that for a rasher of Bobo Callender bullshit."

"It's a scientific fact you ought to know about the earth in case you ever fall into it, Spinks."

Spinks suddenly feeling underqualified for the task he'd set for himself said into the hole, "I plan on checking it out soon's we're back to base camp."

"Keep your coat, Spinks," Callender's voice floated weakly up to him. "You're gonna need it lots more than me."

At a rustling noise Spinks looked up at an animal resembling a large house cat with a mink's pinched face walking at him out of the conifers. The creature stopped walking on the far edge of the kariz and out of green eyes glowing in the semi-dark stared across the open shaft at Spinks. Spinks experienced the odd feeling he and the animal were communicating in some instinctual way beyond either of their capacities to comprehend. He thought of Rebecca's last email to him referencing her and Spinks' vow to always be open and honest with each other before informing him that she was sleeping with another man and hoped Spinks would understand that her decision to stop fighting this thing inside her—she didn't say or even hint at what the thing was—in no way diminished her love of Spinks and that Spinks while they were apart would feel similarly free to fulfill whatever of his needs, be they sexual or otherwise, begged his attention. Iris she wrote had made them both proud at her recent piano recital performing "Fleur De Lis" flawlessly though for several days since then they'd both been down with an exhausting sort of ailment Rebecca was confident was near its end. "Be thankful for your pain," she closed with in apparent reference to Spinks' last emailed news to her about the cracked ribs he'd suffered in a pick-up soccer game. "Feeling nothing is far more painful than broken bones are."

# 8

Spinks made it for a hunting cabin there longer than many of the surrounding trees had been alive. Forest moss coated like a thick paint its log walls. Wire mesh protected a porthole-shaped window in the near wall. English ivy planted around it in years past bearded the sides of the structure nearest the ground. A thick coat of pine needles garbed the pitched roof around a rusted tin chimney. The building faced the direction they'd been walking in though Spinks couldn't spot a road or path—not even a deer trail—leading to or from it. It had the look of having been dropped there between the trees like an abandoned piece of furniture in an overgrown field. The girl stopped walking fifty feet from it.

Spinks followed her eyes to the front door, an unfinished hardwood plank that appeared newer than the cabin overall. A shiny iron bolt was pulled back and away from a steel latch attached to the frame. Recently split firewood piled up by the wall. The girl's eyes might have been tracking a butterfly's uncertain flight through blustery air moving from the door to the dark woods past it and back to the door. She whispered, seemingly more to someone or something she was seeing in her mind or imagining on the other side of the door than to Spinks, "We hid in the trees."

Spinks made his face a blank canvas for her to make of what she would. "You hid from someone in this cabin?"

The girl's eyes widened as if she'd just recognized an identifying feature in Spinks' face or had just recognized in her mind a thought that had been disguised as another thought. She said, "The bear."

Spinks' heart sank. He thought she's worse off than my worst fears warned me she was and when this is over I'll be all alone trying to explain to the world my logic in bringing her out here. He looked again at the open latch, the cut firewood and back at the girl as she whispered, "She reads poetry to the birds and animals." And Spinks again thought of Iris—who she would have been at the age of fifteen.

If you don't save her no one will because it's only you in this whole world knows she needs saving—the thought appeared to him like a flare fired into the night sky.

"Who's there?"

A female voice from the cabin.

Spinks looked from the girl to the cabin and called out, "Jack Spinks—with an injured girl. We'd like to come inside, see to the girl's injuries. Maybe borrow some clothes for her. Trouble you for a drink of water?"

The cabin door creaked open a few inches.

"I promise to pay you later. For the clothes. And the water."

The voice from inside the cabin said, "Injured how?"

"We went off the road in my truck. The girl hit her head. I'm pretty sure she has a concussion—I don't know what all else. She's having trouble making clear sense of her thoughts."

A rifle barrel protruded through the opening. It settled on Spinks. "What road? The closest road's miles from here!"

Spinks said, "Black Cat Hollow Road. People are chasing us. Bad people."

"Bad people would only trouble chasing people through these woods in the middle of the night as bad as or badder than them!"

"We're not bad people, ma'am! We're good people in a bad bind!"

"Keep walking east long enough you'll come to the road you drove off of! Someone there will likely let you use their phone to call the police!"

The door started to shut and Spinks hollered, "She knows you!"

"Who knows me?"

"This girl does!"

The door was eased back open a crack. "Have her tell me. Not you!"

Spinks looked at the girl and found her eyes aimed at the top of the moonlit embankment she and Spinks had just walked down. Spinks looked to where she was looking and felt his stomach turn over. Beneath the trees tall upright shapes he saw two shorter upright shapes. He couldn't make his mind form the shapes into anything but two people—or two creatures resembling people—staring down at the cabin. An urge struck him to wave his arms and yell out at the shapes to see how—if at all—they would react. To see if he was looking at two people, two non-human creatures or two mirages he'd created out of fear and disorientation. He recalled the two upright shapes that had gotten out of the vehicle, the two figures that had walked from the hollow road down to the stream Spinks and the girl had crashed into without once calling out to them or in any way acting as their would-be saviors. They hadn't been mirages. They'd been as real as was this brain-muddled, near naked girl Spinks had made himself responsible for. He hissed to her, "You need to tell this lady how you know her. We need to get inside this cabin!"

The girl turning to Spinks pressed her right index finger to her lips and whispered, "Sshhhh," then, so softly the forest ants might have had trouble hearing her. "The demons can hear near as good as they can see."

Spinks in desperation hollered to the cabin, "She's scared—more than anyone I've ever seen—and her thinking is muddled! Like I told you! She said something about a bear reading poetry out here! That's how she knows you!"

The cabin door creaked farther open letting out a dull light that cast on the forest floor a tall, thick shadow that a medium-size bear standing on its hind legs might have created. A bear pointing a rifle at Spinks.

The door was pushed all the way open. Spinks, taking the gesture as an invitation to come inside, seized the girl by an arm and turned her to the cabin. He looked up at the hilltop for the two upright shapes under the trees and couldn't find them. "Come on, young lady. Let's get you some clothes and food and see if we can't get you back thinking right," he said walking with her at the cabin.

# 9

The woman, aiming the rifle awkwardly at his right knee, watched him as he stepped inside and shut the cabin's heavy wood door how she might have watched an odd-acting animal that had wandered too close to her.

She was dressed in a floor-length gold and white silk robe that, with her mountain of blond cornrows and pale complexion, in the shadowy light of a gas lamp hanging from the ceiling gave her the appearance of an albino Amazonian priestess.

The cabin inside contrasted so sharply with the cabin outside Spinks wondered if the exterior had been intentionally put in its rough-hewed condition to scare off potential intruders. Onto the log walls mahogany paneling had been nailed. Adorning them in twig frames were brief handwritten observances and watercolor sketches of nature colliding with civilization—a deer frozen in a vehicle's headlights, a man sitting on a camel in a row of cars at a red light, a donkey looking out over the city from a church tower. Between two coffin-shaped crates serving as cabinets a pot-belly woodstove was vented by aluminum tubing attached to the chimney. On a handwoven rug a large sectional couch and matching recliner fronted the stove. A hat rack behind the stove served as a perch for a large crow the girl, seemingly taking no notice of the woman, left Spinks' side to quietly tiptoe at. "I let you in only because I could see you weren't going to let the young lady come in alone," said the woman.

Spinks, nervous at the woman's fidgety handling of the rifle, remained standing just inside the doorway. "You know who she is?"

The woman watching the girl, intent only on the crow she

was walking at, said, "I know she's in trouble. A near blind person could see it."

"I told you," said Spinks.

"I'm not convinced the worst trouble she's in is from outside this cabin." The woman jerked the rifle barrel up at Spinks' stomach, Spinks uncertain if her mechanical movements with the weapon indicated she wasn't accustomed to handling it or reflected a want to use it at the slightest provocation. "Who took her clothes off?"

"I came onto her that way."

The woman skeptically eying Spinks down the rifle barrel said, "You come onto her soaking wet too?"

"She crashed my truck into a stream. I pulled her out of it," Spinks said. "You got something she can put on?"

The woman thought and said, "My nephew has some clothes here will fit her better than mine will."

"Where is he?"

"Where's who?"

"Your nephew?"

"In Poughkeepsie where he lives I imagine. You came onto her where?"

"Walking down Black Cat Hollow Road." Spinks watched the girl approaching the crow with her hands out like a beggar asking for money. "I pulled up next to her to see if she needed help."

"It's a big jump from there to here. What's missing?"

Spinks for a moment thought how lucky the girl was to have found some place inside her no one could reach or hurt her at. He said, "She jumped in my truck and damn near killed us both slamming the accelerator to the floor trying to get me to drive away from a vehicle that stopped facing us in the road."

"What vehicle?"

"Was too dark to say. It had orange running lights. Two figures I took for men got out of it."

Nervous fear flushed the woman's face.

"The girl said they wanted her dead. They followed us through the woods to here."

The woman looked at the girl. For all the attention she was paying Spinks and the woman she might have been on the other side of a soundproof screen. The woman said, "What sort of danger have you brought to my doorstep?"

Spinks said, "The girl says it's two demons up on that hill outside."

The woman swallowed hard watching the crow hop from its perch onto the girl's outstretched hand.

"She says they can see in the dark. Not glimpsing even a pinprick of light behind us all the way through the woods to here I can't say she's wrong."

The woman turned back warily to Spinks. "She say why they want her dead?"

"Because she's alive is what she said."

"What sense did you make of that?"

"I made no more sense of it than you likely do."

"She's told you a lot for a girl I haven't heard say a word."

"You ask her a question she might." Spinks watched the girl lean slowly forward until she was eye to eye with the crow. "Her talking comes and goes."

The woman chewed her lower lip moving her eyes from Spinks to the girl and back to Spinks. She was taller and broader than any man not a professional athlete Spinks had ever seen. He supposed her unusual size and appearance had to do with her choosing to share her most intimate thoughts only with an audience of wild animals not likely to judge her too harshly for her thoughts or appearance. He said, "She have it right you're a poet?"

The woman said, "Out here I'm a poet. An artist. An essayist. A chronicler of life. And a spiritual descendant of Henry David Thoreau. In the city I treat the wounds of the mass of human beings living in Thoreau's words quiet lives of desperation."

Spinks made his face a blank mask before her.

"My tools are touch, hypnosis, meditation and a caring ear."

Spinks said, "You want to go get them?"

"Get what?"

"Clothes for the girl."

The woman still intently watching Spinks tilted her head to one side. "I've worked with a few clients like you. They've been my biggest challenges."

"Like me how?"

"So broken apart on the inside you don't even know what pieces you're missing or how to go about putting back together the ones you know about."

The girl was gently stroking the crow's back with a finger of her hand the bird wasn't perched in. Spinks watching her said, "I only did it—carried her through these woods—because she was so frightened—and helpless." He looked back at the woman. "Like a child dying from some disease and you can't help her."

The woman rocked back on her toes and it seemed to Spinks to make her even taller. He thought how intimidating it would be sitting across from her in her therapist's office, her sheer size alone her greatest skill as a human nutcracker. "I wanted to help her."

Spinks was embarrassed to hear his voice quavering.

The woman angling the rifle barrel at a small metal faucet and sink being tube fed by a five-gallon drum against the far wall said, "The water's there. Go ahead."

The floor gave so beneath Spinks' feet he speculated he was walking on the ceiling of a room beneath the one he was in. He took down from half-driven nails in the wall above the drum two metal cups. He pumped the sink's handle until a thin stream of water dribbled out the spigot. He filled the cups with the uncomfortable feeling that at his back the woman was telepathically exhuming like excised body parts scattered across the ground pieces of the girl's story up to as well as after Spinks became a chapter in it. "Her name is Midnight. But her soul is white as snow," he heard the girl say.

And the woman say, "How do you know her name?"

And the girl say, "You called it to her. She was sitting on your shoulder and you said to her, 'What did you think of that, Midnight?' About a poem you'd read to the woods."

Spinks turned the spigot off. He heard the woman say, "And Midnight's review of my poem? Was she kind to it?"

Spinks holding the full water glasses turned from the sink to see on the rug before the couch the woman standing over the girl like a huge foliated tree stealing the light from a frangible sapling and the crow still perched in the girl's hand.

"She flapped her wings and cawed. And you smiled to her and said, "Dear sweet Midnight, you have a soul white as snow."

Spinks walked at them with the odd feeling that they weren't seeing him, that he was visible only to the crow's beaded untelling eyes traversing the room with him. He held one of the full glasses out to the girl and she took it from him without looking at him. Nor did the woman look at him, though she held the rifle out to her side in one hand, still indirectly aimed at him, like a tennis racquet stopped in mid swing. She said, "How long ago was that?"

The girl looked at the crow as if hoping it would tell her how long ago it was. Then she looked back at the woman. "It was daytime. And there were two deer."

"Deer."

"Standing back in the trees. They were listening to your poetry. Like I was. And Midnight."

"You walked here?"

The girl nodded. "There's no road. Just a trail through the woods."

"Did it feel good, the walking? Different than the walking you did tonight?"

The girl got a far-off look as if straining to remember. "He picked some berries and ate them."

"Someone was with you?"

"I was afraid they were poisonous."

"Who was with you?"

"It was one of the rules—always I had to be with him—"

"One of whose rules?"

The girl squeezed her eyes shut. When she opened them again she looked petrified. "Terrible noises and I'm afraid to see!"

"What?"

She turned to Spinks with a desperate look.

Spinks had a vision of her staring wide-eyed at the earth rushing toward her and again had the feeling he'd let her down somehow.

The girl said to him in a haunted whisper, "What am I afraid to see?"

Spinks imagined his brain as the batter in a bowl someone had stuck an electric mixer into. "How would I know?"

"I know how you look at me that you know me. Tell me who I am!"

Spinks stared defenselessly at the girl.

The woman watching him distrustfully placed her hand gently on the girl's head. She said, "We'll unravel you one small step at a time, dear."

The girl stared as blankly up at her as the crow had stared at Spinks crossing the room. Her entire body started trembling. The crow hung in with her until suddenly the girl let out an indecipherable shout and as if hit with an electric cattle prod threw up her arms casting the bird from her hand and into a crazed flight near the ceiling, cawing, banging into the walls. The woman looked from the girl to Spinks and Spinks thought now she's seen what I've seen and doesn't she wish this was Monday morning in her nice, safe office in the city.

# 10

"How did you come to be with this man?" The woman flicked her eyes at Spinks as if he were a half-seen animal darting into the brush off a road she and the girl were driving on. Spinks felt an urge to point something out to her. He wasn't sure what. Something about all he and the girl had been through together to bring them here.

The girl, suggesting again to him what Iris might have looked like at her age, glanced at Spinks then away as if, thought Spinks, she was ashamed to be exposed to him this way and said, "I opened my eyes and he was there."

"He was where."

"With me."

"With you how?"

"Looking at me in the smoke."

"It's in your head the smoke?"

"I can't see things or faces in it. I can't see me!"

"You can't remember things or faces you mean?"

"I only see snapshots—little pictures—that come and go."

"Pictures of what?"

"Darkness. And sounds. Horrible sounds!"

"You're in the darkness?"

"I need my medication and I don't dare get it."

"What medication."

"It's quiet finally. A long time. Still I don't dare leave."

"Don't dare leave the darkness?"

"I'll maybe stay in it forever—then the lights—"

"What lights?"

"Out the window!"

"There's a window where you are?"

The girl absently swiped at her brow. "It's getting hotter—!"

"Hotter in the dark place?"

The girl turned her face up at the ceiling. She shut her eyes.

The woman reached a hand out and lightly gripped the girl's arm. "Are the people you were hiding from in the dark place the people outside my cabin now?"

The girl said in a cold voice, more disconnected even than the one she'd been speaking in seconds earlier, "People dying sound like children crying."

The woman blinked. Spinks could see she was shaken.

The girl lowered her eyes and opened them at the woman. "There are no people outside." Her lips formed a straight line and barely moved when she spoke. "There's demons outside."

The woman nervously chewed her lip more and said, "What do the demons look like?"

The girl looked at Spinks. The woman following her eyes said, "They look like men?"

The girl's entire body started trembling how her lips were.

Then she disappeared again.

Not ranting, not raving, just gone, only her body still there. Spinks could see it haunting the woman how it had been haunting Spinks since he'd first heard the girl talk. How her words at times didn't seem to be coming from her, but from a place beyond her she was struggling to pull them out of. The woman said to the girl or to Spinks or to herself, "The most frightening creatures often aren't flesh and blood. Often they're just shadows in a traumatized mind."

But it was more of a hope than a belief thought Spinks who, moving his eyes at the wall, said, "They're out there—two flesh and blood creatures—on the crest of that hill behind us. I saw them." He looked at the girl wondering if he'd gone completely over into an ethereal world she was living in. "We saw them."

The girl nodded but Spinks didn't know if it was to acknowledge what he'd said or in response to what a voice in her head had said.

The woman said to her, "Let's get you some clothes."

Still holding the rifle she grasped the girl's hand and walked with her to the rear wall. She pushed open a door that until then had looked like just one more piece of paneling to a small room half taken up by an elevated bed life-sized dolls and stuffed animals lay as casually about on as tourists around a hotel swimming pool. Next to it stood a padded weightlifter's bench supporting a barbell loaded down with iron discs the size of motorcycle tires. One wall was plastered with photographs of homes and rural settings vaguely familiar to Spinks. The woman picked up a small wooden chair near the door. She carried it into the center of the room and placed it down and said to Spinks, "They're in a green duffel bag near the opening."

Spinks understanding she meant for him to retrieve the clothes from a space overhead climbed onto the chair and pushed up on the ceiling above him. An internally hinged panel invisible until now moved up then fell with a dull thud into a dark space small, airborne shapes were soundlessly enlivening.

"Bats," the girl said in the blank tone Spinks with an eerie feeling recalled her talking in up at the bats in the night sky over the stream he'd hauled her out of what seemed a lifetime ago.

"They won't hurt you," she said, seemingly intuiting Spinks' fear of bats, borne from his recollection of a boy he'd gone to elementary school with having to go through a series of painful rabies shots after being bitten by a bat.

Spinks, hoping her next words would make more sense to him than her last ones had, said down at her, "You know a lot about bats?"

The girl staring past Spinks, into the space the bats were darting through said, "It's not true they can't see us. They see us with their voices."

The woman said in an even voice Spinks imagined her using with her clients in the city, "These are particular bats you are talking about?"

The girl not answering her snatched up from the bed a stuffed animal—Spinks couldn't tell if was a stuffed kangaroo or stuffed rabbit—and peered with a suddenly angry expression into its furry face as if threatening the animal to contradict anything she'd said about the bats she was remembering.

The woman said in a hushed voice up at Spinks, "Hurry up before they fly out of there."

Spinks going up on his tiptoes stuck his head through the open ceiling into a windowless area a small child would have trouble standing up in lit only by the bedroom light from below. In the three-quarters dark he saw, beneath hordes of flying bats, sealed boxes, trash bags crammed full of things, an old crate with shelves holding books, two worn-looking suitcases, a threadbare mattress. Harsh grunts and a loud gasp floated up to him in the space and he felt the chair shake.

He looked down at the woman frantically shaking the chair in one hand and waving at him to come down in the other.

Spinks, grabbing the duffel bag she'd directed him to, stepped down off the chair and followed the woman's eyes to the girl. She was peering, with her back to them, at the photographs decorating the wall around the porthole window, her shoulders heaving and exhales harshly exiting her mouth as if she'd just run a race or come face to face with a ghost. The stuffed rabbit or kangaroo lay near her feet, its eyes, ears and midsection ripped or cut from it. A letter opener Spinks recalled seeing on an old wood desk against the far wall protruded from the center of the doll's decimated face. Spinks, connecting to unspoken feelings he felt coming from the girl, said quietly to the woman, "It wasn't alive."

The look the woman gave Spinks implied he'd forced his way into her cabin and demanded unspeakable things from her.

"She didn't kill it. It's just a stuffed animal," said Spinks.

The woman started trembling as if the room's temperature had suddenly plummeted.

She pushed the door back into the ceiling.

"A therapist like you must have seen it before," said Spinks.

"I must have seen what before?"

"A person saying in actions what they can't put into words."

The woman hissed to him, "I'm not that sort of therapist. I treat mostly non-violent people with unhealthy lifestyles, anxieties and addictions!"

"She acted sort of that way up on the road," said Spinks.

"She acted sort of what way?"

Spinks inclined his head at the torn-up stuffed rabbit or kangaroo. "I took her for being older then too."

"Older than what?"

"Older than she is."

The woman said, "You know how old she is?"

Spinks said, "She's fifteen."

The woman looked down at the ravaged stuffed animal, as if recalling how it came to be that way, and up at the girl leaning forward, peering intently at one of the photographs seemingly unaware of the hushed conversation behind her. She said in a haunted whisper to Spinks, "Fifteen?"

Spinks said, "It's the age that fits her most times I look at her."

The woman shivered and looked down at the floor.

A hammering sensation started in Spinks' head as if a tiny person were pounding his fists against the inside of his skull. He said to the woman, "Other times I look at her and wonder why when she appeared in my headlights I didn't just keep driving."

The woman raised her eyes to Spinks, looking at him how she might have looked at a possibly poisonous snake she was about to step on. "I'm not sure if you or she frightens me more. You're both wearing masks I can't see behind. I'd like you both to leave my cabin—now."

Spinks nodded at the rifle in her hands. "You ever fired that?"

The woman clumsily raised the rifle at him, but her face told Spinks what he'd more and more come to suspect—she was playacting with it. Same as she'd been playacting with all her talk about wanting to unravel and help the girl.

Spinks reached out and took the rifle from her. He pulled back the bolt. The chamber and clip were both empty.

Spinks raised his eyes to her.

The woman sagged like she'd been punched in the stomach and lost her air. She said weakly, "It's my nephew's. He brings what bullets he needs for it when he comes here in hunting season."

Spinks handing the rifle back to the woman gave her a look meant to embolden her. "If anyone shows up here while I'm gone act with it toward them how you did me. It ought to make them think twice anyway about coming inside."

The woman gave him a desperate look. "While you're gone!?"

"I'll be back for her." Spinks looked at the girl in her frozen posture before the wall of photographs.

The woman made a frightened sound. "You're not leaving her with me!?"

"I can't both watch her and do what I'm going out there to do."

"What are you going out there to do?"

"Hunt whatever's hunting the girl and me."

Spinks tossed the duffel bag on the woman's desk, cluttered with pencil stubs with their erasers worn or chewed off, a bottle of Wite-Out and loose pages of what looked to be hand-scrawled poetry stanzas marred by several crossed out words above which other words had been scrawled. Naked women of all shapes, sizes and ages engaging in artistic pursuits—dancing, banjo strumming, weaving, hatchet-whittling—appeared in crayon drawings on the wall over the desk.

Spinks said loudly to the girl's back, "I'm going out for a while but I'll be back."

The girl turned around at him and Spinks with a start wondered how he'd ever taken her for a teenager. Her eyes, standing out in her pale face like drops of black ink in a beaker of water, struck him now as a mature woman's eyes formed and hardened over decades.

"Kill them," she said, making Spinks wonder if she'd heard and understood his and the woman's entire conversation.

The woman gasped.

Fear marred her face like a rash.

Spinks sorry he'd brought her into the girl's troubles but unable now to save her from them told her, "I'm not back in an hour go out into the woods with her and find a place to hide until daylight. If they can't hear you, they can't find you—even if they can see in the dark."

Then to the girl, "You do whatever this nice lady tells you to do."

The girl said, "Tell me what you're looking at."

"What?" said Spinks.

The girl was peering as intently at him as she had been at a photograph on the wall seconds earlier.

"In my head. What are you seeing through the smoke that I can't see!"

Spinks watching her eyes change back to a seriously messed-up teenager's eyes said, "I can't see anything past your face. You have an angel's face."

"Come see if some of these clothes will fit you," the woman said to the girl. Then, in a hiss to Spinks walking by her for the door, "Hurry back. I'm scared to death being alone with her."

# 11

Spinks eased opened the cabin door and slipped outside. He quietly pulled the door shut then listened to the woman walk back across the floor to her bedroom and her bedroom door shut.

He pressed himself against the front wall and sidestepped along it, in front of the stacked firewood. A hatchet was embedded in the top of the stack. If there was a wisp of truth in the girl's ramblings about the demons pursuing her Spinks figured he could do with a weapon besides his pocketknife. He pulled the hatchet from the log, slipped it between his belt and trousers on his right hip, then stepped around the corner into the dark trees bordering that side of the cabin.

He told himself the girl's words couldn't be taken at face value. She'd been through some sort of trauma—who knew what sort. Or she was flat out crazy. Or delusional. Could be she was delusional from having been traumatized. Her words were distorted interpretations of what had traumatized her maybe. Or they were spoken memories of events so horrifying to her her mind had made them even more horrifying by recasting them with an inhuman bent that had her convinced demons were chasing her. Demons from hell who wanted her dead. Demons who wanted her dead only because she was alive.

Demons who could see in the dark.

That part—the part about them being able to see in the dark—threw Spinks. He shivered involuntarily recalling the few times he'd glimpsed in the woods behind him and the girl indistinct, moving shapes and heard rustling noises the hunter and soldier in him told him were large animals of some kind moving through the foliage. How the girl had kept insisting to him the demons were coming. Telling Spinks to "listen. Just listen." How a feeling the two of them were being followed had grown in Spinks' mind into a certainty of it even as he'd failed to spot any evidence of a light behind them common sense told him anyone in those night-blackened woods would need to find and stay on someone's trail.

And yet they were out there. Spinks had no more doubt of that than the girl did. They—whoever they were—were atop this incline Spinks was making his way up the far side of as quietly as the whitetail buck he'd inwardly channeled trying to keep from being killed those years ago in the Hindu Kush Mountains of Afghanistan would. He'd blacked with ashes from the cabin's wood stove his face, neck and forearms, changed his soaked white jersey for a black T-shirt of the woman's and ditched his broken silver watch for fear of it reflecting in the sky's light as he walked. He moved from tree trunk to tree trunk up the steep embankment his ears alert for the slightest off key note in the night's natural symphony of creaks, peeps, chirps, low-level rustlings. At some point it occurred to him he felt more in control than he had since he'd first stopped on the road to offer the girl help. He asked himself why and realized it was because only now had he chosen the course he would follow. Gone were the uncertainties and ambiguities that had plagued him as he'd grappled with what choice to make. And the helplessness of feeling whatever choice he made he wouldn't be able to save a life he had been made responsible for. Demons from hell—or their metaphorical equivalents—had tried to rip all the sweetness and innocence out of a girl not unlike his own daughter might have grown up to be. What exactly they'd done to her mattered greatly of course, not only to the law and the girl and her loved ones but to the people who would try to help her heal, if she survived, from whatever had been done to her. Not to Spinks though. To Spinks, going to his knees behind a large red maple where the incline leveled out, all that mattered was that this time he not fail to save the life of a person whose care for whatever reason had been thrust entirely onto him.

He heard with his own exerted breathing in the warm night

crickets chirping, a bird or small animal riffling through the branches overhead, an owl hooting off in the woods to the west through which he'd first carried then walked with the girl. His breathing modulated and still he knelt there in the moss and thick leaves listening while imagining two sets of human eyes that could see in the dark trained on him like lasers programmed to fire at some invisible command. He counted silently to a hundred and hearing nothing more than what he'd been hearing lay down and belly crawled to behind a deerberry thicket thirty feet into the plateau. He lay there and listened some more and, aided only by a hint of light from the overcast sky, strained to see anything more than the dark shapes of trees and shrubs and the elephantine boulder at the plateau's far edge he and the girl had walked past starting their descent to the cabin. He started silently counting again. Before he got to ten he heard a groan or growl—he wasn't sure which, or from where—and stopped counting.

And the crickets stopped chirping.

He heard it again. A groan. Not from a tree settling.

He waited a few more seconds, then raised up on his elbows and started slithering toward the top of the incline.

He abruptly stopped slithering seeing a figure move out from in front of the boulder. A tall, rangy figure. A human male figure. Or a non-human figure resembling a man. A man peering down the dark hillside toward the cabin. Making a groan of the sort Spinks had heard earlier the figure raised its hands over its head and bent from side to side the way someone might do stretching to get the kinks out after standing up from a nap or long sit-down. The figure's hands against the near-black sky looked to Spinks to be empty; empty anyway of an object large enough to serve as a useful weapon.

Spinks wondered if the second man—assuming the second figure he'd seen from outside the woman's cabin was a man—was in front of the boulder. And if not, where he was—because Spinks didn't plan to make a move on the tall figure until he knew exactly where the second figure was.

He started slithering again—ahead and to his left—thinking to get parallel to the tall figure and boulder to gain a view of the boulder's front side. Forty feet to the top of the incline. Thirty feet. Twenty. He stopped and looked fifty-odd feet to his right at the tall figure. The figure still looking down the incline had dropped its arms back to its sides. It occurred to Spinks what the tall figure might be looking at. The second figure. Maybe the second figure wasn't on the plateau at all. Maybe the second figure was on its way down the incline to the cabin. Or at the cabin already. And the tall figure was waiting to get the all-clear signal to go down and join it there. The thought filled Spinks with a sense of urgency.

He started slithering again.

He heard a loud snap and froze.

He'd snapped with his elbow a dead twig on the forest floor.

The tall figure appeared not to have heard the snap. Or it had heard it and taken it for a small animal. Spinks was about to start moving forward again when the tall figure cocked its head as if reconsidering what it had heard. A moment later the figure turned around at Spinks and Spinks, seeing in the center of its face where its eyes and nose should have been a thick protrusion suggesting a domesticated pig's snout, felt his heart jump into his throat. The figure raised its arm and pointed it directly at Spinks in the dark underbrush. Then he looked up toward the boulder's top and Spinks, following his eyes, saw crouched up there a figure with the same snoutish face as the other one raising a three-to-four-foot-long object fatter at its base than at its tip toward Spinks. Spinks grabbed the hatchet from his belt and pushed up to his knees and hurled the hatchet at the figure on the boulder.

He heard a grunt and a clattering sound he took for a dropped rifle hitting the boulder then, already running toward where he'd last seen the first figure, saw the second figure fall off the boulder. A loud thump told him the figure had landed at the boulder's base just in front of him. He leapt over the unmoving figure as he saw the tall one twenty feet ahead of him dart behind the boulder. He heard the figure scrabbling around on the loose rock lining the ground at the top of the incline. He sprinted around the boulder and the tall figure was coming up out of a crouch aiming in one hand toward him a pistol. Spinks' instincts told him his best chance to avoid a bullet was to hit the dirt. He dove chest-first onto the ground and started rolling. He heard the pistol go off and a bullet ricochet off the loose rocks as he collided with the tall figure's feet. The figure fell onto its back and Spinks scrambled on top of it and got hold of its gun hand. He slammed the hand against the rocks until the pistol fell from it. Then he balled his right hand into a fist and smashed it into the tall figure's face. He yelped in pain as a sharp object tore into his knuckles. He shook his hand then went back to punching the face lower down, beneath where the sharp object had pierced it and kept on punching it until he realized the figure no longer was putting up any resistance. Then he realized the figure was a man and that the man hadn't been putting up any resistance since Spinks had knocked him down and he guessed the fall had taken the wind out of him. He sat up on the man's chest and reached down to his face and ripped from it the night vision goggles that in the dark had looked like a pig's snout feeling both relieved and foolish for not having figured out way back in the woods why the two men had been able to see in the dark.

The tall man's mouth and nose were bleeding and he was breathing heavily. Spinks in an expulsion of the anger building in him over the last several hours slapped the man's face hard five or six times making it bleed more. The man half-opened his eyes. Then he opened them all the way and looked up at Spinks out of eyes holding tightly to the thoughts piloting them. He had a sharp, angular face that might have been drawn with a carpenter's square onto a plank then cut out with a jigsaw and glued to his skull. Greying blond hair. A blush of veins beneath his eyes. A scar shaped like an open bird's beak on his right cheek. A front molar dangled by a bloody thread from his gums. He said up at Spinks, "Do you even know what you're doing?"

A slightly high-pitched voice with an accent Spinks made if not from the immediate region from somewhere in the vicinity of it. Hearing it from a man he'd half come to believe was a demon from hell chasing him added to Spinks' anger. As did the question the tall man had asked him. Spinks answered the man by slapping him hard several more times. The man winced and spit blood and after catching his breath said, "You can't be stupid enough to think you'll get away with killing me."

Spinks wrapped his right hand around the man's throat and said, "You'll never know if I got away with it if you're dead."

"Good Christ," said the man Spinks taking from his haunted tone he'd seen in Spinks' eyes his own imminent death. Then he realized the man wasn't looking into his eyes. He was looking over Spinks' left shoulder. Spinks wheeled around and saw stumbling out of the darkness at the boulder's edge a man with a hatchet embedded in the center of his forehead through a pair of night vision goggles. Blood and brain matter—though not as much of either as Spinks would have thought in the circumstances—was dripping from the end of the hatchet handle that extended straight up and down over the man's face like a clock hand on the six and twelve. Spinks' first thought was how in the dark from his knees had he brought off such a throw. His next thought was how was the man alive and walking. "Carl?" Spinks heard the man beneath him say.

The man with the hatchet in his forehead looked to be trying to say something back to him but the only sound that came out of his mouth suggested a muzzled dog trying hard to bark. Teetering like a man just stepping from a roller coaster he put a hand out in front of him as if feeling for a solid object to support himself against. He took one more halting step then fell face forward hitting the rock-strewn ground with the sound an axe makes splitting a log telling Spinks the hatchet blade was no longer even a fraction of an inch outside his head and that the man would not be getting up again.

"You've killed Carl."

Spinks moved his eyes back to the tall man. The molar

Spinks had loosened dropped out of the man's gums into his mouth as he said to Spinks, "You just sunk from your knees in shit all the way up to your neck in it."

# 12

Spinks opened his eyes in full night to the sound of a far-off train whistle.

Then he realized the sound wasn't so far off. And it wasn't a train whistle.

It was moaning. Coming from the hole beneath him.

Only there was no hole. Only blackness when he looked down.

As if the earth had devoured Callender, leaving behind only his moans trapped in its core like the pained cries of a spirit embedded there. "You all right, Callender?" Spinks called into the blackness at his feet.

"I can't get my dick out!" Callender's tortured voice floated out of the earth like a trail of verbal smoke from a doused fire.

Spinks from his secure perch above ground shouted what he perceived to be the obvious solution to what he perceived to be the issue, "Just piss in your pants. Fuck sake! You'll wash your uniform later!"

"It felt like more than piss coming out when I tried to! I'm scared of what I can't see, Spinks! It felt like my insides were coming out through my dick!"

Spinks reviewing his limited medical knowledge hollered into the shaft, "Was it blood coming out you think? Are you pissing blood?"

"Something smells like the guts of a butchered hog!"

Spinks couldn't think of a single thing more to say back to Callender, Callender's moans emphasizing to Spinks how over-matched he was by the opponent he was up against. After a lull, Callender's voice again, pained and weak though a modicum less strident, "Drop me down your canteen, Spinks. I can't get at mine under my ass where I fell on it."

Spinks hesitated, then shouted into the well, "I'm not sure it's a good idea. You drinking water."

"You'd sooner I die of thirst?" Callender called up to him.

"If you're bleeding inside I'm saying. It could make things worse."

Callender went silent. Spinks fearing he'd passed out, inclined an ear at the hole and heard a series of weak, skipping inhales, each one like a scratched seventy-eight record bouncing on a turntable, followed by an exhale an embittered old man might make reflecting on one more bad memory near the end of a lifetime of too many bad memories. Spinks thought a drink of water, what harm could it do. He took out his flashlight and shined it into the shaft the beam sketchily drawing Callender as an impressionist artist's view of a turtle sitting on a rock at a murky pond's bottom. Spinks held his canteen over the hole. "It's here in my hand—the canteen," he hollered into the hole. "Can you see it?"

Callender called up to him, "I can't see near anything that light in my eyes. Just drop it—I got one hand to catch it with."

"What about the other one?"

"Snapped—like both my legs I'd bet money on it. I ain't but a bag a broken twigs soaking in my own bloody piss and shit, Spinks."

"It's just bones broken, Bobo. Bones heal."

"Don't do that!" hollered Callender.

"Do what?"

"Call me Bobo when you ain't before! Call me my first name makes me believe you think I'm going to die! You think I'm going to die, Spinks?"

"You're going to get sent home, Callender, then make out to your Five Course Meal By Candlelight you got wounded saving a platoon of soldiers instead of by stepping like a damn fool into a hole."

"Her name's Amy," said Callender. "Amy Hopgood. From Holly, South Carolina. Same as my two boys."

Spinks said, "I don't need to know that, Callender."

"Just in case—I'd like you to," said Callender. "And you already know my boys' names."

Spinks said, "Put your hand up in front of your face. I'm going to drop this canteen. It hits you in the head it's heavy enough to kill you and get me charged with murder."

"Let her go," said Callender.

Spinks with an uncertain feeling opened his hand and watched his canteen plummet down the shaft toward the human shape at its bottom.

# 13

Spinks picked up the pistol the tall man had hoped to kill him with. A Glock Model .380. He pointed it down at the man and told him to stand.

The tall man, with the aid of his hands, slowly got to his feet. Spinks made him to be six-feet-six inches tall if he was an inch. Late forties, maybe fifty, he was dressed all in black—black jersey, black khakis, black belt and holster, black combat boots. His nose was clearly broken, lower lip busted and swollen to twice the size of the upper one, both cheeks puffy and red from Spinks' pummeling of them. He put his right thumb and forefinger into his mouth and, wincing, pulled out a second loose molar and dropped it in his shirt pocket. He lifted his shirttail up in both his hands and wiped blood from his face with it.

He dropped his shirttail. He looked at Spinks.

Spinks said, "You're going to answer some questions, you son of a bitch."

The tall man said, "All right I reach in my shirt pocket first?"

Spinks struck by the odd thought the man intended to pull his molar back out of the pocket in the hope of reinserting it in his gums said, "What for?"

The man said, "I'll maybe save you asking some your questions."

Spinks nodded and the tall man stuck two fingers in his shirt pocket and brought them out of it holding a shiny object several times bigger than a tooth. He held it out at Spinks.

Spinks felt his stomach drop.

The man said, "The one Carl was carrying looks just like this one, except his has the word deputy in front of the word sheriff."

A shiver that felt like he was being shaken by a giant hand went through Spinks. He looked around for the giant it belonged to and saw only the skeletal outlines of the trees haunting the darkness. He couldn't get his mind to stop on any one thought. A few hours ago he'd been driving down the hollow road contemplating whether to have a late dinner at home or eat in town. He took the badge from the tall man's hand and peered at it. It looked as legitimate as any of the few cops badges he'd seen. He looked back to the tall man, gingerly poking with his right index finger at the holes in his gums left by his missing molars. Spinks said, "He would have killed me."

The tall man said, "Who would have killed you?"

"The guy lying dead over there would have!"

The tall man, grimacing, took his fingers from his mouth. "How would he have done that?"

"He tried to shoot me!"

"I didn't hear a shot."

"I'd waited for him to pull the goddamn trigger you'd have heard it! He'd be standing here instead of me!"

The tall man spit and came up short. The bloody globule dangled from the end of his chin like fish bait. He said, "You snuck up on two police officers in the dark. That fact trumps anything that came after it."

Spinks wondered if a trembling in the flesh just below the man's right eye resulted from fear or nervousness or one of Spinks' punches or was a tell of some kind Spinks ought to be picking up on. "She's scared shitless of you!"

"Who's scared of me?"

"The girl down in that cabin!"

The man made a minute shake of his head. "I've never met her."

"She says you and your partner are demons."

"Demons?"

Spinks ran a hand back through his hair. "Why would she say that?"

"You're the one running from the law with her. You tell me."

"What did you do to her that made her so afraid she can't remember who she is!"

"What did we do to her? You sure that's how you want to play this?"

"You won't think I'm fucking playing I put a bullet in your head! You saw what happened up on that road—she jumped half out her mind into my truck when she saw you two and crashed it."

"What I saw up on that road was you drag a half-naked girl into your truck and speed off like a bat out of hell with no regard for the lives of Carl and me or that girl."

Spinks tried to recall what line of rational thinking had led him to here but his memory was like the scenery past a window in a speeding car he was looking out of. He could see only a jumbled blur of images and faces. Even the girl's face, like a picture in a kaleidoscope, in his mind's eye kept changing—her expression going from pained to shrewd, from innocent to conniving, from desperate to cunning.

# 14

He tugged with one hand at the corpse's shoulder, but couldn't get it to roll over. He added his other hand to the first one and pulled the body onto its back and looked down at a pulpy red mess around the hatchet blade severing the man's night vision goggles and his skull beneath them. Spinks had seen sights as bad in Afghanistan but not ones he'd personally made that way. The people he'd killed until now he'd only seen dead in dreams about them well after he'd killed them. He turned away from the corpse gasping for air.

"Carl had a wife and two kids."

Spinks looked over at the tall man—County Sheriff Grey Poncet if the badge he'd showed Spinks was a legitimate county sheriff's badge and belonged to him—sitting shackled in his own handcuffs against a boulder facing Spinks, and said, "I don't want to hear another word out of your mouth about this man. He's dead for trying to kill me. You don't want to be laying here next to him try talking him up some more to me."

He turned back to the dead man.

Blood and brains were pooled around his head like an intricately patterned doily beneath a serving dish.

He'd been a thick, heavily muscled man—a dedicated weight lifter guessed Spinks—a half-foot shorter and generation younger than Poncet.

Like Poncet he was dressed in black from head to toe.

A gold wedding ring on the fourth finger of his left hand.

"In his back pocket," said Poncet.

Spinks, averting his eyes from the mess at the top of the corpse's neck, reached into the dead man's back pocket.

He pulled out a badge.

He held it up to his eyes:

*Carl P. Ames.*
*Devon County Deputy Sheriff*

A string of numbers beneath the words. Spinks put the badge in his front pocket. His hand was shaking and there was blood on it. His legs felt like jelly and his mind like something made of eggshells being rolled over a rocky road.

People lie.

The girl had told him so way back on the banks of the stream Spinks had saved her from drowning in. Even then Spinks had wondered if she'd been subconsciously warning him. Wondered if those two words she'd spoken shortly after opening her eyes at Spinks had been less an accusation aimed at other people for lying to her than they were a confession by a part of her she wasn't entirely in touch with that she'd lied to Spinks.

"The train hasn't left the station yet, son. Listen to me now."

Spinks turned the flashlight beam onto Poncet, his cuffed hands held out at Spinks as if they held a gift for him. "You say you're a good citizen who stumbled into a bad situation—it's a good story and one we can work with. It's a story, son, from what Carl and I saw up on that road that won't be hard to sell. Not especially it won't be with what's bound to come out about that girl."

"What's bound to come out about her? Hell's that mean?"

"You know or you don't know, son. But you for sure know Carl and me weren't on that road looking for random kidnappers."

The thought occurred to Spinks with one jerk of his trigger finger he could, for the time being at least, stop having to wonder if his best instincts had taken him on a road straight to hell. "My father's been dead more than ten years."

"What's that, son?"

Spinks raised the Glock at Poncet's face. "And you don't

look a goddamn thing like he did. Call me son again it'll be the last time you call me anything."

Poncet turned his head to one side and spit more blood. He looked back at Spinks through a macabre mask revealing nothing of the man beneath it. "All right I call you Jack then?"

Spinks feeling as if Poncet without laying a hand on him had thrown him hard up against a tree and strip-searched him said, "You got three seconds to tell me where you came up with that name."

"It's your truck in the stream back there isn't it?"

Spinks was hit with a sinking feeling.

"And your wallet in it?"

Poncet studied on Spinks as if he were rolling something over in his mind.

"And your .308 loaded for bear in the gun rack? And your fish-scaling knife and Colt Defender in the glove box and marijuana stash larger than I'd expect a casual user to have beneath the driver's seat? And your spool of duct tape Carl and me were real curious about your intentions for after what we'd just seen out of you?"

The thought struck Spinks that whatever decision he made from here would be wrong in at least one way if not most ways. He only hoped it would be right in enough ways to keep him for the foreseeable future alive and out of jail. "We'll see," he said.

"We'll see? What will we see?"

"What the girl says seeing you."

"With what you've put that girl through? She's bound to say anything."

"I tried to save her is all I did."

"Save her? Save her from what exactly?"

"I know fear when I see it goddamn it! It's all over that girl!"

"It's some fearful straits she's in being run through the woods at night by a strange man grabs her off the road."

"She jumped in my truck!"

"Like I said, Jack, that's a story we can work with."

"It's no story, goddammit! She was running from something!"

Poncet gave him a long look. "Demons?"

Spinks feeling himself moving farther and farther away from his life of the last thirty-seven years made no reply.

"Maybe she's off her rocker, Jack. Or maybe she's a calculating she-wolf who's played you same as she has many before you. That's someone else's call. I'm just a civil servant was trying to do my job."

Spinks mind did a flip-flop. "What were you two doing on that road to begin with?"

"Police work."

Spinks in a flash realized how unqualified he was and always had been at interpreting motives or character from words or actions.

"What sort of police work?"

"Investigative police work."

Spinks pictured his thoughts as fish in a muddy pond swimming in blind circles. He stepped closer to Poncet and shined the flashlight in his face. His features had a waxy appearance and in the light looked even more as if they'd been designed with a carpenter's square and pencil than they had in the dark. His eyes were pale blue flecked with grey and his pupils statically translucent. Instead of shying away from the light they gave Spinks the impression they were looking right through it and seeing into Spinks' soul and he thought of the girl saying of the demons she said were chasing her "they can see in the dark."

# 15

Spinks, reacting to an eruption of gunfire around him in the Afghan mountains, had fired his carbine at two people he'd barely glimpsed before he'd seen them go down behind some bushes and hotfooted with his team away from the area. Months later his lieutenant had announced to the entire platoon Spinks was being given a commendation for, unbeknown to Spinks until then, killing with his instinctive flurry of shots a man and woman "suspected" by intelligence operatives to be Taliban insurgents. The suspected insurgents later introduced themselves to Spinks in his dreams as gender non-specific Afghan faces smiling warmly in heads atop bullet-riddled bodies Spinks' recognized as belonging to past and present members of his family.

Spinks pulled the hatchet from Carl's head.

Carl's head came apart like a squash severed by a large kitchen knife.

Spinks extracted from Carl's brain a large piece of the night vision goggles the hatchet blade had driven into it.

He tossed it, with the rest of the goggles, into the bushes.

He took off Carl's shirt, wrapped it tightly around the halved head and secured the shirt with a clove hitch knot hoping the head would stay together.

He took a Glock Model .380 from Carl's belt and shoved it in his pants waist next to Poncet's Glock.

He told Poncet to squat down by Carl.

"What now, Jack?"

"I'll lift him onto your back."

"Lift Carl onto my back?"

"You're going to carry him down to the cabin."

"There's one road you can take from here to save yourself, Jack—just one. This isn't it."

"I got on the road I'm on, wherever it leads to, out on Black Cat Hollow Road and it's too late to get off it now."

"That's not true, Jack. But you need to listen to me before it is too late."

"We leave him here about six kinds of animals will be fighting over him. Everything but his bones will be gone by morning. Now get on your knees."

"Carl was a bodybuilder. He weighed over two hundred pounds. Two-twenty-five maybe. How about you carry him?"

"He was your friend. I didn't even know him."

Poncet said, "I'm over fifty years old, Jack, and have a leaky heart valve."

Spinks looked at the corpse again and back at Poncet and said, "I can't carry him and watch you both."

"You'll maybe have two dead cops on your hands you make me carry him."

"You can carry him or drag him and likely leave pieces of his head all the way down this hill. Or we'll leave him here."

Poncet said, "We'll leave him then. It's of no matter to Carl what happens to him now." He started walking down the hill. "The last thing that mattered to Carl was you putting a hatchet in his head."

# 16

"What would I find out about Jack Spinks I asked around?"

Poncet, walking in front of Spinks with his cuffed hands at his waist and head inclined, suggested a contemplating priest as portrayed in an old black and white movie or a man searching the side of the hill they were descending for something he'd lost earlier. He cast not a ghost of a shadow on the ground. Had to be the angle of the moon surmised Spinks supposing that when daylight arrived it would expose a whole host of things he hadn't seen clearly in the dark.

"Ask around where?"

"Criminal data bases, state mental hospitals, drunk tanks. I've got connections everywhere in this state. What part of it you from?"

"Chatham County."

"Chatman County. Must be pretty slow in Chatham County you were up this hell and gone hollow on a Saturday night."

A coyote was baying somewhere. Closer to them an owl intermittently hooted. Branches swayed in the trees overhead more than the slight breeze rustling the underbrush suggested to Spinks they ought to be.

"I was on a business call."

"Selling weed up in here or did you have someone particular in mind to use that duct tape on?"

"Selling insurance."

"Insurance?"

"Homeowner's insurance. People I was selling it to are farmers. Saturday night after dinner's when they have time to see me."

Poncet raised his eyes at a caliginous body winging silently as a thrown object through the night, Spinks thinking what kind of cop leaves his partner's corpse to be devoured by animals. And why hadn't the two of them called out and identified themselves as cops approaching his truck up on the hollow road?

"You don't strike me as the type fella that'd be enough for." Poncet glanced back at Spinks. Two dull lights in a black backdrop all Spinks could see of his face. "Selling insurance."

Spinks said, "Then again you don't know the first goddamn thing about me."

"I'm pretty sure of one thing, Jack. Carl wasn't your first body. Killing him came way too easy to you."

Spinks saw Poncet raise his cuffed hands to his face. He supposed to dab at his busted lip or nose and the thought struck Spinks that shooting him wouldn't make Spinks more of a cop killer than he was now.

"I'm casting a wide net trying to figure what puts you with that girl, Jack."

"I was trying to help someone looked like she needed it. I know what fear looks like and it was all over that girl's face she saw you two."

"Did you look past her face and into her soul, Jack?"

"Did I what?"

"Did you look into the girl's soul?" Poncet dropped his cuffed hands back down below his waist. "Anybody as scared of the law as you say she was must have a reason for it."

Spinks felt his heart turn over.

"She tell you where she was coming from, Jack? Or why two police officers doing their job would scare her into driving your truck off a bank into a stream how you say she did?"

Five hours, four at least, thought Spinks before dawn would cast some light on this dark world he'd wandered into. Unless it was all a dream and everyone in it including Poncet, and most especially the nameless girl Spinks had put his life on the line for, would disappear when he opened his eyes.

"God's truth, Jack, if what you're telling me is true the only demon in these woods tonight is down in that cabin and you're leading me straight to her."

Spinks felt a chill go through him. He tried to summon his memory of the lost, mixed-up girl with a resemblance to his dead daughter he'd stopped on that road to help and in his mind's eye saw only a mature woman with pure black eyes he could no more penetrate than, he'd learned too late, he'd been able to penetrate Rebecca's eyes—

Spinks lunged forward grabbing Poncet by an arm.

He dropped to his knees, yanking Poncet down next to him.

Poncet half-cried out in surprise as much as pain.

"Shut up!" hissed Spinks.

Spinks with a sense of dread pointed to the woods several yards past the cabin. "In the trees. You see it?"

An upright shape in the moonlight moving away from the cabin.

And several yards past it, another. And another.

"Appears you may not be alone in being drawn to that young woman, Jack."

In the scarce light Poncet's badly disfigured mouth opening in his wrecked face suggested to Spinks a dynamited entrance to a mine cave-in.

"Must be something about her has more than one person ready to traipse through the woods in the middle of the night for her."

A formless sense of dread came over Spinks. He'd believed the situation he was in couldn't get any worse. Now the reality struck him—there were no boundaries to how bad it could get.

"Either your interaction with that young woman was exactly what it appeared to Carl and me to be, Jack, in which case you as well can put a bullet in my head right now for all I can do to help you." Spinks looked from where the figures had disappeared into the trees back to Poncet, dangling from one side of his mouth a string of blood-laced saliva. "Or you're the innocent dupe you claim to be and there's no one but me can possibly help you where you're at now."

# 17

Spinks woke with a start having no idea where he was. He stood up in blackness so complete he couldn't see his hand in front of his face. He took a step forward and started to take another one when out of the ground a voice spoke.

Spinks froze in mid-stride. Then he started teetering.

An image of the dark abyss his right foot was poised directly above—the very image he'd always had of the entrance to the afterlife whatever it was to be—blotted out every other emotion, thought and dream in his mind.

Fear alone of the situation he was in nearly caused him to lose his balance. He recalled in the span of a heartbeat standing next to Rebecca at the top of a high overlook—he couldn't recall where or when—and being struck with an irrational urge to jump. Irrational because Spinks was happy and in love and hadn't yet signed up with the Marines and been sent to fight in a war. He'd looked over at Rebecca and the inward look on her face told him that she had no idea. That she was as alone in her head as he was in his and as each person alive was in theirs. It made him feel better—for Rebecca, for himself, for their future—knowing that even as they would be living happily together each of them would be living obliviously alone.

"Spinks! God's sake where you at?"

Merited or not Spinks would come to credit Bobo Callender's panicked shout out to him for kick-starting his survival instinct. Leaning away from the abyss he carefully moved his foot back and placed it solidly on the ground and, his heart racing, collapsed sitting again onto the limb he'd stood up from, firmly discarding from that moment onward the theory of human destiny for a belief that a life's course is as random as the first step a person takes waking up disoriented in the dark.

"I'm here, Callender!" he shouted.

"Was worried you'd run off on me!" Callender's fear-tinged voice told Spinks the death he had been imagining those couple of seconds he'd been hovering on the lip of the abyss Callender had been imagining every second since he'd plummeted into it.

"Guess I dozed off. Sorry!"

"Got blacker down here than hell's rumored to be while you were out. What's the sky like?"

Spinks looked up at a dense-black roiling canopy blotting out the moon and stars. A shiver went through him. Hoping to keep Callender from worrying over what neither of them had a prayer or hope of stopping he hollered down the shaft, "A few clouds rolled in over the moon."

"They must be damn thick clouds!"

"Not so thick." Then, "I'd make them average thick."

Callender made no reply. Spinks imagined he could hear labored breathing floating up through the shaft but guessed it was just an auditory mirage. "Can I get you anything, Callender?"

"Can you what?"

Spinks, realizing how impractical and pointless his last question had been, hollered a new one to Callender, "You holding up all right?"

"I'm wedged in a black hole so tight I can't scratch my balls. How do you think I'm holding up?"

Spinks hesitated, searching for words that would be at once encouraging and not sound asinine in the circumstances. "Relatively speaking I meant."

"Relative to what?"

"To, you know—a while ago."

More silence from the hole.

"Callender?"

Still more silence. Spinks imagined Callender working up his strength to resume their conversation. Then he heard from the well, "Thank you, Spinks."

They were the same words Spinks realized now he'd heard

from the well as he'd been teetering precariously over it a minute earlier. "For what?" he called into the darkness.

"You could have ordered Barlow or Dombrowski to stay here with me—it was your call to make. But you chose to be the one. That says plenty to me."

Spinks wasn't sure why he had decided to stay with Callender beyond that, as the team's commanding officer, he'd reasoned the responsibility fell to him. "Rank has its privileges, Callender. No way I was about to hump all the way back to that village."

"We're good buds. Aren't we, Spinks?"

Spinks had he told the truth would have said he and Callender were at best casual friends and only that by virtue of their serving together in the same unit, but he couldn't bring himself to tell the truth. "Sure we are," he hollered having the odd feeling the night instantly transformed his lie into a more important truth.

"Shouldn't make light of a good friendship, Spinks. It's too rare of a thing in this world."

"Okay," said Spinks.

"Like the love of a good woman. We know that too don't we, Spinks, with our two boss angels waiting back at home for us?"

Spinks thinking of his last email from Rebecca made no reply.

"You're not feeling the love from your boss angel, Spinks?"

Spinks, not feeling the love from Rebecca despite her professing to him it was undying, gazed off at the roiling clouds and tried not to think about what was coming. Callender called up to him, "If you can't tell your good bud who can you tell?"

In the pitch dark like that Spinks suddenly had the sensation Callender's voice was just another pitch of his own voice and that the entire conversation was taking place in his head. "She says she's fucking another man," he hollered into the well. "She hopes I'll understand and will fuck somebody too if I feel like it."

"She wrote you that?"

"In an email."

"Man, that's cold. Unless you all signed on at the start for an open marriage type deal. Did you?"

"We didn't sign on for any deals but the usual ones—to love each other in sickness and health, like that."

"Jesus, I'm sorry, Spinks. That just sucks."

"Yeah," said Spinks. He pictured the cat-like creature that had walked out of the trees earlier to stare at him. Suddenly he had the feeling that from the cover of the trees, now stirring in a stiffening wind, it was staring at him still. He called down to Callender, trying to keep the worry from his voice, "Looks like we might get some rain."

Callender said nothing. Spinks pictured him down there scared shitless and hurting like a son of a bitch thinking if only he'd been walking three feet to the right or three feet to the left four hours earlier. Then he heard from the well, "What are you going to do about it?"

Spinks couldn't think of a good answer for Callender so hollered into the hole, "The worst-looking storms oftentimes just blow over. Or piss a little dribble and move on."

"The rain will be what it will be, Spinks—a drizzle or a hurricane. You can't do a thing about the rain. What kind of a moron would expect you to stop the rain."

Spinks said, "I could cut some pine boughs, lay them over top the hole."

Callender said, "And a few minutes later drenched pine boughs plus whatever's drenching them will be raining down on me. How much of a good bud would I be asking you to try to change God's plan for me?"

Spinks thought, okay, here's Callender trying to keep positive and his mind off things he can't change and asking his good bud for help at it. He said into the ground, "I've got a feeling it's not true."

"You've got a feeling it's not true your boss angel is fucking another man? Even though she told you she is?"

Spinks only nodded but Callender must have sensed that he had and what was in his mind too. "And you see that as a bad thing?"

"It's killing me more than if I thought it was true. I'm all messed up over it, Callender."

"Why would she tell you she was fucking another man if she wasn't?"

"She knows I won't believe it is why—and behind her lie is a truth even worse than the lie, something maybe she's only half aware of herself."

"Like she wants a divorce you mean?"

"No. Not that."

"What then?"

Spinks looked up at the swirling, entwined clouds and thought of the two huge bull elephant seals he and Rebecca on their honeymoon on a northern California beach had watched locked in a violent death match over a female and Rebecca with a far off look on her face saying at the bleeding and mauled animals as if Spinks weren't there, "None of it makes any sense."

"A premonition maybe. She feels something awful coming and can't quite see what it is—or is afraid to—but needs me to know how bad she's hurting from feeling it and this is the only way she knows how to get the message to me. What is the message, Callender—that's what's killing me!?"

A flash of lightning lit up the night and for a moment Spinks saw way down in the ground Callender's face turned up to the sky like a kneeling supplicant's face to a statue of Jesus, his mouth wide open in mid-reply to Spinks but whatever his reply was a crash of thunder deafened Spinks to it.

Suddenly Spinks had never felt so powerless to effect in any way another human life. The future appeared to him as a giant wave cresting to break. He yelled down to Callender, "It'll be all right, Bobo! We'll ride this out together! You and me, good bud!"

In a brief silence before the next thunderclap came he heard Callender say, "It's the thing a person least expects they say will always do him in, Spinks—!"

Then the sky opened up.

# 18

Spinks stood behind a pine tree watching over Poncet's shoulder the cabin's half-open doorway spilling light into the night. He recalled with an anxious feeling the woman telling him the door didn't lock from inside, that until Spinks had come along there'd been nothing she'd felt a need to lock it against.

And the three figures he'd seen walking away from the cabin.

The structure as placid appearing and quiet as the sky above it.

Spinks pushed Poncet out from behind the tree and stepped out after him.

Holding Poncet's Glock in one hand down by his right leg he walked shielded by the tall man to the doorway.

A familiar fluttering sound came from beyond it.

Spinks whispered at Poncet's back, "Go on."

Poncet hissed, "Now wait just a—!"

Spinks pushed Poncet through the doorway and followed him in, scanning the room with the Glock.

The crow named Midnight cawed and loudly flapped its wings from above the fireplace startling the hell out of them.

"Get these goddamn cuffs off me!" hissed Poncet.

"Shut the fuck up," whispered Spinks.

A dull kerosene lamp burned from a stand on the wall by the couch.

The bedroom door was open, its latch hanging by a splinter. A thin trail of blood droplets led from the doorway across the main room, to the front door.

Spinks with a sinking feeling motioned Poncet with the Glock to walk in front of him into the room.

The woman the girl called The Bear was sitting on the floor

against the far wall in a pool of blood yet widening from blood trickling from a deep ear-to-ear gash in her throat and gaping dent in the back of her head exposing her brain. A bloodied ten-pound plate from her weight set lay on the floor near her. A bloodied shard of mirror glass by her right hand. Slash marks marred her face. Her mouth was agape, her arms out to her sides and eyes wide open suggesting her last view of life, or her initial view of what was to come after it, had been at once puzzling and horrifying to her. Spinks was certain if her corpse could talk it would curse him to hell for having brought evil and death into a place where the woman came to escape such things through quiet contemplation, weightlifting and reading her poetry aloud to the woods. He heard a clattering sound and looked up at Poncet picking up from the floor littered with the woman's books, broken pieces of the smashed bureau mirror, barbell, tipped over weight bench, her nephew's 30-06.

"You ready to let me help you now, Jack?"

Spinks wondered if Poncet's handcuffed hands hadn't prevented him from straightening and aiming the 30-06 Spinks would be sitting with a bullet in his head next to the woman. Then he remembered the 30-06 wasn't loaded and was struck with the unsettling feeling Poncet knew it wasn't.

"It's less likely by the second I'll be able to, deep as you've put yourself into this mess."

Poncet lowering his hands dangled the 30-06 crosswise in front of his thighs.

"This poor woman's only mistake was letting that young woman on your say so into her cabin. By my count that's two bodies on your head, Jack."

Spinks for at least the third time that night had an urge to shoot Poncet in the hope doing so would wipe away the last several hours of his life and put him back driving down the Hollow Road in the Durango. "What have they done with the girl?"

"What has who done with her?"

"Who do you think!? The people who did this."

"You think you know who did this?"

"Goddamn right I do. We saw them walking away from here not five minutes ago!"

"We saw three people walking away from here is what we saw."

"Hell are you saying?"

"What this scene tells me, Jack, is this poor woman was clubbed from behind with a ten-pound weight then lying half dead on the floor was carved on for a while before her throat was sliced. My experience investigating vicious crimes tells me a hundred-ten-pound young woman could have accomplished that as easily as one, two or three grown men could have."

Spinks shook his head against an image of himself in the crosshairs of a rifle his own finger was pulling the trigger of.

"Especially a young woman out of her mind how you said she was."

"I said she was scared out of her mind, not that she was out of her mind," Spinks recalling with a tormented feeling the woman staring petrified at the stuffed animal the girl had ripped to shreds with a letter opener and how surprisingly strong the girl was fighting with Spinks in the Durango before she'd wrested control of it from him and nearly killed them both.

"She's for sure out of touch with reality how you described her. Not to mention paranoid."

Spinks looked at Poncet.

"Demons, Jack?"

"I'm not sure what she meant by demons. I'm not sure she was! I only know she was afraid of something— and not thinking right."

Poncet nodded like Spinks had just confirmed his take on the girl, on the woman's death, on the whole shitstorm Spinks had, depending on one's viewpoint, stumbled or charged headlong with his eyes wide open into.

"She kills a woman trying to help her! Why?"

"You didn't know her you told me, Jack."

"I don't know her. I never laid eyes on her before a few hours ago!"

Poncet with his manacled hands pulled back the 30-06's bolt. Finding the rifle empty he showed no reaction. "Then you might as well be screaming at the sky to get you out of this mess you're in as asking why she'd do anything."

He tossed the 30-06 on the bed, Spinks picturing the big woman vainly trying to intimidate with the empty rifle the killers who'd invaded her cabin. Poncet nodded at the bed. "Grab that sheet, lay it over her. Look on her face says she's seen all she wants to of the people she left behind in this world."

Spinks pulled the sheet from the bed and dropped it over the big woman's face and imagined her eyes burning holes through the fabric at him, judging him, accusing him. He moved his eyes up to the wall of photographs of local homes and places, some which he recognized from the roads around—an abandoned three-story farmhouse, a renovated rural schoolhouse, a water tower, a falling down church—recalling the girl with her thousand-mile stare peering at it. Or at one place in particular pictured on it?

"Where were you in the shit, before you were in the shit you're in now, Jack?"

Poncet was holding his cuffed hands out at Spinks in the way of a priest offering the chalice to a kneeling communicant, the tall man's eyes, at once blank as polished stones and seemingly all prescient, telling Spinks nothing about the workings in the mechanism behind them.

"A soldier who's been in the shit can always recognize one like him. Afghanistan was it?"

Spinks not replying, endeavored to show Poncet as little of himself as Poncet was showing of himself to Spinks, but Poncet off some tiny tell he'd detected in Spinks' manner or from his own intuition nodded and said, "I made you ex-military way you snuck up on Carl and me. You didn't learn that selling insurance to farmers."

Spinks said, "Another thing I learned fighting people who looked and sounded just like the people I was fighting them with is to count on more than my eyes and ears to tell the ones on my side from the ones on the other side."

"You've got a sixth sense about people do you, Jack?"

"Comes to knowing what's inside anybody it's all any of us got."

"Your sixth sense what told you up on the hollow road that half-naked young woman was a lost, mixed-up waif nobody would give a shit about if you grabbed and dragged her off into the woods?"

Spinks restraining himself from walking over and busting Poncet in the mouth more said, "Which is it then? I'm a crazed kidnapper and that girl is my victim? Or the girl's a crazed killer and I'm a dumbass dupe taken in by her? You can't seem to make up your mind on that."

"I don't see how either of those things being true excludes the other one from being just as true, Jack. From what I've witnessed so far this evening you might be both a crazed kidnapper and a dumbass dupe."

"Or maybe I'm neither. And that girl is in real trouble that has nothing to do with me."

"You got a wife and kids you've risked leaving without a husband and father jumping into that girl's world?"

"It'll only be my life I fuck up trying to do the right thing," said Spinks, plagued by a recurring vision of a giant hand reaching out of the earth and pulling Rebecca and Iris down into the hell that had consumed Bobo Callender.

"The right thing? Jack Spinks against the whole world but for one girl in it you see walking half-naked down the road? That what you mean by the right thing?"

"She acted to need help. Trying to give it to her felt like the right thing."

"A motive, not an after the fact bullshit excuse, I'm digging for, Jack. Putting your life on the line. Killing a cop. Kidnapping another one. Obstructing a criminal investigation. Nobody goes to those lengths for a girl they don't know the first goddamn thing about out of just a want to do the right thing."

"She was staring at something here like she was in a trance."

Poncet followed Spinks' eyes back to the wall of photographs. What was it the girl had said? People dying sound like children crying?

Poncet walked to the wall.

Spinks walked up behind him.

He followed Poncet's eyes—then Poncet's pointer finger—to one of the photographs.

Spinks reached up and took the photograph from the wall and stared at it.

Poncet watched him staring at it.

"Comes to police work I've learned there are no coincidences, Jack."

Poncet's monstrous face—two front teeth gone, lips split and grotesquely blown up, smashed nose crusted with blood and oozing more of it, black-and-blue eye—recalled to Spinks with a shudder how, against his best efforts to keep a tap on it, the anger he kept bottled up inside on occasion erupted in ways that more often than not led to bad outcomes for whoever it erupted on.

"That where you first met her?"

Spinks felt his stomach turn over.

"Met who where? What are you talking about?"

"The girl. At the house in that photograph."

"I told you, I never laid eyes on her before tonight!"

Poncet as if he hadn't heard him said, "The situation is fluid between the two of us at this moment, Jack. The crowd gets bigger, terms of law enforcement especially, I'm afraid it'll harden around you in ways I can't undo."

Spinks looked back down at the photograph.

A renovated farmhouse, more upscale than most houses on the hollow. A barn transformed into a guesthouse over a large garage. Out back, a pond floating a rowboat tied up to a small dock. A bamboo thicket with a path hacked through it. A mowed strip of field that served as a shooting range.

A stand of blue spruce out front through which the photograph must have been taken. And an overall queasy feeling in Spinks' stomach.

"Put us on the same page, Jack."

Spinks looked up at Poncet.

"You might find your future's not so dark as it looks to you now."

Poncet's non-reflective eyes on him gave Spinks the uncomfortable sensation that, more than just seeing into him, they were divulging skeletons hidden even to Spinks in the dark closets of his unconscious.

"Play your cards right"—Poncet's cuffed hands, mimicking a card shuffling motion in the air, made a jangling sound—"you can walk away from this. Maybe even to a better place than the one you started the evening out at."

Spinks said, "How would I do that? That last part I mean?"

"You tell me what you need, Jack. All options are on the table."

"You're sounding less and less like a cop and more and more like a car dealer trying to sell me a shitty undercoating job."

"I'm a cop who watched his partner get his head split open with a hatchet. We're not so far apart on caring first about staying alive, Jack."

"Tell me what you know about that girl you're not telling me."

Poncet gave him a long look. "It's an odd stance we're in, Jack—you and me. A couple stray dogs running into each other in the woods sniffing each other's asses. After I watch you split my partner's head in half with a hatchet you tell me you're an insurance salesman with a heart of gold. And that's on top of you near running both Carl and me down while speeding away from us with a young lady we watched you drag half-naked off the road into your truck. Now here I am the highest law enforcement officer in the county locked up in my own cuffs with no idea why or what little thing might set you off into another hatchet-throwing rage. Our time together to now makes me skeptical of your account of things, Jack. And more than a little gun-shy of how far up my ass I should let your nose go."

"You'd be coyote feed with Carl up on that hill I was what you say I am."

"I'm not sure what you are, Jack. Only that your do-gooder heart of gold story doesn't fly. How about you fill me in—what is it makes Jack Strange tick?"

"Getting through a day alive. Putting one foot in front of the other."

"That's all of us to start, Jack. And it's never enough. I'm asking what you want out of life past being alive till you're not?"

Spinks since his family had disappeared into that abyss rarely thought about what he wanted. Only about what he'd had and would never have again and how he should have seen more clearly what was coming and done something to stop it.

"Money? Freedom not to have to work to get it?"

"Money to live on is enough for me and I'd trade the freedom I've got now in a heartbeat to have the responsibility for my wife and daughter back."

"You're sticking with the Jesus theme are you? Your only motive for carrying that girl off into these woods is you wanted to save her?"

"Wasn't anybody else around going to."

"Now we're coming to it, Jack. A lonely, guilt-ridden ex-soldier with little left to live for, reduced to peddling home insurance and weed to cow farmers on Saturday nights, driving high as a kite down the godforsaken road he peddles it on when in his headlights appears a pretty, half-naked girl looking as lonely as him—"

Spinks grabbed Poncet by an arm. "That had nothing to do with it!"

"What had nothing to do with it?"

"Her being half-naked and pretty. It's not why I stopped for her!"

"Maybe you believe it's not why you stopped for her, Jack."

"Hell's that supposed to mean?"

"The young woman give you a reason why she was wearing next to nothing when she stepped out in front of you on that road and instead of running away how a scared young woman might be expected to lets you pull up next to her?"

"I told you—nothing she said made a whole lot of sense."

"Scared out of her mind you said?"

"Damn right she was. The only thing certain about her was that. You'd know it too you were with her how I was."

"Here's what I do know, Jack—a young woman fitting the description of the young woman you pulled into your truck and helped to elude two police officers was seen not forty-eight hours ago and five miles from here running from a house fire the bodies of a husband, wife and their eight-year-old child were found in."

Spinks tried to catch his breath and couldn't. Claude Jenkins had told him about a house fire two nights ago on Pinecone Road. A summer place. Claude had heard people had died in the fire but wasn't sure how many and hadn't said to Spinks anything about a young woman seen running from it.

"I'm chancing my life you're the dupe you claim to be and don't know more than I do about the young woman and her involvement in the deaths of that family, who it's about certain were dead before the fire started, Jack."

Spinks feeling a chill in the warm night recalled the girl's crazed behavior and offer to fuck him—"in the ass even"—if he'd drive her away from the vehicle with orange running lights she must have known had two police officers searching for her in it. And her rambling on about smoke she couldn't see through—

"Do you believe they exist, Jack?"

"Do I believe what exists?"

"What the person you carried through these woods had you convinced me and Carl are."

Spinks squeezed Poncet's arm harder aiming to shut him up but Poncet, his face showing no sign of the pain his arm was absorbing, kept talking.

"Demons? Creatures from hell without consciences or feelings living in this world disguised as human beings?"

Spinks said, "They don't come from hell, the ones I believe in."

"Wherever they come from, Jack, the question is—can a normal human being recognize one when he comes across one? You know, out and about? Drinking a beer next to him at a bar? Shopping in the same store as him? Walking like a half-naked Eve in The Garden down the side of a hell and gone road he's driving on?"

If some people, as Spinks had heard, had a gift for reading faces Spinks wasn't one of them. He couldn't read a damn thing in Poncet's face. All he could see looking into it was evidence of his own violence as the tall man's bicep fluttered in his hand like a bird in quicksand beating its wings. "Those three shapes we saw heading into the trees away from a cabin got a woman with her head bashed in in it? What do you make them to be?"

His opaque eyes again blocking Spinks from glimpsing what was behind them Poncet said, "Three people let's call them. I'd say that's most likely."

Poncet pulled his arm free of Spinks' grip and gave it a shake like he was trying to get blood moving in it again. "There's only one person in this cabin could give us a better description than that of them and she's dead."

Spinks dropped his eyes like hung corpses cut from a tree to the woman's shrouded body wondering if he'd go down in local lore as the decorated Marine vet who, a few years after his wife's and daughter's tragic deaths, went off Rambo style on a battalion of police officers after he'd kidnapped a teenage murderess he'd fallen under the sway of. "She called her The Bear," he said.

Poncet followed Spinks' eyes to the woman's hummocky

shape resting beneath them like a life-sized sculpture waiting to be unveiled. "Easy to see why. And to conclude from it tonight wasn't the first time she'd been here."

"She'd spied at least once on the woman from behind a tree—watched her read her poetry to the birds and animals in the woods."

"The young woman told you that?"

"She told it to this woman with a cut throat."

"She tell her why she'd do a weird fucking thing like that?"

Spinks shook his head. "It felt magical to her watching her in secret. That'd be my guess. She said she walked here with someone—a him—she was supposed to always be with."

"Someone?"

"That knock on her head took most of her memory."

"Or her memory's fine and she was real good impersonating the girl you hoped for her to be."

Spinks recalling the girl, after he'd told her she was Iris's age, asking him in a barely audible whisper "How old?" The scant weight of her. The heat of her body. Her blind reliance on him to carry her through the woods to a safer place. He said in a reflective whisper, "In my arms she felt innocent as any kid."

"A man-eating tiger can make itself feel like a tame housecat it needs to."

Spinks looked back at Poncet. "She said the demons want her dead because she's alive."

"Sounds like the groundwork for an insanity defense to whatever crimes she ends up charged with."

"Maybe she saw something she wasn't supposed to see. Something the people who came in here and bashed this woman's head in want to make sure she never tells anyone she saw."

Poncet looking down at his cuffed hands said, "I'm just a cop, Jack, a not particularly smart or competent one. A cop who allowed a guy claiming to be an insurance salesman to disarm me and kill my chief deputy. I don't know every fucking thing there is to know. I'm about two light years out of my depth on this case." He looked back up at Spinks. "But here's what I do know—if you hope to ever again sell insurance or do any other goddamn thing in the free world past the end of tonight you'll get these fucking cuffs off me so I can get back to my job in which I promise you I aim to find out if there are in fact demons—human or otherwise—prowling these woods or just one evil and/or out of her mind young woman you've fallen in thrall with for reasons I'd be afraid to see deep enough into your psyche to find out about."

Spinks, as if speculating on an old friend's spiral into insanity, absently wondered which of several good intentioned missteps he'd made that evening had been most crucial in bringing him to a point where he was deciding if to leave locked up in a cabin in the woods or unshackle and keep a sharp eye on a county sheriff he'd beaten to a pulp and kidnapped after he'd killed his chief deputy with a hatchet. "Show me your hands."

Poncet held his hands out at Spinks.

Spinks got the handcuffs key out of his pocket and unlocked the cuffs. He stood back and watched Poncet take the cuffs off, snap them shut and attach them to his belt. He held his hand palm-side up out at Spinks. "The key?"

Spinks put the key in his pocket.

Poncet kept his hand out at him. "I get my gun back at least?"

Spinks didn't answer him.

"I'm going to need my weapon, Jack."

Spinks nodded down at Poncet's Glock in his belt. "I got it right here."

"I'm going to need it on me I mean."

Spinks walking for the door said, "I'd be a damn fool to arm a cop who believes I'm a kidnapper."

# 19

Poncet peering down in Spinks' flashlight beam at blood drops on the pine needle blanketed ground past the cabin doorway said, "This one won't make it far without a better tourniquet on."

He looked up at Spinks. "Who's your money on for the bleeder?"

Spinks raised the beam at the dark expanse of trees the blood trail led into. "Whichever one the sons a bitches the woman stabbed with that shard of mirror glass by her hand trying to keep them from taking the girl."

"Two kidnappers and the person they kidnapped is who we saw walking away from this cabin? That your theory?"

"Only way I make sense of it."

"Your theory doesn't pass the eye test."

"I don't even know what that means."

"They were separated by a good fifteen, twenty yards those three."

"So?"

"How's that make sense if one of them was a prisoner of the other two?"

Spinks tried to recall the alignment and size of the three human shapes he'd seen from up on the hill and couldn't. His memory wouldn't even recreate them as definitively human. It showed him three upright shapes was all. Shapes that could as well have been three upright black bears as three upright people. "Maybe she got away from them during their tussle with the woman. And they're out there chasing her now."

"Who's out there chasing her?"

"Whoever broke in here and killed the woman!"

"There were three of them you're saying now? Not two?"

Spinks shook his head against dark thoughts about the girl creeping into his mind.

"A young woman you claim you had to half-carry through these woods got away from three bloodthirsty killers? How'd she do that?"

"Out the bedroom window when they were breaking in maybe."

"A housecat with a good shove could about fit through that window."

Spinks' memory flashed on the girl calmly standing over a stuffed rabbit or kangaroo doll she'd brutalized with a letter opener sticking out of its face. And on the woman with a petrified look telling Spinks to hurry back, she was scared to be alone with the girl.

"Here's a more likely theory, Jack—two people broke into this cabin and three people, after cutting up and killing the woman lying on the floor in there, walked out of it together."

Poncet's eyes reflected as blankly at Spinks as black water hiding a centuries old lake bottom.

"Or this—three people walked into this cabin and found just what we found in it."

Spinks pushed Poncet toward the woods. "Or maybe you got reasons of your own for wanting me to believe bad things about that girl!"

"She's worked a spell on you Jack."

Spinks aimed his flashlight back at the ground.

"Made herself into a young woman Jack Spinks needed or wanted to see."

Spinks located the trail of blood heading into a denser stand of pines.

"You're the only one I know of has seen the young woman you've described to me—so tell me, what is it about her has made you ready to throw your life away for her?"

"The world has made me responsible for her, I don't why," said Spinks following Poncet and the blood trail into the trees.

❧

A pretty young woman.

Half undressed.

Alone, on a back road.

Night time.

Only the moon, stars and God watching.

How off kilter had he been?

Two Jack shots dropped into beers at Claude and Cindy Jenkins's house over the couple hours he'd failed to convince them to add life and long-term health insurance riders to their homeowner's policy. A quickly downed Budweiser in his truck before he'd left their driveway chewing on the disappointment of losing out on two seventy-five dollar commissions he'd been counting on on top of the fifty dollars he'd undercharged Claude for a bag of weed. Another Bud—or most of one—in the mile before—

Plus the joint he'd smoked with Claude and Cindy—

Goddamn Sheriff Grey Poncet, conjurer cop, disguised demon or both, had put in his head baseless doubts about Jack Spinks' character.

He would have, Spinks assured himself, done the same goddamn thing out on that road stone cold sober for a fully dressed ninety-year-old hag.

He imagined time as background music that had stopped playing.

How long had it been—days? weeks? months?—since the girl had stepped out from the woods in front of him and with her hauntingly familiar eyes drawn him into accompanying her into this indecipherable black world parallel to and unreachable from the world she'd drawn him out of.

Stars sporadically winking through the trees and his and Poncet's weak flashlights angled down at the root- and rock-marred ground they were walking over provided scant illumination under a sky showing not a hint of dawn light.

Recalling his stopped watch he wondered if time had

stopped everywhere. Or if in this parallel world he was trapped in time didn't exist.

He pictured an anchorless pendulum steadily swinging in a black abyss that had no beginning or end or anything in between. A space there was no forward, backward, up, down or sideways in. A place the same endlessly. A sticky spot on a giant piece of flypaper for infinity.

Poncet abruptly stopped walking in front of him.

He turned to the woods left of him and aimed his light deep into the night.

In the white beam two eyes gave off an impenetrable sheen.

Unblinking eyes.

Eyes in a stoic, bearded face. "You reckon it's a sign the whole world's been turned upside down time we've been in these woods, Jack?"

"Hell you talking about?"

"It's like seeing up for down and down for up. It's not normal."

"Seeing an owl in the woods at night isn't normal?" said Spinks eyeing the huge bird standing as still as a woodcarving placed between two trees so far off the trail Spinks had the eerie feeling Poncet had known it was there before he'd put his light on it. Poncet turned his eyes, as opaque and unreadable as the owl's eyes, onto Spinks. "Standing flat-footed on the ground instead of perched in a tree, Jack? When's the last time you've seen that?"

Spinks pretty sure he'd never seen it didn't say so.

Poncet tightened his battered lips in a cryptic frown toward the owl.

The after dark predator soundlessly rose up and flew into the night.

Poncet looked back at Spinks. A quiver in one corner of the tall man's lips maybe bespoke some inner emotion—humor, deceit, fear, anger. Or maybe was a lingering effect of Spinks' pummeling of the area. "I wonder if we ought to be up in the trees looking for the young lady, Jack. For all the traces of her down here on the ground she might have sprouted wings and flown right past her demons on their way into that cabin we found the woman butchered in."

Spinks felt as lost peering into Poncet's eyes as he had hours earlier peering into the dark underbrush for the source of the sounds coming through the night at the girl and him. "Suppose that's it, Jack? She can change forms? Make herself into one thing, then another? Or one young woman, then another, so that even looking straight at her a man is never sure if he's seeing the young woman she actually is or a young woman in his mind she's made herself look like to him or a mirage that isn't of flesh and blood at all?"

The thought struck Spinks like a hard slap in the head he, not the girl, had been knocked unconscious crashing the Durango; he, not her, had come to by that stream in an eyes-wide-open nightmare he was walking through even now.

"What would you have done different, Jack?"

Spinks shook his head to clear it. "What?"

"If Carl and I had called out we were police officers walking up to your truck out on Black Cat Hollow Road? Would you have done anything different than you did do?"

Spinks didn't have an answer to the question so didn't offer one. He shoved Poncet's pistol, then Carl's, deeper into his pants waist. They were following a zigzagging path of underbrush matted down by what might have been human, bear or deer footsteps and sporadic drops of blood through a thick stand of oak, maple and elm trees that, as near as Spinks could tell, was headed deeper into the woods rather than back toward the road.

"You resting easy with it, Jack?"

"Am I resting easy with what?" Spinks thinking he hadn't rested easy with anything or in any way since he'd laid eyes on the girl.

"Killing Carl. Any smudges of doubt showing up in the picture you framed in your mind of how that went down?"

Spinks said, "I've got no doubt he'd of killed me if I hadn't killed him. I'd just as soon though his boss and friend hadn't decided to leave his body out there in the open for animals to chew on."

Poncet's studied frown told Spinks Poncet couldn't find a sensible answer in Spinks' reply to the question Poncet had just asked him.

"It'll all get sorted, Jack. Tonight will."

"I hope to hell it will."

"We'll all have our say on it. Everybody a part of it will. Course Carl will have to do his talking on it without words, though what one look at him with his head split in two up on that hill will say is likely to have lots more sway on how it gets sorted than any of us will from all the hours of grilling we'll be put through."

Spinks said, "I reckon that woman therapist back in her cabin with her head bashed in and throat slit will have something to say on it too. And so will the fingerprints on the weight disc that bashed her head in."

Poncet moved the light beam up at Spinks' face. "I'm right here with you in having stepped into something way over our heads, Jack. The difference between us being I know something about negotiating the terrain we're in and you're as lost as a blind mole in a sunlit maze. That, and I'm wearing a sheriff's badge and you're a guy claims to be an insurance salesman driving a truck loaded with weapons and dope enough to supply half the residents of this hollow with."

Spinks reached up and pushed Poncet's light away from his eyes. "You see any more owls, on the ground, in the trees or flying through the air, don't waste your time showing them to me." He shoved Poncet in the back to start him walking again. "I know damn well the sorts of creatures native to these woods and the sorts not and the second sort and that girl are all I care about finding."

# 20

A near naked young woman he'd first taken for a mirage walking along the road's shoulder.

No.

That was wrong.

He was recalling it incorrectly.

She wasn't walking along the road's shoulder when he first saw her.

When he first saw her, a hundred-odd yards ahead of him in the Durango's headlights, she was emerging like a ghostly forest nymph out of the woods onto the shoulder.

Only then did she start walking along it.

Walking along it in the direction Spinks was driving in.

Walking along it without even glancing at the Durango's advancing headlights—because she was in shock and not thinking clearly as Spinks had guessed at the time? Or because, as Poncet had tried to make Spinks believe, she had seen his headlights from the woods and then stepped out of them aiming to look to him lost, half-naked and vulnerable?

Ridiculous.

How could she have known who was in the vehicle coming at her?

Maybe it hadn't mattered to her who was in it as long as the vehicle was heading down the hollow, rather than up it.

Meaning what?

Meaning maybe she was confident that trouble on that road would only come at her, from the direction of the highway, and not from behind her on a road that dead-ended in a mile or so at the Jenkins place.

That would square with why she'd panicked seeing a set of

headlights framed by orange fog lights coming up the road at her and Spinks.

Had she recognized the vehicle as a police cruiser with sheriff's deputies in it hunting her for her connection to a triple homicide on an adjacent road off the highway?

It doesn't jive Spinks told himself.

Not with his read of human nature it didn't jive.

It didn't jive that the lost, brain-scrambled young woman he'd carried through the woods and who'd brought to his mind his dead daughter was a calculating she devil involved in murdering a family and burning their home and torturing to death a woman who had taken her into her home and tried to help her.

The young woman he'd carried through the woods wasn't the young woman he'd stopped for up on the road.

The thought struck Spinks like a physical blow—

Her before and after selves shared the same body was all.

The head injury she'd suffered crashing in the Durango had left her with only scant fractured memories of who she had been before then. When she came to at the bottom of that embankment Spinks told her two people with flashlights were chasing her down she was lost in about every way a human being is capable of being lost in—physically, psychically, in spirit, in purpose—and wholly dependent on the person whose arms she had woken in from an interrupted nightmare in which she was being chased by people she saw in her delusional mind as horror story demons from a place she interpreted metaphorically as an Old Testament-like hell.

No one in his or her own nightmare is ever the demon.

One is never the victimizer in one's own horror dream.

The dreamer is never the evil one. The dreamer is never the chaser.

The dreamer is always the one being chased.

Could the young woman he'd help guide through the woods in her hollow far-off voice have been speaking to him out of a semi-conscious, phantasmal nightmare in which the police she was trying to elude for crimes she'd committed in this world were demons in a dream created hell wanting to kill her only for being alive?

What did he know about that young woman's life before she'd hit her head and had most of her conscious memory wiped out? A young woman marred with what looked to be scratches from the woods she'd emerged half-naked out of onto the road in front of him, scared, desperate and on the run from someone or something? A young woman he'd spent scarcely five minutes with before she'd forcefully taken control of his truck and crashed it nearly killing them both? A demanding, foul-mouthed young woman more violent than any female he'd ever encountered? When Spinks had first pulled alongside her she'd moved her eyes at him in the way of what? A tethered horse maybe trying to read the face of a stranger she had no choice but to let climb onto her? Or a wild bronco taking the temperature of a stranger she'd made up her mind to take for a ride?

They came out of the dense hardwoods into what looked to be an old farm meadow hijacked by alders, berry bushes, crab and thorn apple trees, onto a narrow, moderately beaten down path heading through an area of thick brush and coppiced trees growing over the stumps of larger logged trees. Spinks made the path for a deer trail likely ending at a pond or stream. A few yards along it Poncet stopped walking and crouched down. His pummeled features in the dancing half-light evoking a special-effects-created monster's mask he reached with an index finger into a splotch of fresh blood he'd highlighted in his flashlight, lifted the finger to his face and, with a reptilian dart of his tongue from between his swollen lips, licked the blood from it. He savored what he'd licked with a cogitative expression.

Spinks with an unearthly feeling said, "Jesus Christ."

Poncet got to his feet. He showed Spinks his bloodied teeth. "We're on the right track still."

“Hell you talking about?”

“We haven’t veered off onto the trail of a wounded deer or coyote.” Poncet spit the blood he’d licked from his finger at the blood on the ground he’d swiped it from. “The same lingua cells hypersensitive enough to tell me that’s human blood cause my tongue to about burst into flames I even touch it to the mildest of spicy foods.”

Spinks half-hoped he was lying unconscious by the stream he and the girl had plunged into and that the life he felt he was experiencing so intensely was only a chain of nightmarish images playing in his comatose brain.

“The answers to the more confounding questions will have to wait until we catch up to the person leaking their life out into these woods,” said Poncet.

“What more confounding questions you talking about?”

“Man or woman? Adult or adolescent? Victim or perpetrator?” Poncet wiped his bloody fingertip onto his pants leg. “There’s no age, sex or quality discrimination in the taste of human blood. It all tastes the same.”

He lowered his light back to the path and started walking up it again.

# 21

Living hell could have gone on there and no one on the hollow road would have seen a flicker of it. Or heard a peep of it.

At the end of a long winding drive that stand of blue spruce was a visible and audible shield in front of the house and its three outbuildings.

Seeing a photograph of it on the dead woman's wall Spinks had flashed on his one visit there and suddenly feared he'd been wrong about his never having laid eyes on the girl until tonight.

He recalled the girl peering at that wall of photographs and his fear grew.

Sebastian Poe's face floated into his thoughts like a pitch-black cloud in an already threatening sky.

He'd met Poe at Claude and Cindy Jenkins' house thanks to Claude puffing Spinks' illicit wares to Poe despite Spinks having told his fellow former marine, friend and insurance client he wasn't actively looking to expand his secondary business borne after the death of his family out of despair, boredom, a search for meaning in what had suddenly felt like a meaningless existence and to put to use again the horticultural skills he'd developed working with Rebecca and Iris in their half-acre vegetable garden he'd let go to seed after their deaths.

Burly, mid-forties with a Cossack's beard beneath a buzz-cut and forearm tats Spinks guessed he hadn't paid more than cigarettes to have done Poe rented the fields around the house to Jenkins to grow corn on. He supposedly owned the place with a few other people occasionally seen driving in or out of the place but Jenkins had only ever spoken to Poe who told Jenkins he worked in Albany during the week in the security field, whatever the hell that meant, and like Jenkins and Spinks was an ex-marine, though had done his time in the first desert war not the second.

Amiable with a manner that at the same time made it clear he was certain his time was more valuable and overall place in the universe more significant than anyone else's Poe told Spinks he wanted some of that good shit he'd sold Jenkins at the price he'd sold it to Jenkins for.

Spinks told him Jenkins got a cut-rate price on his good shit for buying insurance from Spinks and asked if Poe was interested in pursuing a similar arrangement. Poe said he cared fuck-all for buying insurance and Spinks, germinating a dislike for Poe, doubled the already inflated price he'd meant to charge him for the couple ounces he had on him. Poe, ponying up from a wad as thick as his forearm, inquired what other goodies Spinks could sell him and Spinks told him home, life or auto insurance. Poe called Spinks an interesting fellow and slapping him on the back like they were fast friends requested Spinks bring him as much of the good shit as he could get ahold of. Spinks told him that he dealt in ounces not tons and that the price would include a transportation fee and Poe, who would have slapped him on the back again if Spinks hadn't moved out of the way, said, "Just be sure to give me a heads up first."

He'd been shooting skeet by the house when Spinks had arrived, launching the pigeons from a thrower next to him with one hand then raising a twelve-gauge he was holding in the other and firing at them. A few men somewhat younger than Poe and with similar buzz cuts and bulked-up bodies were listening to southern rock at low volume and drinking beer in a make shift lean-to nearby. They nodded grimly to Spinks then returned to conversing in the sound vacuum of the music. Poe offered Spinks a go with the twelve-gauge then suggested they have a shoot off with Poe getting the weed for free if he won and paying double for it if he lost. Spinks didn't miss a pigeon and Poe who only missed one afterwards pursed his lips as if struggling mightily to keep a vile creature from slithering out between them and angrily stalked off at the house. Spinks after searching the beer drinkers faces for a cue and getting back only blank looks followed Poe.

Poe made a loud whistle as he approached a large garage/ guesthouse before the main house. Two bay doors in the garage were open and a car in each space. The Lexus SUV Poe had driven to Jenkins' house sat next to it on a patch of grass. Poe whistled sharply again and Spinks saw a door in the guesthouse above the garage open and three young women in mid-thigh-length T-shirts and apparently nothing else walk in single file out of it onto the deck and, standing at the rail, wave to Poe like parade contestants on a passing float. Spinks couldn't see them very well. He registered mostly they were young, looked much alike and dressed alike to the point they were dressed at all.

Poe glancing behind him as if to verify Spinks' eyes were on the young women waved back to them and kept walking.

Spinks at the house heard growling and music playing but couldn't see the source of either. He looked up at the second floor and there were blinds over all the windows. Poe pushing through a door leading to what looked to be a kitchen said tersely over his shoulder to Spinks, "Hold your dick a minute." Spinks stood waiting on the porch with two of the men who'd ambled over from the gun range until Poe came back out holding a six-pack and smiling toothily as if he'd spit out into the kitchen sink the vile creature he'd been struggling to hold in his mouth. He handed Spinks a wad of bills adding up to his fee times two and said, "Let's talk."

"About what?"

"Whatever's in the air. Like I said the other day you're an interesting fellow."

"Interesting how?"

"You're a dude past caring about consequences for one thing. That's plain as day."

"Why's that interest you?"

"Because I'm the same way and gravitate toward others like me."

Spinks got the idea Poe was on something stronger than the

weed he'd sold him. He said, "I doubt we're much alike."

"Oh, I don't know—we've both been through some god-awful angering shit we're still carrying around and keeping a cap on so far by blowing it off a little at a time right? The thing is anger's of no use without containment and control. Containment and control until it's time for the boom, man—I see that in you like it's in me. When I say I see it in you I mean I read it in you—it's your life force writing the words, man. Containment, control, boom. The trifecta, baby. It's in you and that interests me."

Spinks told himself Poe was touched in the head or up on something and he ought to just leave. At the same time he found himself drawn to listening to him the way someone startled awake in the middle of the night is drawn to listening to the wind at his window or creaking floorboards outside his door.

He took a slug of beer and looked out toward the guesthouse. The young women had gone back inside. Spinks' memory of them showed him only a flight of colorful songbirds fluttering around a single feeder with a perch big enough for only one of them to eat at.

"You'd like a closer gander at them?"

Spinks looked back at Poe, watching him closely.

"See if they'll stand up to your hopes for them?"

Spinks said, "I don't have any hopes for them. I don't even know them."

Poe pulled a pack of cigarettes from his shirt pocket. He drew one out with his lips and held the pack out at Spinks. Spinks ignoring it said, "Who are they?"

"Their names you mean?"

Spinks unsure what he meant said, "Do they live here?"

Poe rubbed his chin, seemingly puzzling on the question, then not answering it said, "Would you like me to introduce you to one of them?"

"What for?"

Poe shrugged. "Maybe you'll give me something back on the weed?"

Spinks looked at him for a few seconds and said, "I'll keep the cash."

Poe slapped him on the back how he had at Claude Jenkins's house. "It's in you, man—the trifecta. If you know it or not—it's in you. And you can shoot too. Better than me even—I've never seen that before. Have you seen that before Sledge? Arno?"

He turned to the two other men and they shook their heads, no they'd never seen it before.

Spinks said, "You're some kind of criminal? Is that it?"

Poe finished his beer and crushing the can said, "No, man. Didn't Claude tell you? I'm in the security field." He popped a fresh beer. "And you sell insurance, right?"

Spinks took another swallow of beer gazing again toward the guesthouse and seeing a curtain in it slowly draw across the window nearest the door. "Right."

"You want I can have them come out again? They won't look how they do now forever—or maybe even tomorrow. Old time she's a flying for all of us. Have another look, see if you're drawn to one more than to the others."

Spinks shook his head. He had the idea Poe had made a point of showing him the young women to test him about something. But about what exactly? And the young women responding like well-trained dogs to his whistle. An angry simmering started in his gut and he wasn't sure exactly what it was aimed most at. "They free to leave?"

"Of course they're free to leave. Man, this is America. We fought for that right, you and me, right?"

"So they're what? Your tenants?"

"Room, board, free run, with certain restrictions, of the grounds and surrounding countryside. Factoring everything in it's a better deal for them than a hotel, man."

Spinks finished his beer and placed the empty on the ground by his chair. Poe popped him another one. The other two men sitting a few feet away on the steps hadn't said a dozen words between them. Poe handed Spinks the beer. "You're calm as a windless day on the outside, man, but inside—it's loud as shit yeah? A churning that never stops under all that containment and control?" Poe nodded to Spinks. "And the question's always there right—how long before the boom?"

Spinks said nothing having briefly left Poe's company for a waking nightmare in which Rebecca was standing still as a statue in a black nightgown and huge black sun hat that hid her face nearly to her chin over Iris's bed as she slept.

"Here's what I don't get about insurance, man—once a thing is gone it's gone. A house, a car, a life—you're never getting back what you had and paying all those premiums betting you're going to lose a thing you picked out for its special qualities and end up with cash to buy some shitty replica of it is just—you know it's like, it's like communism, man. It's saying one thing is like another. Your wife, your car, your kid. I tell you—no lie—I'd murder my wife or kid before I'd bet on them dying to make me rich. And the one thing that can be exactly replicated? Money, right? Cash is cash. And fuck, man, why insure money when you can just go out if you lose it and grab or steal more of it."

Spinks looked at Poe and Poe said, "I know you know I mean no disrespect, man. We all do what we gotta do to get by. You, me"—he nodded up at the guesthouse—"the ladies up there."

Poe clicked his beer can against Spinks' can. "Cheers, man. It's a pleasure talking to somebody who understands."

They sat in deck chairs watching dozens of ducks lounging on the pond Spinks suspecting Poe was taking Spinks' pulse on selected subjects with outlandish out of the blue statements such as that a number of his acquaintances had been born Black and through a series of homemade remedies he'd been denied a patent for Poe had turned them white and that twice a year he had several friends over to join him in a mass shotgun slaying of the ducks his daily feedings lured to the pond and that once the blood scent was out of the air he put out feed to attract new ones, his underlings, Sledge and Arno, wordlessly nodding without ever as much as cracking smiles to indicate Poe might simply have been trying out an off-center sense of humor on Spinks.

Spinks decided he didn't need the money he got selling a few ounces of weed bad enough to do further business with Sebastian Poe who, in Spinks' memory of him as he walked on edge through a swampy patch of brush and briars exhaling an insidious pulpy scent, had horns growing out of the back of his head. But then, when he closed his eyes, and more and more even when he didn't, he saw the same sort of horns growing out of the back of Grey Poncet's head floating in the near dark at eye level in front of him like a small planet dropped out of its constellation. Spinks, with a growing sense of dislocation, wondered if in this night that felt to him less like an interminable stretch of time than it did a locked room full of horror house special effects his brain was coming apart like a rag doll a dog's been at? If his mind had been so frayed by the night's events it could no longer tell the difference between internal images and external realities? He'd been through a war—he'd been through far worse than a war losing Rebecca and Iris and, worse even than losing them, the beyond human comprehension horrible way of how he'd lost them—and knew stress together with fear, grief and anger in a human mind could make black look white, evil look good and the act of dying look like a corridor down which lay blissful life.

And what, he wondered, might that lethal combination of emotions done to the images in the girl's mind?

Was that house owned by Sebastian Poe a hell she'd managed to escape from? Or was it a hell she'd created? Or was it a house Sheriff Gray Poncet had drawn Spinks' attention to believing Spinks—and possibly the girl—was involved with activities at it far more sinister than peddling a little weed?

# 22

A rhythmic flowing sound in the darkness ahead.

Less forceful in its pitch than the rushing water he'd pulled the girl unconscious out of his crashed Durango in.

A spot upstream from that spot?

Or a different stream altogether.

In different woods than the woods he'd carried the girl through.

Or hadn't he carried her anywhere at all?

Was he still with her on that stream bank next to his crashed truck and the sound he was hearing was in his dreaming or awake and fracturing mind—?

A gunshot sent him belly-first to the ground.

He slithered for the cover of the nearest tree.

"Throw me one those pistols!" hissed Poncet, on his belly behind a tree just in front of him.

Spinks switching off his flashlight, cocked an ear at the woods. He heard flowing water—real water, real woods, the memory of a real gunshot in an otherwise silent void. He whispered to Poncet, "I throw you one who you going to shoot it at?"

"Hell you think? Whoever shot at us!"

"You sure someone shot at us?"

"You deaf?"

"I heard a shot. Hard to say what it was aimed at. Or where it came from."

"Stand up and step out from behind that tree you'll likely find out what it was aimed at."

"Better that you do."

"Better that I do what?"

"Stand up. Holler out, 'I'm the county sheriff, don't shoot no more.'"

"I don't believe I'll do that."

"You're not worried someone out in front of us would shoot a cop are you?"

Poncet didn't answer Spinks nor comment on his ironic tone. Nor did he holler out at the woods.

Spinks cocked an ear at the stream and heard what sounded like a whisper or moan. Before he could ask Poncet if he'd heard the same thing Poncet hissed, "Something—or someone—is between us and the water."

Spinks drew Poncet's .380 from his belt and, holding it in one hand, peered ahead at clumps of dark underbrush like rolling waves on a blustery sea beneath a fractured ceiling of still maturing spruce and pine trees. Nothing moving he could see. No chirps, chatters or peeps he could hear, as if the birds and animals native to those woods had called time out to watch this conflict between human invaders in their home play out. The sound again. A moan not a whisper. All animals in certain straits it struck Spinks sound alike. And every living creature when hurt and feeling threatened is at its most dangerous. "Call out who you are," he hissed to Poncet.

Nothing from Poncet.

"You hear me, Poncet?"

He saw Poncet's head turn toward him. He waited a few seconds for him to say something but, Poncet not saying anything, turned his head back around and started slithering out from behind the tree away from Spinks and vaguely parallel to the water.

"The hell?! You think I won't shoot you?" hissed Spinks mulling doing so.

"Who's there!?"

A male voice. High-pitched and weak at once as if its owner were struggling to keep a few hundred-pound weight he was holding up with both hands from crashing down onto his head.

"I'm here—by the stream. I'm in bad shape!"

Spinks wondered if it was possible he and Poncet had stumbled onto someone in these forsaken woods with trouble unrelated to the trouble that had him and Poncet in them.

"Answer me goddamn it! I know someone's there!"

Spinks looked to where he'd last seen Poncet and didn't see him now. Nor did he hear anything from that direction. He looked toward the water again and was just as blind there. He called out, "Who are you?"

After several seconds the voice came back hesitantly, "A guy hurt bad!"

"What are you doing out in these woods?"

"I—camping—Jesus, come help me…!"

Spinks hollered, "That you who took a shot at us?"

"I shot in the air—to grab your attention—I saw your flashlights," the voice weaker still.

"You alone?" hollered Spinks.

"It's just me! Please, I'm bleeding bad…"

Spinks hollered, "Step out into the open where I can shine a light on you! Watch you throw your weapon into the woods!"

"I can't hardly sit up, never mind stan…"

The answer ended in a muffled gasping sound.

Spinks hollered, "Shine a light show me where you are!"

No light came on. And no voice came back to Spinks.

Spinks waited several seconds and hollered, "I'm not coming over there till I can see you and that your hands are empty!"

No answer.

"Hello?" Spinks yelled. Then, "Poncet!? Where you at?"

No answer.

Spinks waited a few more seconds and slithered out from behind the tree. He stood and in a half crouch ran a few feet to his right then straight ahead several yards at the stream. He stopped and went to his knees behind a clump of bushes. He heard the stream directly to his right and a slight rustling to his left. He peered through the darkness to his left and saw in dark outline near the base of a large tree a hunched-over figure. He watched the figure rise up into an upright position. He aimed the .380 at the figure and yelled out, "There's a pistol aimed at your head and a crack shot aiming it! Don't move!"

The figure froze.

"Turn a half-circle to your left! Slowly!"

The figure made a slow turn toward Spinks and called out, "He's dead!"

Poncet.

Spinks was a moment taking in what he'd said. "The guy who was just talking to me is dead?"

"Half his insides are here on the forest floor."

Spinks got out his flashlight and turned it on. He got to his feet aiming at Poncet the light in one hand and the .380 in the other.

Poncet stood near a large pine tree. His hands were clasped behind his back and head tilted to one side, a man contemplating his or another's predicament. Hunched forward in a sloppy sitting position against the pine tree's trunk was a dark shape Spinks took to be the body of the man he'd been conversing with through the woods. He said, "He was plenty alive a couple minutes ago."

Poncet straightened his head. "Used up his last strength must be hollering to you."

Spinks holding the .380 on Poncet took a few steps at him.

Poncet's shirtfront and pants legs were bloodied. He nodded at the dead man of whom Spinks could see only two legs in blood-soaked jeans stretched out from the base of the tree on blood-soaked pine needles. "He's draining through a deep gash in his stomach. A guy claims to be camping without camping gear."

Spinks in mind of the muffled gasp that had ended in mid-sentence the dead man's last shout not long before Poncet had gotten to his feet over the man's corpse was reminded how in over his head he was in a world he hadn't known existed until a few hours ago.

"You make him the bleeder from the cabin?"

"Not likely to be more than one person in these woods tonight with a puncture wound in the gut. Appears his partners got tired of having him for an anchor and left him here to bleed out."

"Left him armed with a pistol from the sound of that shot we heard."

Poncet nodded. "A Jericho automatic. Why I came in quiet on him."

"What is?"

"To keep him from shooting one or both of us."

"Him dying ended that risk."

Poncet didn't say anything.

"That the Jericho you're holding behind your back?"

"I'll put it in my belt you do the same with my .380."

Spinks shook his head.

"Trust is a two-way street, Jack."

"It's a street you and me aren't close to being on."

"No offense, Jack, but my most charitable view of you is you're a little off upstairs and more than a little unpredictable. A less charitable one is you're up to your eyeballs in criminal activities tied to that girl and will do me how you did Carl when it suits you. The point being I can't operate effectively as a police officer or comfortably as a private citizen worrying over the potential harm could come to me with you being armed and me not."

Spinks nodded, indicating he'd heard Poncet, and said, "Drop the Jericho and move your hands at waist height and palms up slowly out in front of you."

Poncet said, "No can do, Jack. Believe me it will look better for you when this all comes to an end us being on even footing how we are now as opposed to the hostage like situation we were in."

"You're holding a pistol behind your back. I'm holding one pointed at your head and a finger on its trigger. How do you see that as even footing?"

Poncet, shuffling his feet, shifted his shoulders forward slightly.

"It'll be the last mistake you ever make attempting what's going through your mind right now," said Spinks.

Poncet neither dropping the Jericho nor altering his stance any gave Spinks' words a few seconds thought and said, "I'm of that sect of Christians who believes life is a scrum watched over by a God willing only to help those of us who help ourselves."

Spinks keeping the .380 aimed between Poncet's eyes said, "You could have said all that in another language for all it means to me."

"It's like a free for all."

"What is?"

"A scrum. It's a rugby term. I'm saying I can't by myself pull you out of the pile of shit you're in, Jack. You have to hold a hand out for me to grab hold of at least."

Spinks said, "I'm getting tired of waiting."

A subtle drop in the tall man's shoulders told Spinks that Poncet had made up his mind to not test the odds. He heard the Jericho hit the ground. He shoved the .380 in his belt and walked to Poncet at the base of the pine tree.

The dead man sitting against the tree might have been a passed out drunk a prankster had poured red paint on below his chest. His head rested lazily on one shoulder, his mouth agape. Blood oozed from a gash in his abdomen like oil oozing from the ground in a natural oil field. His black fatigues were drenched in it. Spinks seeing the blood-drained face tried not to alter his expression but Poncet evidently picking up on some subtle tell in his manner said, "How well did you know him?"

Spinks deriving no more about Poncet's core from looking into his eyes than he had every other time he'd looked into them said, "I didn't know him."

Poncet frowned. "None of us really knows anyone you're saying? That happy horseshit?"

"I had a couple beers with him and a couple other guys. I didn't exchange a half-dozen words with him."

"Where?"

"You pointed me to a picture of the place in the woman's cabin. My guess is you know a lot more than I do about it and the people connected to it. My guess is too this man here was alive when you got to him a few minutes ago."

The dead man slid like melting snow from a pitched roof off the tree's trunk and onto his back on the forest floor. The landing opened his eyes and pushed a loud gasp out of his lungs and fresh blood like a jet of eel's ink out of his mouth. Poncet lifted one of his feet up over the corpse's face and with the toe of his boot shut its eyes again. He began tapping the boot rhythmically up and down on the dead man's forehead as if to a tune in his head.

Spinks thought hell kind of a policeman acts this way and said to him, "Maybe there's something you wanted to be sure he didn't tell me?"

Poncet said, "What I wanted was him not to shoot me. It's possible he quit breathing some sooner than he would have without him putting the effort he did into wrestling with me over the issue."

The truth? A lie? A fuzzy merging of the truth and a lie? As with everything that Spinks had witnessed or been involved in from the moment the Durango's headlights had found the girl a case could be made for or against any of those possibilities. He moved his eyes from Poncet's boot laying a beat on the dead man's head to a winged shape in the dark sky and recalled Poncet saying maybe they ought to be looking for the girl up in the trees. He looked back at the tall man's wrecked face with its non-reflective eyes and the thought struck him that whatever internal mechanism externalized a person's being to the world was as far removed from Poncet as was the winged creature Spinks had seen flying above the trees from the image it had drawn in his mind of it. "Talk to me, you son of a bitch."

Poncet tilted his head at Spinks.

Spinks pointed down at the dead man. "That, or I leave you here cuffed to him."

Poncet lifted his boot from the dead man's face. "Be better you talk to me first, Jack. No sense me telling you what you already know."

Spinks said, "I know the guy lying here went by the name of Sledge and worked for Sebastian Poe and that Poe owns that house."

"He why you were on the hollow road tonight?"

"Who?"

"Poe. He your boss too?"

"The only boss of me is me. I sold Poe a few ounces of marijuana one time is all. I did it against my better judgment and only because Poe didn't turn me down when I quoted him a price that was more than twice what I would have charged someone I liked even a little bit for it. The whole scene at Poe's place gave me a bad feeling. Most of all he himself did."

"I don't know, Jack."

"You don't know what?"

"I don't know that I believe to Jack Strange Sebastian Poe is just a gentleman farmer he sold weed to one time"—Poncet wiped his bloodied boot sole on the forest floor—"any more than I believe Jack Strange is just an insurance salesman who happens to be an expert at killing people and while driving down a desolate road just happened upon a young woman works for Sebastian Poe."

"Works for him how?"

"I've been trying to figure out if you know the answer to that question ever since you put a hatchet in Carl's head."

"What I know about that girl is what I told you."

"If that's true you haven't got the vaguest idea the trouble you've made for yourself."

"Seeing I'm the only one of us holding a gun I'd make you to be in deeper trouble than I am."

A pinecone fell to the ground between them. Poncet peered a few seconds at it then, stepping the foot he'd just taken from Slade's face onto it, said, "Poe's organization is the target of a three-state RICO Investigation focusing on prostitution, loan sharking and strong-arm jewelry store robberies in New York, Massachusetts and New Hampshire." He tapped his foot on the pinecone in the same rhythmic way he'd tapped it on Slade's face. "The Feds brought my office into it to help them with certain local aspects of the investigation."

"And the girl?"

"She's a part of the local aspects."

Spinks gazed up at the sky for the winged creature he'd seen earlier and saw only a disintegrating grey streak like a trail of exhaust left by a passing jet. His mind took him away from his earthly nightmare, into the self's realm and memories of an even darker place and time. He lowered his eyes to Poncet straightening up from his waist holding Slade's Jericho in one hand.

Spinks front-kicked Poncet in his forearm.

The Jericho flew several feet into the woods.

Poncet shook his kicked arm—"Son of a bitch! Feels like you broke it!"

His eyes to Spinks' eyes were two chunks of lusterless coal.

"I was only going to hand it to you!"

Spinks pistol-whipped Poncet.

Blood and part of a tooth flew from Poncet's mouth.

Poncet spit out more of the tooth and said, "Insurance salesman my ass!"

Spinks saw sprouting from Poncet's head the two horns he'd been half-certain he'd seen sprouting from it before Slade's gunshot had forced them to ground. He pressed the .380 to the tall man's forehead foreseeing both ridding the world of a demon that preyed on teenage girls and clearing his mind of a lot of negative thinking about his trip into these woods that had cast him from an outer circle of hell into a place a lot closer to its core. "Blink," he told Poncet.

A slight twitch near the tall man's blackened eye offered the only hint of how he was feeling having a gun pressed to his forehead. He said, "You kill me you'll kill the only chance you've got of getting out of this night alive and a free man."

Spinks pushed the .380 barrel into Poncet's skull just above his nose. "Blink, you son of a bitch. Or I'll figure no one's in there."

Poncet shut his eyes. He opened them. Not really a blink. "You telling me you didn't know the girl is one of Poe's, Jack?"

Spinks, noting Poncet's eyes after shutting and opening hadn't changed their appearance any, said, "One of his what?"

"Robots."

"Hell you talking about!?"

"He gets them at the age of eleven or twelve—has them grabbed off a city street or imports them from Eastern Europe through his underworld connections. Word is he locks each new girl in a room and allows all manner of cretins to have at her without ever showing himself to her until after a couple of months he breaks into the room and saves the girl from the man he'd just sent in to rape her—Feds have heard he's even shot a couple of the rapists dead—and becomes in her eyes her savior. After that they'd do anything for him."

Spinks felt near as sick inside as he did every time he pictured Iris sitting next to her mother in their minivan on the last day of their lives.

"He has close to fifty of them whoring for him in upstate cities and little towns like this one and a few especially psychotic ones, whose loyalty to him knows no bounds, he employs in more deadly ways such as having them make a diamond dealer and his family appear to have died in a fire in their summer home after the diamond dealer, to avoid going to jail for washing Poe's dirty money, flipped on him to the Feds..."

Spinks shot his eyes up into the tree overhead, searching for the source of a girlish shriek piercing his heart like a frigid shard of ice fired into it.

A giant winged shape took flight from the tree painting him with its shadow.

Iris and Rebecca flying.

On a carnival ride designed by the devil.

Iris shrieking, against having the life she wouldn't get to live stolen from her.

Against the worst sort of betrayal an offspring of man or animal can feel.

And Rebecca?

A million—maybe a billion—times he'd replayed it and always Rebecca was silent and stoic as the death she was flying to; posture upright and erect, her mouth in an unreadable line as straight as the road they'd flown off of.

Too long his soldier's instincts told him. Too long his mind had been in another world and his eyes in the trees.

He looked down.

Poncet wasn't where he'd left him. He wasn't there at all.

Had he ever been?

Spinks suddenly didn't feel confident in either the accuracy of his perceptions or the reliability of his memory.

Had the big woman and her cabin existed outside his mind?

Had he only imagined splitting open with a hatchet the head of Deputy Sheriff Carl Ames?

Had he encountered in these woods two policemen at all?

His brain felt like a damp shirt a weightlifter was wringing dry.

The only memory he was certain of was the girl. Her otherworldly proclamations about demons and hell. The petrified look in her eyes. A buried and truer self hinted at in her body's heat against his arms carrying her. His feeling from the moment she'd stepped out in front of his headlights—and not anyone else's—that she'd become his responsibility. That if he didn't help her no one would.

He looked at the base of the tree and saw a dead man lying next to it. He was relieved and as troubled as he had been the first time he'd seen it—how long ago was that? Five minutes? Fifteen? An hour—by the thought that the dead man had been abandoned alive here less out of callousness than out of purposefulness.

A cool breeze touched the back of his neck in the same instant that his instincts told him, for the second time in however long that he'd been in this spot, he'd been too long removed from the physical world. He wheeled around—

In the tree nearest him a large branch bounced steadily up and down where something had just lifted off from it.

He looked around with his light under the trees until he found the dead man's Jericho.

# 23

A heavenly water tank tipped over onto the earth.

Jagged bolts of lightning on top of sonorous thunder like high voltage laser shots directed by an angry God.

Spinks above the deluge could scarcely hear his own voice screaming into the hole, never mind it reaching Callender at the center of the earth.

His desperate shouts turning Callender's name into a hopeful question.

"Callender!?"

Offering him pointless instructions.

"Keep moving your arms and legs to stay above the water!"

Nothing—not even a groan or splash—came back to him from the hole.

The sixty feet between them could have been a million miles.

Spinks' disembodied voice, even if it was reaching Callender, of no more use to him in that earthen tub fast filling with water than his shattered limbs or loaded carbine were.

A scuba tank to breathe through about all that would help Callender now, or—

Spinks sat down by the hole.

Fast as he could he took off his uniform boots and trousers, looped the trouser legs around his neck, tied them in a secure knot, took the looped trousers off over his head and made sure the fly was unbuttoned.

"Put these around your neck, Callender!" he shouted with little hope Callender could hear him or, even if he did, would in his dire straights recall his water survival training on self-made floatation devices or have the mental acuity or strength to put to use what he'd been taught.

He dropped the trousers down the hole.

"Use your cupped hands to fill the legs with air—!"

A loud explosion as a towering spruce tree overhead burst into flames.

Spinks, aiming to become less of a target, instinctively dropped face-first to the ground, the tree's limbs crashing to earth around him as if they'd been sheared off by two giant knives chopping straight down on either side of it.

Realizing not artillery fire but a lightning bolt had exploded the tree, Spinks leapt to his feet, snatched up his boots in one hand and ran seeking cover from God's fury into the woods the cat-like animal he'd made eye contact with had disappeared into.

Spinks getting drenched crouching half under the cover of a massive boulder sticking out like a sore thumb amid a thick stand of spruce trees as if the world's designer had randomly tossed it there after throwing up his hands on finding a more suitable place for it.

Callender drowned or drowning a hundred-odd feet from him in a hole with a wide-open faucet running into it God alone had the power to turn off and so far had shown no intention of doing.

Powerless.

The word like a hammer striking solid rock over and over again in Spinks' head.

The word evolving into an all-encompassing feeling devouring every other feeling he might have been experiencing.

Powerless as a weak finger to stop, slow down or divert the giant ball that was the world's momentum.

Powerless against God's fickleness.

Powerless against Mother Nature's whims.

Powerless against emailed words disguised to remove them of their plain meanings.

Powerless against the intentions behind those words.

Powerless against the distance from Afghanistan to Upstate New York.

Powerless against a loved one's lonely or stressed mind.

His thoughts coming at him harsh and merciless as the storm.

Attached to them all the overwhelming reality of his own powerlessness against a certainty of something beyond terrible looming just beyond his sight.

# 24

Tracking the stream on a winding path through the woods Spinks realized the person he'd been until he'd pulled up next to the girl and helped her into his Durango was extinct. No path he could take from here would get him back to that existence. If he managed to stay alive through this seemingly endless night the Jack Strange who came out the other side of it wouldn't be the Jack Strange driving near-drunk and stoned down the hollow road near the start of it.

No matter what sort of life would be left to him—or if no life at all would be—knowing it wouldn't be the life he'd been violently thrust out of earlier that night he found oddly comforting.

The possibility occurred to him that he had created the situation he was in in response to a prompt from some unconscious part of his brain that understood if not forcibly ripped out of it he would have stayed forever in the life he'd been living since the love of his life had driven her Subaru Forester off a thousand-foot cliff into the ocean.

With the other love of his life strapped into the front passenger seat.

On a clear day, in a mechanically sound SUV witnesses to the crash said had veered across the centerline and sped straight for the drop-off never showing its brake lights.

THIS IS THE ONLY WAY she'd written on a note taped to their refrigerator.

Her family, her closest friends, least of all Spinks—had no idea of the meaning of those five words.

Or how a woman who had somehow found in them logic for taking her life had also found in them logic for taking all those unlived years away from an innocent as the driven snow eleven-year-old girl who'd called her Mommy and had, literally, loved her to death.

The only possible attempt at an explanation or goodbye Spinks in looking back could credit her with was the assertion in her last email to him that though her love for Spinks and Iris was as strong as ever she was fucking someone else and Spinks should feel free to do likewise. Spinks after returning to the States could find no evidence her assertion was true. There'd been no other man. There'd been as far as Spinks was able to divulge no grave or terrible secrets she'd revealed to her close friends or coworkers. No suggestions of a physical, mental or spiritual disease hinted at to her doctor, pastor, family members. No clue picked up by anyone Spinks had spoken to that her life was spiraling out of control and her mind being taken over by a deranged, hallucinogenic and/or evil force.

"It's the thing a person least expects they say will do him in, Spinks—!"

The last words to reach him before the start of a hellacious storm from Private First Class Bobo Callender out of the bottom of a sixty-foot-deep hole he appeared unlikely to get out of alive, doing his best to console a good bud to take his own mind off the least expected thing coming for him.

Less a life Spinks had been living these four years than a trial.

A trial repeated every day, without a beginning or end.

His thoughts like a satellite endlessly circling in space.

A trial to get out of bed in the morning. A trial to get through each day working or, lacking the will to work, doing not much of anything past getting drunk and/or high to varying degrees. A trial lying awake in bed each night going over the same questions without answers while churning with anger, grief, remorse, guilt over how he'd closed his mind to the warning signs that the darkness he'd always known existed in Rebecca's mind had taken it over completely before lapsing finally into a state of fitful unconsciousness haunted by dreams filled with more anger, grief, remorse, guilt and unanswerable questions.

Hating himself for missing Rebecca even after all she'd destroyed.

Missing Iris the most though. Missing her nonstop. Wondering who she would have become. What she would have been like at the age she would have been at whatever point in time he was thinking of her at while his life to no discernible purpose unwound like a ball of string rolling down a hill.

Tributaries flush with late spring rains added to and strengthened the stream on its serpentine path through a forest of virgin pine man-made tools had never touched. Dead or rotting trees pushed over from past storms had in a number of places fallen across the water creating a series of small ponds behind half-effective dams over, through and around which water rushed in forceful jets. Holding the cloud-shadowed moon and a few misty stars peeking through the high trees the night to Spinks, half-blindly making his way through it, was as infinite and unchanging as a painting he'd been made a living part of and couldn't get out of. His light picked up, lodged between two rocks in the current, a body being forcefully waved side to side like a surrender flag. He moved closer and made it out for a juvenile deer, still with spots on it. He crouched down and lifted the body out of the water. Wet as it was it was still warm. Spinks guessed the fawn wasn't dead more than a couple hours. He pictured it crossing the water with its mother before slipping on the algae-coated bed and being drawn under the current to drown in stages between rocks holding it like a vice. He laid the body above the stream on a bed of damp pine needles and sat down exhausted next to it. Thinking about the inequity of the world he felt his eyes moisten. Innocence trampled as evil soldiered on. Angels ravaged, drowned, cast off of cliffs; demons, if they let them live at all, poisoning them with their demon blood to kill the angels in them. He could no more stop his tears flowing than he could stop the stream. He felt the fawn's unblinking eyes on him like two questions asked shyly with little hope of being answered. At a sound like a random wind gust moving through dead branches he looked up.

A human female figure standing in the trees beckoned to him.

Obscured by night she might have been dressed only in darkness.

Her hair a single piece of soft fabric falling gently around her ears.

She'd been lost and he'd found her. Or the other way around. He'd been lost and she'd found him.

Spinks got to his feet and walked at her.

She disappeared like mist blown by the wind.

He stopped walking and wiped his eyes.

She'd been as real as everything else in this night. He was certain of it.

Relief of the sort that finally having a tooth pulled after weeks of gnawing pain washed over him accepting the fact that there was no possibility of his going backward into the life he'd jumped out of. The only possible path for him was forward—even if that path led to his imminent death or life in prison. The girl, whatever her name, whatever her past, whatever her crimes, in his arms had felt to him like Iris had felt at every age he'd ever held her at—warm, not cold. A little angel.

# 25

The light beam divulging like a third eye the trees and bushes ahead of him suddenly was only a white spot in an empty black sea.

Spinks abruptly stopped walking. He angled the beam down at the ground at his feet.

He'd halted just short of stepping off a cliff where the trees ended. He flashed on his memory of Bobo Callender's voice floating up out of the earth to stop him a step short of plummeting down on top of Callender trapped and broken at the bottom of a sixty-foot deep kariz.

Rebecca and Iris soaring in Rebecca's minivan off a thousand-foot cliff onto seaside rocks.

From cradle to grave the course of entire lives determined by a few steps taken or not taken.

By the placement or misplacement of a foot. By a guiding hand steering or mis-steering a vehicle's course on a mountain highway.

To his right the water fell in twin streams on two sides of a boulder sitting mid-creek as if intentionally placed there to force the onrushing water into choosing its course to the bottom.

He gazed out over the darkened woods below at the flowing water dully winking in spots where the sky's pale glow sporadically reached it through the dense foliage not for the first time wondering which particular moments, memories and thoughts from a lifetime of them flooded the minds of a mother and daughter plummeting through a thousand feet of nothing toward their deaths. He hoped for the countless time Rebecca and Iris had both left the world with their minds awash in only their best moments, memories and thoughts at least a few of which had included him. Off in the distance something flickered in the trees. A light or reflection of light. Seconds later he saw it again and made it for a flashlight beam moving at the direction of an unseen hand toward where, from what he could see of its meandering course, he figured the stream would be. It vanished again and didn't come back but stayed as implanted in his memory as the female figure who'd earlier beckoned to him from the trees.

He veered left, away from the cliff, and started walking again, hunting with his light for a passable way down the hill.

A few hundred feet lower than where minutes earlier he'd started his descent, and several times that far from the stream, he walked back to his right, through oak, elm and maple trees towering over thick underbrush, until he again reached the flowing water, his only marker in a black maze of trees that might have been as big as the world or small as a prison cell.

A finger pointing crookedly through the dark night toward a vague promise of a destination borne of something more than hope.

He crouched down by the stream and with his cupped hands scooped into his mouth water as untainted and fresh as an infant's first view of the world. He washed his face in it, then submerged his entire head in it, Bobo Callender calling up to him from the bottom of a hole that would soon fill up with water his fear of death had left him like a sweated-out fever after he'd been dunked in a river by a Baptist preacher and accepted Jesus into his life.

Spinks shook the water from his head and didn't feel any less alone or, except for being cooler, any different than he had. He looked up through the trees and saw only a few stars struggling to be visible and a hint of the moon through thick clouds.

He got to his feet and resumed following the stream on its indomitable path.

Older trees gave way to younger, scrubbier ones. Sporadic

boulders popped up among them like dropped after thoughts. Burgeoning underground creeks sporadically dampened the ground, making homes for loud peepers and tree frogs that went silent at his approach and resumed chirping at his back. The stream's current, ever stronger and more determined, in his ears was like a voice he'd heard and couldn't quite place. Its sound and the terrain's vaguely familiar feel told him he'd walked through these very woods in the opposite direction with the girl in his arms though his recollection of doing so was as hazy as the lost details of a dream or long ago trip the passage of time had blurred. The thought occurred to him for not the first time that what he believed he was experiencing and remembering of these woods was entirely a figment in his unconscious mind. Rounding a corner minutes later he recognized the shape of his crashed pickup truck fishtailing in the middle of the stream telling him with the certainty of a hammer strike to the head he was squarely in reality and that this night would end because only in dreams do nights go on forever. The sun would rise on a new morning. A day would follow it. The light would find Spinks a hunted man in a world the night had turned inside out. He went to his knees seeing a light flicker seventy-five feet downstream, near the Durango. He turned off his flashlight.

The light near the Durango flickered again.

No. Not near the Durango.

In the Durango.

A flashlight beam.

Moving about in the truck's half-submerged cab.

Spinks got back to his feet and walked stealthily along the high-grass covered shore at his half-drowned truck he was still a year's worth of payments from owning. He stopped walking on the shore, directly across from the night-darkened Durango swaying in the swirling water like a huge misshapen tail casually swatting at flies. He could hear splashing sounds from someone moving in or around the cab in water he recalled to be hip deep or so. From the light beam's location and movements in the cab he surmised the light-holder was leaning into it through the far side passenger window Spinks had pulled the girl out of. From every encounter he'd had that night he surmised whoever the light-holder was wasn't peering into the Durango's cab out of concern for survivors of the crash still possibly in it and was more likely to reach for and turn a weapon on Jack Spinks than willingly answer questions from him.

And Spinks had questions he intended to have answered.

He figured anyone interested enough in his crashed pickup truck to wade through a raging stream to get to it was a good candidate to put his questions to.

What he'd need to do to get them answered didn't much matter to him anymore.

Drawing Poncet's Glock he stepped carefully into the half-way to knee-deep water closest to shore and walked as quietly as he could at the truck, the steadily deepening water tugging at his legs like coarse vines blanketing a jungle floor he was struggling to traverse. It felt to him like a lifetime ago—or like an incident from someone else's life entirely—he'd carried the girl in the opposite direction through this water, unsure if she was alive or dead. He recalled as if it were being recounted to him about someone else's life, laying her unconscious body on shore and a few minutes later her eyes opening and, more than any words she'd spoken to him before or since then, begging him to save her. A little angel's eyes. If he'd looked into the eyes of the girl he'd stopped for up on the road would he have seen those eyes? That face? Was the half-crazed, violent girl who'd jumped into his truck up on the road and nearly killed them both the same girl he'd watched come back to life in his arms on the stream bank, lost and afraid as his own daughter had to have been flying off that cliff next to one of only two people in the entire world she'd trusted her life to?

Hail hit the water in three or four places near him.

On such a warm night? And no threatening clouds overhead?

Spinks was mulling the unusual conditions for hail when his

ears detected a popping sound the raging stream was largely muffling.

A panicked feeling came over him.

Hail wasn't hitting the water.

Bullets were hitting the water.

Spinks swiveled his head about, searching for the source of the shots, knowing from having peered out at the darkened stream from both its banks earlier that standing where he was he was as visible to the shore as an enshadowed bear hunting fish would be.

He dove beneath the water still holding Poncet's Glock in one hand. He struggled against the current, painfully forcing water up his nose, toward the truck ten feet away. Bullets sliced noiselessly through the water right of him. He pushed off the bottom hard to his left and came up hugging the Durango's driver door. The cab, under water halfway to the door windows, swayed against him in the current. Spinks, leaning to his right, peered through the open driver window and saw through the passenger window the stream moving like a giant black snake through a nearly as black world. The Durango's glove box was open and, from what he could see of it, empty. His .308 wasn't in the rack above the seat. A blurred face appeared in the opposite window. The face disappeared and two hands clasping a small object pushed through the open window. Spinks jerked his head back from his window a moment before a bullet whizzed through it. Then another one. Spinks powered his way two giant steps upstream to the near edge of the windshield. He peered around the windshield, past the Durango's partially submerged hood, searching for the shooter.

He saw only a pinprick of light in the darkness halfway up the opposite bank.

A bullet from a shot he didn't hear hit the water behind him.

Another one slammed someplace into the Durango.

Spinks, certain both shots came from farther away than the stream on the other side of the truck but with no idea from where, dove into the stream again.

He resurfaced from his chin up realizing he'd lost Poncet's Glock. He reached to the back of his belt for Carl's Glock and found it gone too. Staying only far enough above the stream to breathe through his nose he started slowly working his way around the front of the cab. He rounded the cab and saw not five feet from him a darkened human shape raising what Spinks had no doubt was a pistol fired at least twice at him already. Spinks, aided by the current now at his back, pushed mightily with his legs forward into the shape as the pistol fired and a bullet whizzed past his left ear. The gunman fell backwards with Spinks on top of him, one hand wrestling him for the pistol. Then the pistol was gone, lost to the stream as Spinks and the gunman, pummeled and pushed downstream by the current, awkwardly wrestled to reach the surface as much as they did with each other. Spinks got his hands around the gunman's neck and, holding them there, managed to pop his head out of the water and gulp in some air. He went back under the water and took to choking the gunman in earnest, aiming to drown or strangle him. In not very many seconds the gunman's body went limp and Spinks suddenly realizing how small it was stopped choking it. Overcome with a sick feeling he pulled the body out of the water.

He turned it over onto its back in the stream and stared down at it. "Oh, Jesus, God, no!" he gasped.

Her eyes were closed and she wasn't moving. Like every man Spinks had encountered that night she was dressed all in black. An empty holster hung on one of her hips. A sheathed knife was strapped to her right calf above her boot.

Spinks, holding her head above water with one hand carefully placed beneath it, dragged her with the other hand as rapidly as he could manage through the enraged waters to shore. He lay her body down on the damp grass. He tilted back her head, forced open her mouth and with both hands pushed hard a few times on her chest between her breasts, then leaning forward put his open mouth on hers and exhaled three or four deep breaths into her lungs. He went back to pushing on her chest, begging her to breathe but she didn't. He breathed more air into her lungs and pushed again on her breastbone. Water burped out between her lips. She coughed and more water came out of her mouth. Her chest moved slowly up and down. Her eyes opened lazily and Spinks said down at her in a breaking up, hoarse whisper, "I'm sorry, Angel. I'm sorry I wasn't here before."

The girl gazed up at Spinks through darkness obscuring her bloodless features like a thin sheet cloaking a corpse. She coughed out more water. Spinks pushed her hair off her face, the familiar female face that was a constant fixture in his mind subtly changing form like the moon moving in and out of the clouds. He wiped spittle from the corners of her lips. The girl in the way of a kidnap victim who's just had a blindfold removed after hours of sightless travel rolled her eyes right, at the rushing stream, left, at the wooded hillside, up, at the darkly lurking trees and back at Spinks crouched at the top of her head. She coughed more.

"You didn't kill her?"

The male voice behind him recalled to Spinks the gunfire raining from afar onto the stream at the same time the girl had been firing a pistol at him; and that both Glocks Spinks had been armed with were in the stream. "I saved her life," he said not turning around though doubting keeping his back to the speaker would keep him from shooting Spinks if that's what he meant to do.

"Odd that," said the voice, the girl's eyes—they might have been glistening black pebbles pulled from the stream from what Spinks could see of them in the night—rolling toward the voice like a dog's eyes toward its master's whistle. "After you about killed her."

"To keep her from killing me," said Spinks, making the man to be ten-odd feet behind him, aiming a high-powered rifle at the back of his head and unable from where he stood to see more than Spinks' back and the bottom of the girl's legs extending out in front of him.

"She took you for a bad man."

"She took me for someone else then." Spinks' eyes traveled the length of the girl's darkened body, to the lump he recalled for a knife strapped to her right calf. He moved his right hand in the air over the girl's leg slowly at the knife. The girl's eyes rolled away from the voice in the darkness, to Spinks' hand.

"You're not a bad man?"

"Not next to a lot of men walking around."

"Just a man in a bad situation?"

"It doesn't feel to me like a good situation having my back to someone who's just tried to shoot me dead with a high-powered rifle."

A crunching noise indicated the rifle-wielder was stepping closer to Spinks. "I'd wanted to shoot you dead you'd be dead."

Spinks' hand reached the sheaf and grasped the knife handle. "Dodging bullets in that stream I sure felt like you did."

"The bullets were to tell you your life is no longer in your hands—it's in my hands—and Gracie that a dude from out the woods armed with a pistol was headed her way. Where is that pistol?"

Spinks slowly drawing the knife from the sheaf said, "In the stream."

The girl might have been a block of ice watching him. He slipped the knife under his soaked shirt. "Gracie?"

The girl's eyes rolled like drops of water on a barely tilted pan from where the knife was secreted beneath Spinks' shirt, back at the speaker.

"He a goddamn liar?"

The girl's mouth opened in the semi-darkness like a small bay door to an unlighted space. "He no have a gun."

A voice from another world. Or from another continent anyway.

Spinks wondered if his memories of his little angel were like cataracts clouding his vision.

A flashlight beam aimed down over his shoulder partially exposed a young woman with his little angel's bob-cut dark hair and spare body begging for a good meal.

But not his little angel.

Spinks gasped.

The truth was in their eyes.

His girl's eyes—Spinks had come to think of the girl he'd lost in these woods as his girl, not in a romantic or possessive sense but as a young life he'd somehow become responsible for—had a lost look begging to be found. The eyes he was looking down into now had a look beyond lost, with no memory of ever wanting to be found. A look behind which Spinks imagined only a black void stripped of whatever memories it might once have held.

Eyes that scared him. Eyes that at the same time saddened him.

"Can you stand?" said the male voice at Spinks' back.

"I think yes," said the young woman the voice had tagged Gracie.

"Do it," said the voice.

Gracie shakily standing, dripping water in a post-drowned fog, brought to Spinks' mind a stunned animal, after being knocked down by a bullet, instinctively struggling back to its feet. A young woman who'd never been young. A young woman formed not from her history but from implanted thoughts. Or were Spinks' perceptions muddled again? Every sight, sound, touch he experienced colored by his memory of the first young woman he'd pulled near-dead from this stream and that memory colored by his always present memory of his dead daughter.

"I was dead," the young woman said into the air over Spinks' head.

"Dead's forever. No one comes back from dead"—the cold metal impacting the back of his neck Spinks' only assurance that more than a bodiless voice had responded to her.

"I saw me lying here in the grass like empty dead corn husk."

A scoffing sound behind Spinks. "You saw yourself dead?"

Gracie moved her eyes up at the dark sky. "From up there."

"How'd that work? Being up there and down here at the same time?"

"Was only my body down here. I not in it."

"No fun that I bet."

"I no need that empty shell no more where I was. And I no want it back. It would only have weigh me down."

Spinks from his unending hope that Iris and Rebecca were happy wherever they were now wanted to ask her more about the place she was at when she was looking at herself dead but worried the rifle wielder would react badly to his intruding on their conversation.

"Then I open my eyes and I back in my body. Back in this fucking life. It no feel like I fit here no more after I spend time in nicer place to come after."

The man applying pressure to the rifle barrel against Spinks' neck said, "See how bad this life you got now strikes you when you're dead for real with no man around you can fuck or bribe to bring you back to it." He pushed Spinks onto his stomach in the wet grass at Gracie's feet. "You'd still be in whatever fuck afterlife you think you were in wasn't for this dude breathing life back into you. Course he's who killed you in the first place, so the question for you is if you should kill him, fuck him or fuck him and then kill him."

He told Spinks to roll over. Spinks did and looking up at the second of the two gofers he'd met at Sebastian Poe's house said, "You don't know how to swim?"

Arno—that was his name—poked the rifle barrel into Spinks' mid-section as if Spinks were an animal he'd run down in the road he wasn't sure was alive or dead. "Jesus Christ. The goddamn weed salesman!"

Spinks said, "'Cause if you can swim how do you defend sending a hundred-pound girl into a raging stream while you sit your ass on shore?"

Arno raised his eyes to Gracie. "Jack Spinks is making you out for a fucking lightweight, Gracie. Tell him how much you weighed last we checked."

Gracie looking down at Spinks said in a tone as inflectionless as the voice on a GPS, "One hundred twenty-two pounds,"

Spinks wondering if she was seeing the man who'd killed her, the man who'd saved her life or a man in her eyes as alike to every other man as one knife to another in a matching set of silverware. And why she hadn't said anything about the knife he'd taken off her?

Arno said, "That weed you sold Mr. Poe weren't close to what your buddy gave us a sample of. Didn't even taste like the same shit."

Spinks said, "Mr. Poe got the leftover chaff from last year's crop I'd have thrown out I hadn't found a sucker to buy it off me for top dollar."

"On your feet, motherfucker."

Spinks got to his feet facing Gracie, his eyes, seeing her in the light, telling him she wasn't a young woman in any measurement other than years. He said to her, "If you were looking to clip my marijuana stash from under the front seat of my truck two sheriff's deputies beat you to it." Gracie stared at him as if he were nothing in the night's darkness.

Arno said, "We found you though. Ain't that the tits."

Spinks turned around at him. "You're not curious about the sheriff's deputies?"

"Why you think we're out here?"

Spinks remembering the vehicle the girl had run his Durango into said, "You followed them through the woods to the woman's cabin?"

"Mr. Poe doesn't take anything for granted, asshole."

"Hell are you saying?"

"It's not sheriff's deputies holding a gun on you is it?"

The inside of Spinks' head felt as if a high wind had just blown through it. Arno jabbing the rifle into his stomach said, "Beats the shit out of me what Mr. Poe saw interesting in you past an angry, half off the wheels son of a bitch. But hell, that's ninety percent of the world. An angry, half off the wheels son of a bitch not on a man's team ain't worth a shit to him."

Spinks, doubled over in pain, took in a couple deep breaths trying to decide if he could get Gracie's knife out of his belt and blade-first into Arno before Arno could shoot him. He concluded he couldn't. "Was it you tortured to death that poor woman, you miserable, cowardly fuck? Or was it your fellow ass-kisser Slade you left to bleed out back there in the woods?"

"I could see from the start you weren't no team player. You're one them thinks nobody might know more than you do."

Spinks straightening up said angrily, "What was the purpose in it?"

"We asked her a few simple questions. Instead of answering them she got physical with us and it cost her dying slow instead of quick."

"She didn't know anything about whatever you were asking her. What did it gain you to kill her?"

"Fuck you mean gain? She stabbed Slade in the gut."

Gracie said flatly, "She no mad about it no more. She watching us right now."

Arno gave her a look both threatening and befuddled. "Fuck you talking about?"

"This life—it all ugly from where she's at." She raised her eyes at the night again. "Breathing, talking, fucking. They all glad to be free of it up there."

"Don't fucking open your mouth again until I tell you to. And get your goddamn eyes out of the sky," Arno said to her.

Spinks said, "I had a couple firearms, some insurance forms, my wallet and just short of a quarter pound of marijuana in my truck. Any of that not there that those sheriff's deputies didn't take likely got washed away by the stream."

Arno jabbed him with the rifle again.

Spinks caught his breath and said, "You had her looking for something other than that you're going to have to tell me what it is."

"You know damn well what she was looking for."

"How would I know what she was looking for?"

"You been running through these woods for your health that it?"

"I've been running through them trying to save the life of a scared girl jumped in my truck."

Arno looked at Gracie. "You think he's bat-shit crazy, Gracie? Or just a liar?"

Gracie didn't say what she thought. She might have been a stone statue erected there.

Spinks said to Arno, "What did you do with her?"

"Do with who?"

"The girl I left in the cabin."

"You better get your eyes checked."

"What?"

Arno looked at Gracie again. "I think he's just a liar."

Spinks imagining his sanity as a living thing weakening under a barrage of punches said to Gracie, "You're her friend? The two of you are roommates?"

Not a sound, blink or facial tic from Gracie.

"You're all built the same—and have the same hairstyles—you and her and another young lady Sebastian Poe has living over his garage?" Face and body still as quarry water, lips tightly closed, hands clasped behind her back Gracie might have been looking at something faraway in the darkness or at nothing at all. "I didn't understand that day you three came out and waved to me what you were trying to tell me. I should have tried to help you only—!"

Arno said to Spinks, "It's only the trees that are listening to you."

Spinks looking from Gracie to Arno and back to Gracie suddenly wasn't sure he wasn't the one flesh and blood person standing there. The one flesh and blood person in those entire woods. He had the sensation watching Gracie's frozen features in their expressionless gaze her head was being dangled before him on invisible strings in the grasp of an invisible hand. A sharp pressure in the center of his chest led him to look down at a rifle barrel being pressed hard into his sternum.

"Where are they?"

He looked up at the moonlight-distorted, deeply cratered face of the man applying the pressure. "Where's what?"

"I asked your friend the same question and she gave me the answer you just did. Think about where she is now."

"Friend! What friend?"

"And of all the time we took putting her where she is now."

"You talking about the woman you tortured to death back in that cabin? She was a therapist in the city came out here on weekends to write poetry and take photographs! Tonight's the first time I laid eyes on her!"

"You want to walk out of here alive and pretty much in one piece you got three seconds to come up with those diamonds."

"Diamonds!? Hell you talking about? What diamonds?"

Arno looked at Gracie and back at Spinks. "If your invisible girl is holding them you best snap your fingers real quick, make her cough them up."

Spinks shook his head and saw colors. "I don't know what you're talking about. I don't know anything about any diamonds."

Arno jabbed Spinks harder with the rifle barrel. "You tried to drive away from those sheriff's deputies for having a little weed in your truck?"

"I didn't try to drive away from them at all! The girl did."

Arno shook his head in disbelief.

"She jumped into the space beneath the steering wheel and slammed the gas pedal to the floor!"

"You think I'm stupid?"

"I think your dumb as shit if you think I stole Sebastian Poe's diamonds!"

"Where is your scared girl now? Think hard, asshole."

"You all would know more about where she is than I do after you broke into that cabin and murdered the woman I left her with."

Arno pointed at Gracie.

"Look at her."

Spinks looking at Gracie had the sensation of peering into a pond of murky water at a drowned corpse with a once beautiful, hauntingly familiar face.

"She look grateful to you? Like she'd maybe cut you some slack for saving her life?"

"Why do you let this asshole treat you like you're dead?" Spinks said to Gracie, her closemouthed expression and still as stone posture unchanged since he'd last looked at her.

"Where would you like her to start?"

"What?"

Arno jabbed him again. "She's especially good at carving a man's cock and balls into strips so thin you could package and sell them for bacon."

Spinks, flashing on the dead woman cut up in her cabin and Poncet calling the girl Spinks had carried through the woods Sebastian Poe's robot, felt sick to his stomach. And overwhelmingly sad. "You don't give me the answers I want right now I'll have her cut on you in enough places and enough different ways the bullet I'll put in your head after she's done won't hardly matter."

Spinks let out an internal scream formed from bone-deep agony and blind rage.

He said to Arno, "I ask you a question first?"

Arno carefully watching Spinks said, "What is it?"

"How many times a day does Sebastian Poe have you wipe his ass?"

Arno angrily jabbed the rifle barrel at Spinks' midsection and Spinks, ready for it this time, in one motion with his left hand grabbed the barrel and pushed it away from him. The gun went off as Spinks with his right hand pulled from his belt beneath his shirt Gracie's knife. He jammed it up to its hilt into Arno's lower abdomen. He grabbed the handle with both hands and forcefully leveraged the blade up, through Arno's stomach, pancreas, liver, until it hit bone. Arno dropped the rifle. Spinks withdrew the knife. Arno made a choking sound as blood and intestines poured from his gaping midsection like weed-infiltrated water from a tipped bucket. He teetered then fell forward onto his stomach, made a slow-motion sort of slither, then lay still in his pooling insides.

Spinks stood over him shaking. With anger. With fear. With sadness.

He was drenched in blood. He knew his mind wasn't right but wasn't sure if his thinking was severely off or if he was only disoriented from all he'd been through. Absolute sanity in the world he was in struck him as a place as far off as the small, mostly empty house on ten acres of mostly barren land he'd called home for four years leading up to today. He told himself he would find the girl, his girl, if it took him a thousand nights as long as this one that wasn't yet over to do it. And before or after he did he would find Sebastian Poe and kill him. With as many good people in the world who died unjustly every day Sebastian Poe—a demon on earth who turned pre-pubescent girls into robotic killers—should not be allowed to live another minute in it. He looked down at his shaking hands. He was still holding the knife. The knife that had carved up the woman in the cabin. The knife that Gracie after coming back from the afterlife had wordlessly watched Spinks take out of its sheaf on her leg and put into his belt. Had she foreseen—or only hoped—what Spinks would do with it?

He turned around.

She was peering up from her back at the dark sky from where before coming back to life on the stream's bank she claimed to have been staring down at her dead, discarded body. If she'd been up there, staring down at her earthly flesh during those few minutes she wasn't breathing, she was up there now for eternity.

The bullet had entered her chest exactly where someone would draw a heart in diagramming its location in the human body. Spinks looking down at what Gracie had called her empty husk wanted to believe with all his heart she was looking down at him looking down at it. The face looked younger than it had when she'd been behind it. The eyes, emptied of their dark history, lighter, nearly pellucid and shockingly like the eyes of the girl he'd carried through the woods. The body like a collage of twigs with flesh over it carefully placed on the grass, the sight of which made Spinks positive she'd lied to him about weighing more than a hundred pounds. Feelings like those he'd felt sitting over the drowned fawn back in the woods welled up in him. His sadness now though was less for a life cut short than for a life not lived at all. Whatever she'd been in the years she'd inhabited the body lying at Spinks' feet—Whore? Temptress? Torturer? Murderess?—Spinks was quite certain Gracie, or whatever her real name was, wouldn't have been in a life she had chosen to live. The life she might have lived had she been allowed to choose it would forever be a mystery. The one she did live had belonged to Sebastian Poe. And what of the life of the girl Spinks had carried through the woods? Spinks with a glimmer of hope recalled the look in her eyes—lost, yes, but not, like the look in Gracie's eyes when she'd been alive, gone past all memory of being lost or hope of being found again.

In her pockets he found a lighter, cigarettes, a pencil stub, a tiny notepad. No photographs, identification, cash, good luck charms. The notepad's pages were three quarters taken up with infantile pencil stick figures—the sun, birds flying, a dog fucking a woman, an angel smiling, a man who looked to be screaming with a knife sticking out of his forehead—and one syllable words—pig, dog, cunt, eat, smile, shit, laugh, fuck, love—in large looping print of the sort a small child first learning how to write might make. She had a small tattoo of a set of puckered lips framed in a heart on the back of her neck. Another on her right wrist of a single half-closed eye without a lash.

Arno was strapped with a Colt nine millimeter and bands of ammunition for it and for the rifle he'd sprayed the water around Spinks with and one too many times jammed into his midsection—a Panther .308 semi-automatic. A walkie-talkie hung from his belt. Red Man chewing tobacco, a set of car or truck keys, an all-purpose fishing knife, two packets of Beef Jerky in his pockets. Spinks put the keys and knife in his pocket, the ammunition band for the Colt around one shoulder and the

Colt and walkie-talkie into his waistband. He dragged the body off into the trees and propped it sitting up against the trunk of a large white pine where anyone walking that way down to the water would be bound to find it. He placed the Panther in the body's lap and Arno's hands around it knowing Arno's gutted body and the staging of the scene would make it clear someone had walked away from the scene while satisfying himself that the one guilty party was holding the only murder weapon involved in the killings.

He couldn't tolerate the thought of Gracie's body resting in sight, throwing or even shouting distance of the body of a man who, if he hadn't been her direct torturer and indoctrinator, had certainly been one of her enablers and handlers.

He picked her up and carried her several yards in the opposite direction and placed her face-up on her back in a soft patch of sweet flag grass where the sound of the flowing water muted the noises of the woods behind her. Her features appeared to be getting younger the farther away from life she traveled, ivory white skin unblemished, a little girl's button nose, pouty lips. He pictured her, as so often he did Iris, laughing at the sheer joy of being a kid alive in the world. Rolling playfully about in that grass. He took the sheaf from her leg and threw it and the knife in the stream. He pulled up several armfuls of bluestem grass from the bank nearest the water and covered her body with it hoping any nocturnal scavengers would leave her alone and that he'd be alive long enough to give her location to the police or someone else able and willing to carry her out of the woods and give her a proper burial.

He walked into the stream up to his knees and as best he could washed the blood from his clothes, hands and face.

He looked blindly up the incline he and the girl—his girl—in his Durango had plummeted down several hours that felt like a lifetime ago and wondered if he was trapped in a time warp the exact length and dimensions of this night, from which death, arriving with the first rays of sun on a new day, would be his only escape.

# 26

Stepping out of the woods at the top of the incline onto Black Cat Hollow Road, he pictured himself stepping back into the world from an alternate universe he'd created in a dream state after being knocked unconscious crashing his Durango into the stream.

The illusion wouldn't hold.

The truth resisted his mind's attempt to obliterate it.

The world he'd just stepped out of was the same world he'd just stepped into.

He'd been as awake inside those night-shrouded woods as he was now walking up this badly paved road he'd driven dozens of times in the past.

Every horrible thing he remembered seeing and/or participating in, every place he recalled being, every person he remembered encountering beneath those trees existed outside his head and in the same world he'd been bumbling aimlessly through ever since his wife had murdered his two reasons for living.

He dropped to his knees at the road's edge and raised his arms at the same obscured moon periodically unmasked by blowing clouds he'd imagined winking at him—in humor? Judgment? Approval?—as he'd blindly carried through those woods a young woman whose real or imagined silent cry for help had rung in him a bell of the sort he'd failed to hear or respond to for his own young daughter.

One world. Inside and outside the woods. Inside and outside his mind.

A world he was now a killer and likely fugitive in.

He'd gone into the woods as one person and come out of them as another.

The world looking at the man he was now would see

what?—A murderer? A fool? A bad man? A kidnapper? A cop killer? A deranged lunatic?

He started walking up the road again thinking if he could look back on himself as a decent man whose life had gone to hell for trying to do what had felt to him like the right thing to do he'd maybe rest a little easier in eternity anyway.

The moon's dull glint caught a metallic glow in the forward darkness.

In a few more steps he made out a dark-colored SUV.

A mud-brown Ford Explorer.

Parked on the dirt shoulder near where hours earlier a dark-colored vehicle with orange running lights had come to a stop facing Spinks and the girl in Spinks' Durango.

A dark-colored vehicle the Durango had careened off of before plummeting down the embankment and crashing into the stream.

A dark-colored vehicle Sheriff Grey Poncet and Deputy Carl Ames had gotten out of to follow Spinks and the girl through the woods.

Spinks took from his pocket the keys and key fob he'd taken off Arno's body.

He pressed the fob.

A beep from the Explorer as its fog lights flashed orange.

Spinks, with a disoriented feeling, walked several slow circles around the Explorer.

Not a dent or scratch on it he could see.

A coincidence? Two dark-colored vehicles, both with orange running lights, appearing in the same location—only hours apart—on this desolate road?

One of them the transportation for three murderous criminals.

One of them the transportation for two county police officers.

Two vehicles, transporting a total of five people.

Five people arriving, within hours of each other, at this same remote location where Spinks had encountered a scared to death young woman being chased, in reality or her mind, by demons in a dark-colored vehicle with orange running lights.

Five people who, on this interminably dark night, all found their way through miles of mostly uncharted dark woods to the same secluded cabin the young woman had, through happenstance or design, led Spinks to.

Five people all dead now—except possibly County Sheriff Grey Poncet who, like the young woman Spinks had first encountered on this road, had vanished into the ether.

Spinks' head spun.

He flashed back to the last time he'd seen Poncet. Poncet, under the cover of Spinks' Glock, standing across from Spinks over Slade's bled-out body slouched against a pine tree trunk by a moderately rushing stream—

And then?

A blood-curdling screech overhead and Spinks, against a gut-churning feeling warning him not to, raising his eyes toward the sound and—looking down from the night sky at where his Glock was aimed at an empty spot in the trees he last remembered Poncet standing in.

The tall man had departed Spinks' sphere as quietly as a puff of air. Had he retraced his steps out of the woods, back to his damaged cruiser? If so, where was he now? And if he had made it back to the cruiser he'd abandoned on this road and was the upright cop he claimed to be why hadn't he radioed every police agency in the state to dispatch all available officers to the hollow to search for the man who'd killed his deputy and the suspects in the brutal murder of a New York City therapist?

Spinks the entire night had seen only two cops and more and more suspected they might not be cops. Or, that they were cops in pursuit of an agenda up this hollow other than enforcing the law and likely against the law.

An agenda to do with the traumatized young woman Spinks had first encountered on this piece of road.

An agenda that risked exposure if legitimate police officers were to apprehend, interview or take a statement from the young woman and/or Spinks.

An agenda Poncet was involved with Sebastian Poe's crew in.

"Why do you think we're out here?"

Arno's words reverberated in Spinks's consciousness like waves of sound from a giant struck bell. *Walkie-talkies.*

Arno and Poncet had both been carrying one in this backwoods hollow a cell phone signal couldn't be found in.

A walkie-talkie doesn't require a signal. Walkie-talkies are functional up to a few miles in any terrain or conditions.

Push a button to talk. Let it off to listen—

Had Sebastian Poe's three stone cold killers been guided by Sheriff Grey Poncet's voice through those dark, tangled woods to the woman's cabin?

The sheriff and his deputy—or two men impersonating the sheriff and his deputy—were working with, or for, Poe?

Spinks envisioned Poncet on his walkie-talkie directing Arno, Slade, and Gracie to the woman's cabin, even as the girl, peering terrified up the hill at the sheriff's and his deputy's upright shapes under the trees, whispered to Spinks, "The demons can hear near as good as they can see."

He stepped to the Explorer's driver door and opened it.

He climbed into the driver seat.

Tobacco, tobacco smoke, stale beer, cheap fried food smells.

Over the rear window an empty gun rack Spinks supposed the Panther had rested in. A camouflaged hunter's cap hanging from the rack.

A fuzzy go-go dancer doll dangling from the rearview mirror.

An opened cigarette package on the dash.

Loose bullets, empty store-bought pastry wrappers, fast food cartons, a large manila envelope on the seat.

Spinks picked up the envelope.

He pulled out of it a blown-up photograph.

He placed the photograph in his lap and peered down at it.

He was aware a period of time had passed but not of its dimensions.

Longer than a moment, shorter than the remaining night.

He sensed he'd ventured far while going nowhere and that the space he'd taken up doing it was the exact size of the last four years of his life.

Darkness was still a constant. He pictured it as a mind-altering drug, more powerful than years of uninterrupted daylight, he'd drunk too deeply of. And the elongated night a length of rubber being stretched apart from both ends to cover a greater distance, space and time than God had designed it to.

It occurred to him peering out the windshield at the cloud-draped moon that it hadn't become more or less cloud draped or changed its position since he'd first been aware of it that evening, however long ago that had been. Also, that his perceptions might not be entirely trustworthy. Reality in his current view of it was a greased pig he was unable to get a firm grip on.

Questions evolving out of shreds of his memory appeared as ghostly figures on horseback galloping out of the fog in his brain.

Who in this infinitely long night besides the young psychopath named Gracie had he dragged out of the stream and breathed life back into?

The girl I carried through the woods. The girl without a name, answered Spinks.

The girl without a name, the ghostly horsemen disdainfully reminded him, vanished like smoke into a dark sky the moment you took your eyes off her.

Like Iris vanished, while you were fighting a war. Remember?

She didn't vanish. She was murdered! The woman I loved murdered her!

And then, halleluiah, you found her again, saved her life a second time after nearly killing her a second time?

Who are you talking about!? Found who!?

The girl without a name.

No. The second girl I pulled from the stream only looked like her in the half-light.

Looked like Iris?

Looked like the girl without a name! I was certain I'd found her again—

Certain until Arno's flashlight beam shining down at the half-drowned female face looking up at you from the stream bank showed you a set of eyes you were positive you didn't know?

Spinks nodded. Gone eyes. A killer's eyes. A walking dead person's eyes.

Not the lost eyes of the girl who'd flooded your mind with memories of Iris.

Not the eyes of the girl you as much as gave up your life to help rescue.

Not the eyes that first opened at you on that stream bank after you'd pulled the girl you'd stopped for on the road from your crashed Durango.

Spinks nodded more.

The ghostly figures stared stonily at him.

What of the eyes of the near-insane girl who jumped into your truck, attacked you with her fists, and drove your truck off the road?

What?

Do you remember what was in her eyes? Did you even let yourself see what was in them?

I don't know what you mean.

Or in the eyes of the young woman who ripped to shreds with a letter opener the rabbit or kangaroo doll at the woman's cabin?

Did those eyes and the eyes that looked up at you in Arno's flashlight beam belong to two different young women?

Or has every set of female eyes you've looked into this evening belonged to one small dark-haired young woman now lying dead from a bullet in her heart beneath handfuls of bluestem grass near the bank of the stream you twice pulled her half-drowned body from?

You're out of your mind—are you saying I can't tell one young woman from another?!

More stone-faced stares from the ghostly figures.

For Christ sake—it wasn't Gracie I carried through the woods to the woman's cabin—!

More silence from the ghostly figures.

The girl I left in that cabin wouldn't—couldn't—have done what was done to that woman—!

Where then, if it wasn't Gracie, is the young lady you believe you did leave with that poor woman?

Spinks stuck his head out the driver window and screamed into the night.

His mind, he feared, wasn't entirely right; it felt to him like a series of rotting steps he was trying to negotiate in the dark toward a closed door to an unknown room.

He had gone into the woods feeling lost and was even more lost after finding his way out of them. He'd been feeling lonely and powerless and was even more lonely and powerless after trying and failing to help a young girl he'd decided on no sound evidence was even more lonely and powerless than he was. He'd been holding in four years of target-less rage and was even more enraged at what he couldn't see after killing two people he hadn't known.

He looked back down at the photograph in his lap.

A former rural schoolhouse converted into a weekend home. A photo of the same home was in a photo collage on the dead woman's cabin wall. Only in that photo the home's doors and windows weren't circled in magic marker and hand-drawn arrows didn't point from the home to the road a hundred odd yards to its front, to the woods to its rear, to the garage directly to its left. *Master Br* wasn't printed over a downstairs window, *safe* over a window next to it, *kid?* over an upstairs window.

The photograph of the converted schoolhouse on the woman's cabin wall had been directly next to the photograph of Sebastian Poe's sprawling house and grounds Sheriff Grey Poncet had directed Spinks' attention to from which Spinks concluded the Poe house photograph was the photograph the girl had been peering intently at.

She could just as easily have been peering at the photograph in his lap.

Spinks recalled Arno saying, "Mr. Poe doesn't take anything for granted."

And Poncet telling him about a house fire a jeweler working with the Feds in their investigation of Poe, the jeweler's wife and their eight-year-old child were killed in that a slightly built dark-haired young woman was seen running away from.

Slightly built and dark-haired like the girl without a name Spinks had picked up on the road and carried through the woods to the woman's cabin.

Slightly built and dark-haired like the girl who'd disappeared from the cabin after Spinks left her in it with the woman to go hunt the girl's demons.

Slightly built and dark-haired like the girl he had a few hours later breathed life back into after nearly drowning her to keep her from shooting him.

Slightly built and dark-haired like the girl Arno had shot in the heart and Spinks had left buried under armfuls of bluestem grass down by the stream.

A slightly built and dark-haired girl Spinks had pulled out of the stream not one, but two times? The only girl he had seen or interacted with that night?

A girl Poncet had called "one of Poe's girls"? A severely damaged psychopathic girl brainwashed by Poe?

Or one of two girls Spinks had brought back to life on that stream bank? Two girls who, in his tortured, frayed memory, had become one and the same girl?

A girl who hours that felt like a lifetime ago had ignited his memories of his dead daughter and buried anger at his dead wife and started him on a blind, unthinking odyssey through the woods to try and do what he had failed to do for Iris—save her life.

A therapist his family physician had convinced him to see after his wife and daughter's deaths cautioned Spinks that if he didn't allow himself to forgive Rebecca and grieve for her as well as for Iris he would sink deeper and deeper into the darkly phantasmagoric world their deaths had seemingly left him in, a world existing on a potentially devastating mixture of depression, confusion, alcohol and rage. What does she look like when you think of her? he'd asked Spinks of Rebecca.

"A hat," said Spinks.

The therapist nodded for him to continue.

"A wide-brimmed sort of sun hat with a black veil that comes down to where the top of her neck would be."

The therapist nodded more. "How do you see the rest of her—beyond the hat?"

"There is no rest of her. She's just a hat on a head with no face."

The therapist wrinkled his brow and nodded more. He asked Spinks what Iris looked like in his mind.

"An angel," Spinks told him.

"You see her up in heaven you mean?"

"I've never been to heaven. I see her in town. Or on a road I'm driving on. Or hiking in the woods. Or in my backyard. I saw her for a few seconds in the parking lot outside your building. Her lips are always moving but no sound comes out of them. She talks to me with her eyes."

"What do her eyes say to you?"

"Always the same thing—'Don't you recognize me, Daddy? It's me, your little angel. Please catch me before I hit the rocks.'"

Two sessions were all his insurance would pay for so he'd stopped going. Plus he'd already known he was angry and depressed and drank and drugged too much and speaking to a stranger about his wife and daughter had felt to him more and more like he was betraying a secret between the three of them, him and the ghosts of Iris and Rebecca whom he had grown increasingly certain were in the therapist's office listening in on his sessions…

☙

A crackling sound jerked his mind back into the Explorer's front seat.

He darted his eyes out its windows.

To either side of the road enshadowed trees swayed in a gentle breeze like intoxicated dancers on a darkened cruise ship deck.

More crackling—from inside the cab. Or from inside his body.

He jerked his eyes down to his waist.

The walkie-talkie on his belt was enlivened with static.

And in the static sporadic words.

He took the walkie-talkie from his belt.

He stared at it uncertainly as a voice said out of it, "You there? Over."

A male voice. Garbled yet oddly familiar.

Spinks hesitated, then pushed the walkie-talkie's talk button and said, "Yes."

He let the button go. A moment later he pushed it again and said, "Over."

A couple seconds static from the walkie-talkie then: "I hope you've got good news. Over?"

Spinks pushed the button and said, "About what? Over."

"About this fucking mess of a night we're having. Over."

Spinks pushed the button and said, "Negative. Over."

"Hell you saying!? The mess isn't cleaned up? Over."

Spinks pushed the button and said, "Not from where I'm sitting it isn't. I'm dead. It's only been a few hours and already I'm sick of it. Over."

"What's that you said? Over."

Spinks thought more and said into the walkie-talkie, "My

body's down by the stream the dude we've been chasing through the woods ran his truck into." He let go of the button and right after pressed it again and said, "It's sitting up against a pine tree but I'm talking to you from my new permanent home in hell."

He heard a few seconds of static, then, "What's that about the dude who ran his truck into the stream? Over."

Spinks pressed the button and said, "He gutted me like a fish. Looking back on it I can see he had cause. It's too late to say I wish I'd made better choices in my life but conditions being what they are down here I'll be wishing it forever anyhow."

Several seconds of static then the voice said choppily, "The dude still got my merchandise? You worthless fuckers leave him in the wind with it?"

Spinks said into the walkie-talkie, "Word is the merchandise never left the Pinecone Road House. The dude is a clueless fuck."

An angry burst of unintelligible words came out of the walkie-talkie.

Spinks said into it, "Slade's down here with me. We've got a place saved for you. Over."

"Repeat from when you said the merchandise never left the Pinecone Road house. Are you chewing on marbles? I can't hardly make you out. Over."

"Negative— Reception down here—really—bad—"

Spinks switched off the walkie-talkie and lay it on the seat.

He sat looking at himself in the dash mirror haunted by the familiar-sounding voice he'd heard and couldn't quite place coming over the walkie-talkie.

He opened his mouth and slowly said to his reflection, "Over."

❧

He found himself sometime later still at the wheel of the Explorer.

Only now the Explorer was moving.

Five miles down the hollow, maybe six, to the main road.

A left.

Less than a mile to Pinecone Road.

Left again.

He had the sensation the Explorer was driving itself and he was floating in the air above it, his unconscious thoughts guiding it up a long stretch of road unwinding like a haphazardly tossed rope through hilly dark woods interspersed with pasture land sporadically haunted by prone and standing four-legged shapes.

He was consciously aware of where he was going only when the smell out his window informed him he was there.

Two plus days later and wisps of smoke still floated above and around the half-gone structure. That, or the near translucent tendrils were the lingering souls of the man, woman and child the conflagration had consumed.

Police tape enclosing the house and yard.

A kid's charred bike, blackened croquet stakes, an easel with a miraculously undamaged dilettante's half-finished painting of a horse or cow on ash-strewn grass out front.

A burned minivan in the drive under a basketball hoop the flames had eaten the net of while leaving the pole and rim untouched.

The severely drooping branches of a willow tree near the house suggesting in the darkened yard survivors of the blaze doubled over with smoke inhalation.

Spinks stepped out of the Explorer and heard a mewling sound.

He recalled the girl saying people dying sound like children crying.

He took a few steps at the house and the mewling stopped.

He crouched down and stared a number of seconds into the forward darkness, his mind lighting up like a bottle rocket exploding in the night with years removed images.

A movement as vague as a shadow at the edge of an exposed photograph caught his eye.

"It hurts like hell I know," he said softly into the darkness.

"Nothing will ever take the sting out of it. Just know that every creature that lives long enough will learn that life isn't fair and that most of us decide to keep living it anyway—"

A medium-size dog nearly the same shade as the darkness it appeared out of walked at him dangling from its collar metal tags soundlessly colliding.

A family pet orphaned by the fire is what Spinks saw.

He couldn't make out its breed—or if it was a mix of several.

It made not a sound walking past him into its unknown future.

"I reckon you will too," he whispered at the vanishing image.

He stood and walked at the house, as alone as he had been since he'd walked out of the woods.

Parallel lines of police tape spanned the gaping front doorway.

Spinks bending down sidestepped between the bottom two lines.

He took his flashlight from his belt and turning it on stepped into a large, open fire-damaged room still damp from the water that had doused the flames and showing traces of white chemicals that had aided the effort.

A goodly sum had been laid out making the old schoolhouse into the upscale weekend home the fire had destroyed—upscale to Spinks anyway. Ash-blackened white marble flooring underlay the space. Two walls of built-in ceiling-to-floor hardwood bookshelves and their contents ravaged by the flames. A melted wall TV the size of a bedsheet faced a recessed area equipped with what appeared to have been reclining leather seats for six. A still-standing granite bar separated the space from a large kitchen area. Spinks leaning down near the bar picked up from the floor a gold frame holding a photograph enclosed in scorched glass: a man and woman Spinks' approximate age and a boy six or so on the man's shoulders dressed for summer fun on white sand fronting a stretch of unoccupied ocean.

Grief, fear and anger like the symptoms of a recurring flu

he couldn't shake overcame Spinks. Time and space abandoned him to a wilderness without markers past those plotting the scarcely charted nether regions of his unconsciousness.

He turned his face up at a blurred female face looking down at him from beneath a dangling fan-light in a piece of darkness radiating more warmth than the overall darkness.

Memories hit him like a reservoir of tears rushing through a broken dam.

The face came apart and dissipated like seedpods in the wind leaving him with a jumbled memory of three familiar female faces.

He looked back down at the photograph and now saw in it, over the heads of the boy and his parents, a jumbled human face comprised of parts from the three shadowy faces in his memory.

The jumbled parts evolved like a developing picture into a single recognizable face.

For the first time since he'd lost her, he saw her clearly.

The lost, frightened girl running from demons he'd stopped for on Black Cat Hollow Road.

The amnesiac girl he'd left with the dead woman in her cabin several hours ago.

Not the young woman who much later had tried to kill him and was now dead with a bullet from Arno's rifle in her heart under handfuls of bluestem grass near the stream Spinks had pulled her from.

How could he have even contemplated they were one and the same girl?

His certainty beyond a doubt that the girl he'd risked his life coming to the aid of existed separate and apart from any other female in the world or in his imagination, mind or memory heartened Spinks.

And confused him even more than he had been already.

What was she doing in this fire-destroyed house?

Had it been her ghost looking down at him from beneath that fan-light?

If it was her ghost and she'd died in the fire that would mean the confused girl he'd picked up a day later on Black Cat Hollow Road was—

He turned his face upwards again at—a blackened solid plaster ceiling.

A hope that he wasn't in that house, that he was lying unconscious on the stream bank next to his crashed Durango took a firmer hold in him.

But he knew it was a false hope.

He wouldn't be smelling the fire's aftermath if he was unconscious. He wouldn't be seeing charred evidence of the conflagration on his fingers after touching them to the walls unless he was wide awake looking at them.

He lay the photograph on the bar.

Wherever she was now physically— his girl—he was certain of one thing—she was here, in this house, in some form.

He could feel her presence around him in the smoke-tinged air. He looked through the kitchen and down a hallway, at a stairway charred midnight black but miraculously still standing. Beyond it, the area of the house the hand-drawn map in the Explorer's glove box placed the master bedroom (*Master Br*) and safe (*safe*) in was completely destroyed. It was clearly where the fire had begun. Spinks pictured firemen discovering in a room down that hallway three bodies—belonging to two adults and one child—so badly burned they couldn't be identified let alone determined to have been killed before the fire had been intentionally started to cover up the manner of their deaths.

He walked carefully down the imploded hallway to the stairway.

He shined his light up the collapsing, blackened stairs recalling on the hand-drawn map the room on the second floor labeled *kid.*

And Arno saying, "Mr. Poe doesn't take chances. He covers all the bases."

Maybe they hadn't expected the boy in the photograph to be

here. Or maybe they hadn't cared if he was or wasn't here. They had prepared themselves for either case.

Or maybe they had made certain he would be here.

Had the jeweler's son two nights ago made his last trip down these stairs, seeking comfort in the safety of his parent's bed after waking in his bedroom upstairs from a bad dream?

Had he been asleep at the far end of the first-floor hallway between his mother and father at the start of the family's real-life nightmare?

Or had he been sleeping in his own bed when the noise from the real-life nightmare had roused him and prompted him to rush downstairs in a frightened dazed state? Had his parents screams wakened him to the last horrifying moments of his and their lives?

Or hadn't he walked downstairs of his own will?

Had he been hiding, petrified, in or under his bed when Sebastian Poe or one of his hired psychopaths found and dragged the boy out of his bed and downstairs to let the jeweler know in his final stage of pre-death suffering that ratting Sebastian Poe out to the feds was going to cost him more than just his and his wife's lives?

Spinks put a foot on the stairway's lowest step.

He tested it with his weight.

The fire-damaged wood, giving without breaking beneath his foot, had a trembly feel. After the second and third steps supported his weight in the same shaky manner as the first one had Spinks began walking up the stairs with the careful precision of a soldier walking through a minefield.

# 27

A night Rebecca was driving them home from a party they'd both drunk too much at a tire blew on their Jetta. A backcountry road enlivened by indistinct rustling noises from woods to one side and a pasture past a picket fence to the other. The hot, sultry air, rife with bats, breathed a scent of farm animals and cultivated crops. Rebecca watched Spinks get out the jack with her hands on her hips and a tight-lipped expression Spinks in their two years of marriage had learned to not guess at the meaning of or thought behind.

She wandered off as Spinks pried off the blown tire's hubcap. He was twisting off the last of the flat's lug nuts minutes later when she reappeared holding a bouquet of wild flowers. She pulled from the bouquet two stems of butterweed and placed a stem behind each of Spinks' ears. She stepped back and, framing him in her encircled thumbs and forefingers before her eyes, clicked her tongue and said, "I'm going to frame that shot and hang it in my mind." Then, as if resuming a discussion they'd been having when the tire had blown, said, "It's a nice spot to make a baby," Spinks as surprised as he was thrilled at her bringing up a subject she'd always shut down his attempts to broach.

Rebecca handed him the bouquet.

"Do you mind if I call you Robert?" she said.

"What?"

"I see it printed there above your shirt pocket."

"Robert?" said Spinks, following a befuddled pause.

"I take it you're on your way home from work, Robert?"

Spinks showed her a crooked smile. "From the gas station in town. Yes."

"Well, I don't know what I'd have done if you hadn't stopped to help me. A woman alone in the middle of the night—on this desolate road—"

"My pleasure," said Spinks.

"Well, Robert, I'll leave you to it."

She walked off into the darkness.

Twenty minutes later the spare was on and Spinks couldn't find her.

He shut the trunk on the flat, jack and lug wrench and was still alone. He'd become accustomed to her ghostly behavior. Of her stealthily vanishing and just as stealthily reappearing in one of her many different personas. She'd walk away from Spinks into woods or up a city street or mountainside, disappearing to him gradually like a pill dissolving in a glass of water or in the blink of an eye around a bend or through a doorway. A full day after she'd secretly walked out of a New York City hotel room they'd rented for a weekend getaway she'd walked back into it in a black wig and hotel maid's outfit. Before Spinks could ask where she'd been, get angry or say how worried he'd been she broke out in sobs before confiding in a heavily Latin American accented voice that she'd been forced to flee her home country and take any kind of work she could find after government terrorists had murdered her husband and parents and gang raped her and, on her maid's income alone, she couldn't properly feed and clothe the innocent child borne of their brutal act and wondered if the nice mister could possible pay her a few extra pesos for personal services beyond cleaning his room?—her recounting of the fiction so disarming Spinks he'd neglected to ask what she'd been doing the past twenty-four hours beyond purchasing a black wig and maid's attire.

He called her name into the night.

The peepers went quiet, seemingly listening with him for a reply.

None came.

He stepped at the woods and called to her again.

In the ensuing silence he heard, "I'm afraid I haven't any

cash, Robert. Would you be amenable to accepting payment in kind for your services?"

Spinks turned around.

Rebecca was peering at him out of the darkness astride a large horse a few yards on the other side of the pasture fence.

She rode the horse up to the fence revealing to Spinks, as the darkness parted for her, she was as naked as the horse was.

Her lithe, dancer's body in the moonlight bone white against the horse's midnight black. Her auburn hair a shimmering veil framing her face above pointed globes intricately sculpted to fit perfectly into Spinks' hands. The horse stretching its head over the pasture fence. Rebecca's right hand gripping its mane. Her left hand's fingertips on her thigh lightly grazing her pubic bush glistening with a hint of dampness.

Spinks hadn't even known she could ride, her equestrian ability only the latest hidden side of her she had arranged to reveal to him in a dramatic way. He was certain at that moment he was the luckiest man alive to be loved by her and doubly so that the Jetta's tire had blown by a field lived in by a gentle natured horse with a spirit as game as the spirit of its knock dead gorgeous rider.

In the role of the good Samaritan she'd chosen for him Spinks told her he'd changed her tire out of the goodness of his heart and was happy to accept something good out of hers in return.

Rebecca put a finger to her lips and her eyes on the moon in apparent thought on the matter then proposed Robert get out of his clothes and onto a soft patch of grass between the fence and car and allow her to compensate him for his kindness using her wiles, imagination and physical dexterity.

Spinks aka Robert, half out of his clothes already, told Mrs. Spinks' her offer was more than generous and he was more than willing to accept it.

Her fingers had barely brushed his cock before Spinks fired off in her hand. She moved down on him and he came a second time. Then he moved down on her and came from the excitement of her coming. Rebecca at long last guided his cock into her and ordered 'Robert' to give her his load. When he did she laughed and said, "Now you've done it." Then made him do it again in case the first shot was a dud.

Serenaded by cricket chirps and whickering from the dark pasture they lay in the dew-moistened grass, entwined from their toes to their necks, whispering intimately to each other about the beautiful life they'd just created together and of the boundless future that lay in front of he or she and them.

Hints of a less than stellar day to come darkened the early morning they woke to hungover and groggy.

Spinks under a gathering storm drove for home while Rebecca stared silently out the passenger window. When she'd started crying he'd thought it was from happiness over the baby hours earlier she'd ecstatically told him she was one hundred percent certain was growing inside her. But when she'd turned from the window to him he realized whatever she was feeling it wasn't happiness. She appeared grief stricken and afraid and radiated across the car at Spinks despondent anger he had no idea the root of. "You don't know me at all!" she raged.

"How don't I know you?" Though Spinks knew she was right. He didn't know a part of her she would occasionally and inadvertently show him a glimpse of that he sensed she herself didn't know and that, when Spinks allowed himself to reflect upon, troubled him how a rustling in the underbrush or far off wolf's howl troubles a camper in the woods sleeping under the stars.

"You wouldn't have done what you did to me if you knew me!"

"What did I do to you?"

"As easy for you as stepping on a bug and squishing it under your foot!"

"Baby, please slow down. I don't know what you're talking about."

"Stop acting so fucking innocent because it's in you like it's in me—it's the reason we found each other in the loony bin. I see it in your eyes. I feel it up inside me when you fuck me!"

"What do you feel? What's in me?"

"A black spot—a mysterious black spot in us both—we don't dare look straight at."

"Rebecca, baby, you're scaring me. I love you, but you're scaring me."

"This world"—and now in her face Spinks saw only the grief and, even more than that, the abject fear—"it's not fair—not right—to bring a child into this world…"

But they did bring a child into it, and they'd loved her with all their hearts. Or so Spinks believed they both had. Never again had Rebecca brought up the mysterious black spot. Or lost it so completely as she had that night the two of them had begun Iris's life. Never again until the day she'd driven her and Iris off a thousand-foot cliff while Spinks was thousands of miles away in Afghanistan doing all he could to keep a man he hardly knew, but knew better than he knew his own wife, from drowning in a sinkhole.

# 28

Spinks pictured a mammoth enflamed serpent slithering up the stairway, disintegrating the steps and enclosing walls, before, from the platform at the top of the stairs, darting its fiery tongue down the second-story hallway charring and blackening everything it touched.

Standing on the platform he shined his light down the hallway.

Four doorways along it, two on each side, their doors missing or open into the black spaces they fronted; a gaping hole into the night at the far end where a window had been broken out; impossible to tell if it had been broken from the outside—maybe by firefighters trying to access the burning building—or broken from the inside by someone looking to escape the conflagration through the window.

The hallway floor appeared sporadically thin as ice on an early spring pond and pulpy everywhere but on the two-by-eight beams supporting it.

Spinks stepped onto one of the beams.

He walked carefully along it like a gymnast on a balance beam. Lined up neatly on the floor by the first doorway, as if carefully placed there by a mother's hand, his light found a blackened pair of child's dress shoes so incongruous to that scene it caused him to gasp and create in his mind a formal outing the family had planned for the day following the fire. He stepped through the doorway into a small bedroom. A half-burned kid's bed. Charred stuffed animals, a pillow on its gutted mattress. Singed posters like rotting bark on the walls. Neatly folded and miraculously untouched by the fire on the charred dresser a tiny pair of black slacks, white dress shirt, a small boy's undershirt, underpants and socks creating a gut-wrenching image of the woman in the photograph downstairs placing them there just ahead of or just after kissing her son goodnight in the hours before the start of the family's waking nightmare.

Had the killers killed the boy in front of his mother and father?

Or visa-versa?

Which of those intolerable options would a parent choose if forced to?

To watch their child killed to spare the child having to watch them killed?

Or to be killed in front of their child clinging to the slight hope their killers would relent after killing them and spare their child's life?

A pained cry shattered the room's silence.

Spinks was a moment understanding the cry had come from him.

He couldn't under any circumstances imagine having chosen to have had Iris die before him.

A sound as quiet as a slight breeze rustling a dead tree's branches made him certain he wasn't alone in the room.

He raised his eyes to a sun hat fronted by a black veil in the air over the bureau.

Sad, he whispered, how black your mind must have become.

"You have no idea," said Rebecca.

A skeletal hand lifted the hat's veil, then turned to dust the ashen air consumed.

Her face was a block of granite with features carved into it. Spinks in the shadowy light couldn't make out the expression forever frozen on it.

He moved closer to it and, instead of Rebecca's eternal stone face, saw looking out of a mirror hanging above the bureau a creased, drawn face.

The face blinked when Spinks blinked. Frowned when he frowned.

Two tears rolled down its cheeks from its half-gone eyes.

"No way you're me," Spinks whispered to it and the face whispered the words with him.

Poor guy, he thought, has aged decades in a single night.

He strained to remember where he was—in the burned house of a murdered family he hadn't known—and what had led him here.

Two girls had led him here—Iris and the girl without a name.

He pointed his light upward hoping to see a dangling fanlight and saw only a blackened plaster ceiling.

He stepped out of the room and onto the floor beam he'd walked to it along. He took a giant step across the hall to a beam running parallel to the one he'd been on.

He walked a few feet along the beam to a second empty doorway.

He stepped into—a bathroom.

The wallpaper, charred and peeling, festooned with cartoon characters Spinks didn't recognize. A half-incinerated wood cabinet decorated with kids' stickers standing next to a bath/shower stall, its glass door in pieces on the floor inside it. The toilet scarcely two feet high. A granite countertop, holding the sink, only a foot or so taller than the toilet. A mirrored wall cabinet a standing child could reach above the sink. Two half-melted toothbrushes clinging to a ceramic holder next to the cabinet; two metal rinsing cups on the floor; two charred bath towels and washcloths…

On the shower floor shards of broken glass, three or four oozing splotches of plastic Spinks recognized as melted shampoo, rinse and body wash bottles—the molten remains of a shower cap and woman's metal razor.

In a bathroom used by one little boy?

He stepped to the vanity cabinet and opened it. On the bottom shelf, untouched by the fire, a tube of bubblegum toothpaste, banana-raspberry shampoo, bubble bath, fish-shaped scrub brush. On the shelf above it Crest whitening toothpaste, hand cream, Secret deodorant, hairbrush, small box of tampons.

The boy's mother perhaps, on nights the boy had been afraid to sleep alone, slept with him and used the upstairs bathroom that had been designed for him?

Or had someone other than the three people in the photograph downstairs been staying in the house? A woman or girl old enough to be in need of tampons and a razor? A woman or girl Poncet hadn't known about? Or had known about and didn't tell Spinks about?

A rapid clicking sound started Spinks' heart pounding in his chest.

He darted his light around the room and saw nothing to explain the clicking.

The clicking continued.

Spinks' mind's eye showed him a faceless human-figure scoldingly clicking its tongue watching Spinks fumbling around in the remains of the conflagrated house for clues from a world only the dead could access.

He drew Arno's Colt from his belt and stepped into the hallway.

He sensed more than saw something moving rapidly toward him.

He ducked his head against a rapidly clicking shadow whizzing by his right ear.

He aimed his light after it and saw a small creature dip down from up near the ceiling and disappear out the broken window at the hallway's end.

He stepped onto the supporting beam and started walking up the hallway.

A second small shape—then a third—darted out of the last doorway on the hallway and out the broken window at its end.

His light showed him a room half the size of the boy's room containing a single bed, bureau, schoolroom-type wood desk and chair.

A half-open door to a narrow closet in the far wall.

Something about the room seemed off to Spinks. He wasn't sure what.

The walls were smoke stained in places though from what he could see the furnishings, beyond being water-soaked, were undamaged, signifying the fire, after expending its fury in the front part of the house, hadn't made it this far.

The room appeared to have been hosed down mostly as a precaution.

He stepped through the doorway, to the bed.

Impossible to tell if it had been made up or not before water from a fire hose had hit it. Its damp sheets were speckled with flecks of paint the hose had loosened from the nearby wall. On the wet floor near it lay two stuffed rabbit dolls, a pillow, what looked to be a sketch book floating in a thin puddle in a crease in the floor, a paperback book.

The paperback was entitled PERSONAL DEMONS.

The picture on its cover was of a young woman peering warily over her shoulder at two partially obscured men lurking in dark shadows.

The bureau had only a knocked-over cheap plastic clock on it. Spinks pulled opened the top drawer; a young woman's panties, two bras for a small-breasted woman or girl, a few socks neatly folded in it. The drawer beneath it held a pair of girl's shorts, jeans, two jerseys, a one-piece bathing suit. A hidden object was creating a small bulge beneath the clothes. Spinks reached beneath the clothes and pulled a bulky manila envelope from the drawer.

Two rubber bands were wrapped tightly around it.

PRIVATE! STAY OUT! DO NOT TOUCH!! hand-printed in black Magic Marker on its front.

Spinks removed the rubber bands and shook out of the envelope onto the bureau a sealed plastic baggy holding upwards of two dozen similarly shaped polished pebbles that might have been picked up off the road out front or off any other number of roads.

Pebbles, Spinks intuitively understood, that were unremarkable to everyone but to the person who had collected them.

He experienced a stabbing pain in his heart recalling how shortly before his second Afghanistan deployment he'd unearthed several bird feathers in Iris's desk drawer while searching in it for a pencil to write her a note for her to discover under her pillow after he was gone. The feathers were in an envelope hidden beneath a coloring book in her desk drawer. The envelope said *My private feathers* on it.

Nine years old and already she'd been keeping secrets. Like her mother had.

Spinks respecting her want to have something all her own, hidden from the rest of the world, had never told Iris he'd discovered her cache.

He sat down on the bed, breathing heavily, seeing his little angel's face at that age. The age he'd last seen her alive at. The age she would never grow any older than except in Spinks' mind.

In Spinks' mind Iris had a birthday every year.

In his mind she was, as he sat there, the age the girl who'd been staying in this room was from the clothes in the bureau and the tampons in the bathroom cabinet.

A girl well into puberty.

A girl well into puberty with a secret pebble collection of the sort a girl six or seven years younger than her was far more likely to keep?

Spinks looked again at the little kid's stuffed animals on the floor.

In his mind's eye he saw a girl sometimes nine years old and sometimes fifteen years old.

He stood up and stepped to the desk.

A water-soaked laptop rested amid scattered sheets of damp papers atop it.

A white paper sheet was taped to the wall above it. Spinks aiming his flashlight at the sheet made it out for a printed list of some kind largely obliterated by water and smoke. Peering closely at it he was able to read only the list's top four entries the firemen's hoses had somehow avoided:

> 6:50 a.m.—Get up. Look in mirror—smile, frown, nod. SEE ME. 10 sit ups, 10 squats, 10 pushups, 60 second plank.
>
> 7:00 a.m.—Take meds, make bed. Get dressed. Brush teeth.
>
> 7:10 a.m.—Wake Nicholas up. Feed Balboa. Read activity list for day.
>
> 7:25 a.m.—Make Nicholas' breakfast from menu list on refrigerator—

Spinks shined his light at the water-damaged papers on the desk. They looked to be mostly sketches and drawings of creatures and beings one might see in fantasy and horror films. He opened the desk's top drawer. Inside were pencils, yellow pads, prescription pill bottles and a carefully folded paper that looked to be a letter of some kind.

Spinks picked up the paper—a letter, yes.

He unfolded it onto the desk.

It was addressed to Angel J. Olivet and Lydia Olivet Gans, court appointed guardian of Angel J. Olivet. The short letter was written by Dr. Emanuel Rios of the New York-Presbyterian Psychiatry Hospital in White Plains, New York. It was dated a week ago. It stressed the need for Angel to follow the list of instructions given to her on her discharge from the hospital and Lydia's duty to call a twenty-four-hour phone number listed in the letter if her sister stopped following the instructions or taking her meds or started showing serious indications of a relapse of the mood disorder symptoms, anxiety and/or hallucinations that had necessitated her admission to the hospital. The pill bottles belonged to Angel. One held a prescription for Risperidone. The other for Lithium—

Spinks reacting to the clicking sound that had startled him

earlier jerked his light up at a bat darting out of the closet's semi-darkness. He watched the furry creature fly out the room doorway into the hallway, recalling a female voice whispering, "They see us with their voices."

Angel Olivet searching for pieces of her pulverized memory in the living darkness over the stream that had nearly killed her.

"They were there. They know what I can't remember," she'd said up at the bat-infiltrated night.

Spinks' heart started beating faster.

He walked at the closet.

Another bat, then another, flew out of it.

He shined his light into a space that wasn't big enough for a person to sit down in. Water from the fire hoses, evidently aimed from the room doorway, had barely dampened the inside of the closet.

He couldn't see any bats in it or where the ones he saw might have come from. Only a limp-looking blue, mid-thigh-length dress and girl's button-down shirt hanging from a metal bar above a pair of running shoes, black dress flats, and a slightly wet suitcase still with a few clothes in it opened against the back wall.

He guessed Angel hadn't been here long enough to fully unpack yet.

A week at most by the date of her doctor's letter that accompanied her discharge.

Her big sister, Lydia, maybe brought her here straight from the hospital. Lydia and her money-laundering, diamond-dealer husband's country home a perfect setting for an emotionally troubled young woman to re-acclimate herself to the world in. A piece of rural paradise free from the many harmful distractions available to a troubled mind in the city. At her little school desk she would make the imagined pictures that darkened her thoughts appear less threatening by giving them artistic forms. Under her sister's loving and watchful eye she would follow a structured schedule and be a caretaker for her little nephew—making his meals, reading to him, playing with him—

Accompanying him on berry-picking ventures into the woods on which she was never to let him out of her sight.

Then the demons came.

Poe's people maybe hadn't even known she was staying at the house given the short time she'd been at it.

"People dying sound like children crying."

Angel Olivet in her haunted voice had said so at the dead woman's cabin.

Had she heard the butchery going on downstairs and, paralyzed with fear, shut herself inside this tiny closet with its door opening straight onto her bedroom?

It would be one of the first places a person searching the room would look for people hiding in the house.

Suddenly Spinks realized what it was about the room that was off. It was smaller than it ought to have been. The hallway outside the room was a good ten feet deeper in the rectangular-shaped house than the side of the room with the closet in it was. And the closet wasn't more than three feet deep. He stepped into the closet, to the rear wall. He reached down to the open suitcase and pulled down its top—a bat flew up from behind it startling him.

Spinks watched it fly through the shadowy room like the image from a half-remembered dream through his consciousness.

He closed his eyes.

He opened them on a hinged door, three or so feet high, in the closet wall behind the suitcase.

The door's bolt lock was unlatched leaving between the door and closet wall an inch-wide ingress and egress for the bats. Spinks pushed aside the suitcase and dropped to his knees. He pulled the door fully open and, holding his light out in front of him, crawled on his hands and knees into an unfinished attic half as big as the bedroom and, like it, largely spared from the fire that had eaten through the home's front section. Moonlight through an open window in the far wall landed on empty suitcases, cross-country skis, sleds, winter clothes hanging on wall hooks, a bicycle, standing file cabinet, toboggan, several boxes sealed with masking tape. Spread out in a small open area of the floor near the window was a partially shredded blanket. Spinks pictured Angel Olivet lying, kneeling or sitting on the blanket shaking and more afraid than she'd ever been in her short, traumatized life. He saw her with her fingers in her ears unsure if the horrible human sounds she was trying to not hear were coming from downstairs or inside her head. He looked up and saw a fanlight dangling from the rafters above the blanket and, clinging in a dozen-odd places to the rafters, the bats that Angel, stripped of most of her memory on that stream bank she'd regained consciousness on, had remembered.

The bats that she had said knew what she couldn't remember.

Spinks stood and walked to the blanket.

He looked down at strands of Angel's short dark hair on it and in his mind saw her lying on her back on the blanket afraid to leave the attic even to get her medication in the next room she had known—or sensed anyway—she was disassembling without.

Peering up at the bats peering down at her.

Seeing in their wizened faces insight well beyond her own and compassion greater than that possessed by mankind or demons.

"They won't hurt you," she'd assured Spinks.

Spinks wondered how long she'd lain in this dark space battling fears borne of horrific human sounds and her own imagination by ascribing wisdom and compassion to an attic full of bats.

And what had finally given her the courage to leave?

Or had a fear greater even than the one that led her to take refuge in this attic in the first place chased her from this house she'd called hell into the woods?

"It's quiet, finally. A long time," she'd said to the dead woman.

"Then the lights. Out the window." And. "It's getting hotter!"

Spinks walked at the attic window wondering if the killers had left after they'd murdered the jeweler and his family and only later they—or someone—had come back to the house and set fire to it to cover up the crime.

He looked out the window over the front yard at Pinecone Road how Angel must have done after seeing lights through it two nights ago and saw a set of headlights between orange running lights coming down the driveway at the house.

He couldn't hear an engine. He couldn't hear any sound at all from the vehicle, not even when it drove into the yard and stopped beneath him, near Arno's Explorer.

The vehicle's running lights blinked off and came back on, blinked off and came back on again like monstrous orange eyes adjusting to the darkness or blinking away some irritant that had gotten into them. Or as if the brain receiving their messages was trying to envision a family summer home from the gutted structure standing before it.

The running lights went dark a third time and didn't come back on.

The headlights blinked off.

Moon-filtered darkness covered the vehicle like a thin sheet dropped over a corpse at a murder scene.

The driver door opened as soundlessly as an obsessive thought endlessly repeating in a diseased mind.

A large male figure, garbed in the night's darkness, stepped out of the vehicle.

The figure raised its face at the fire-gutted house.

The enshrouded man put his fingers in his mouth and made a high-pitched whistle that reached Spinks not as a sound, but as a blinding, disorienting pain like that brought on by a migraine headache.

Spinks' view of the world out the window shimmered in undulating waves of darkness.

He watched the male figure make a one-handed summoning

motion at the vehicle's passenger door and out of it, in obeisance to the motion, emerge three wispish female figures that in Spinks' pain-altered vision might have been the same young woman replicated three times. Spinks, groping for an explanation for what his eyes were showing him, surmised that he had in the accident that had put his Durango in the stream been thrust out of the physical world into an abstract world where gut feelings and intuition had taken the place of his five senses.

His memory told him he was looking at three doomed—or already dead—young women he'd last seen waving to him from the second-floor deck of Sebastian Poe's guest house, dressed in mid-thigh-length T-shirts identical to the T-shirt Iris's all-but-unrecognizable body had been found wearing over athletic shorts in the passenger seat of a Subaru Forester at the bottom of a thousand-foot cliff.

He bent forward and powerfully exhaled a lungful of the air that had been poisoning him for four years. He watched it dissipate into the quavering night like a cloud of toxic smoke from a radioactively infected factory. It occurred to him that in the entire world there couldn't be more than half-a-dozen female body types and that the pain of human grief is a projector programmed to play in an afflicted brain different versions of the same enduring image over and over again ad infinitum.

And that there were as many vehicles in this part of the world with orange running lights as there were without them.

And that as often as bad men were replicated in the world innocent children died in it.

Another loud whistle, which he experienced only as a dull knife stab to the memory portion of his brain, prompted the three little angels in the yard to robotically raise their right hands and wave at the window he was standing in.

Spinks pulled Arno's Colt from his belt.

He leaned out the window putting the pistol's sight between the eyes of the man standing in kingly fashion between three waving females in thigh-length T-shirts, feeling how he'd felt every time he'd jumped out of an airplane. Like he'd found nirvana plummeting at a hundred-plus miles per hour at the earth and in those few seconds hoped his parachute wouldn't open and take him out of his enlightened state. He put his finger on the trigger, certain after the physical and mental slog he'd been through in the preceding hours the male figure standing in the yard needed to die even if his doing so wouldn't save the lives of all the little angels he'd brainwashed and enslaved.

"The hell was that gibberish you were saying over the walkie-talkie about Gracie being dead and you and Slade in hell?!"

The voice came from the yard or from his head. Spinks wasn't sure which. He wasn't sure he wanted to know.

"Goddamn it, I see you up there, Arno! Answer me!"

Spinks pulled the trigger once, twice, three times.

The three sharp reports, echoing in the night, revived him like hard slaps to his face.

He shoved the pistol in his pants waist then turned away from the window and walked out of the attic. He made his way carefully back through the upstairs hallway, down the stairs and out into the front yard.

# 29

Drenched and shivering under the scant cover of the trees, Spinks was impotent to do more than hope for the best for Callender, against a fear that, not a hundred feet from him, the private first class was suffering an excruciating death in a deepening pool of rainwater slowly robbing him of every ounce of his oxygen, self-respect and dignity.

He recalled Callender telling him that a few years back he'd found Jesus and been born again and Spinks wondering what good being born more than once into a world that had him trapped and crippled in a sixty-foot hole rapidly filling with water was doing him and that he would have been better off if he'd foregone his second birth for swimming lessons.

And Callender hollering up to Spinks they were good buds weren't they?

His voice pained and needful.

A physically and mentally shattered man ensnared like a fly in a spider's web, afraid of dying hidden from the world in multi-tons of dirt and stone, alone and uncared for.

Of course we're best buds Spinks had hollered down to him, that white lie the only thing he'd been able to do in all the hours he'd sat atop that hole to in any way lessen Callender's pain. Spinks wasn't sure at what point the lie had become the truth. At what point Callender had transformed from Spinks' casual friend into a trusted confidant he found himself unburdening buried thoughts and fragments of his life to. Memories, he had hardly been aware of, attached to concerns, worries, fears he'd never let himself admit to or examine, let alone given voice to. At what point Callender's invisible presence and non-judgmental ear had become to him a God Spinks had always hoped for but doubted existed. A God, disguised as a crushed human form barely discernible from the earth's surface. A God to whom Spinks confessed he'd known, since back when they had fallen in love as troubled teenage patients at New York-Presbyterian Psychiatry Hospital, Rebecca was unstable and prone to hallucinations. That her mind, populated with sad, manic, overpowering, seductive, depressed, dangerous, and nefarious characters, too often excluded the beautiful, wondrous woman he was in love with and was Iris's loving, attentive mother. He'd known that a part of her didn't want to be a mother, for fear of being the sort of mother who'd birthed her, that she'd refused to look at the first daughter she'd given birth to and surrendered to the state when she was fourteen. A part of her didn't want to be alive at all. A part of her believed Spinks had the same dark spot on his soul she was certain existed on her own. On that last point Spinks feared she was right. He often felt like a powder keg on the verge of exploding, though no one but her he was certain could see it. Just as no one but him could see her in a constant battle to stay anchored to the world she shared with Spinks and Iris. He said down into that hole, to God or Callender, that he feared from her last email Rebecca intended to do—maybe had done already—something so unspeakable and irreversible Spinks couldn't say it aloud, not even to God or Callender. Something any attentive parent and worthwhile husband would have foreseen as a possibility long before he found himself sitting in the rain over a hole entrapping a fellow soldier in woods six thousand miles from where he could do anything to allay his fears for the only two people in the world that made his life worth living. That he loved her only made it more inexcusable that he'd allowed his mind to consciously remember only the ninety-five percent of the time she was his Rebecca and Iris's mom and block out the five percent of the time she was someone neither of them recognized. Staring down into that black void that he hadn't in hours heard a voice or peep from, he prayed to God to save them both—his wife and daughter. And he prayed to Him to save Callender too but that if He was able—or willing—to save only two of the three please, please, please save his family and if he was able or willing to save only one of the three, dear God in heaven, please make it be my little angel who has the most to lose in terms of potential life yet to live.

# 30

The psychiatrist he saw two times told Spinks he was damaged.

As if it were some deep insight only a man with a PhD could see.

He compared the damage he saw in Spinks to someone with a broken leg who after refusing to wear a cast or stop trying to walk on the leg has developed a permanent limp he only notices half the time anymore. He pointed to a framed painting on the wall and said, "What color do you see most of in it?"

"Black," said Spinks.

The psychiatrist said, "If I told you I don't see a speck of black in it what would you say?"

"I'd say we're not looking at the same painting."

Patches of mist like dust spirals shaken from a rug had intruded on the yard in the time he was winding his way down from the attic, through the home's ravaged bowels, to the front door.

Static mounds half-hidden under translucent patches evolved in his mind into people, images, possibilities needing only the light of the world to be fully borne.

One of the mounds moved slightly.

A lump the size of a small tree amputated of its branches near the home's front wall.

It moved again and groaned as Spinks walked to it.

Spinks looked down through the white shroud covering him at Sebastian Poe.

Poe said, "Who is it?"

His voice was weak and staticky. Like it was coming from a radio station in hell, thought Spinks. Spinks said, "It's Jack Spinks."

"Who?"

"Jack Spinks. I sold you that good shit you wanted, remember?"

A sputtered cough and Poe said, "Help me up, man. I'm hurting bad."

Spinks said, "You had me out to your place to shoot skeet and watch the ducks on your pond?"

"Give me a fucking hand, man! I'm bleeding bad."

Spinks leaned down at Poe. "What's happened to you?"

"What?"

"Why are you lying here on the ground? Did you trip over something?"

"I been fucking shot, man!"

"Shot? You mean like someone shot you? With a gun?"

"Yeah, with a gun! I don't get to a fucking hospital soon I—"

"Where?"

"From up in that window. Motherfucker shot me three times—!"

"I mean where on your body did he shoot you?"

"I don't know where, man. Feels like fucking everywhere!"

"I can't know if it's safe to move you without knowing where you've been shot," said Spinks. He took Arno's Colt from his belt and, leaning in at Poe, shoved the barrel through a bloody hole in Poe's pants, two inches into his left thigh. "Does it feel like you were shot here?"

Poe made a squealing, pain-drenched snort and Spinks drew the barrel out of his thigh and pushed it three-quarters of its length into a bloody hole in Poe's shirt over the left side of his chest near his shoulder. "And here?"

Poe gasped out a string of bile onto his chin.

Spinks drew the barrel out of Poe's chest and shoved it into a jagged, bloody hole in Poe's shirt just left of his belly button, torqued it hard to the left, then to the right and said, "And this has to be the third place. Yes?"

He shoved the Colt up to its handle into Poe's guts and wiggled it.

"There's just three bullets? You're sure?"

Poe made a helpless, pain-drenched squawk Spinks imagined a kidnapped child being raped might make.

He pulled the Colt out of Poe's abdomen and wiped it on Poe's pants leg.

Poe making little half-rocking motions in the grass sobbed and moaned.

Spinks said, "Jack Spinks. We had some beers out on your porch, you, me, Arno and Slade, and you shared with me your opinion on the insurance business and offered to pay for the weed I sold you with one of a few young women looked to be in drug-induced zombie states and barely out of puberty you had imprisoned over your garage? You thought I was an interesting fellow on the way to going boom?"

Poe groaned louder. He rolled his eyes at Arno's Explorer and back at Spinks and hissed through his teeth, "Where's Arno?"

Spinks said, "Last I saw him he was sitting up against a white pine tree in the woods off Black Cat Hollow Road. He didn't look like he was readying to leave anytime soon."

Poe murmured, "It was you talking that crazy shit over his walkie-talkie?"

Spinks said, "What walkie-talkie? What crazy shit?"

Poe, appearing as a cheaply made bargain bin rip-off of the shotgun toter spouting nihilist bombast Spinks had overcharged for a quarter pound of marijuana, recalled to Spinks how intense pain, of both the physical and mental sort, withered the mind and psyche along with the body. "Slade and Gracie?"

Spinks said, "They're in the woods in the shape Arno's in, which is to say your operation has an opening for three psychopaths. Though the young woman who Gracie was before you grabbed her off the street or paid some trafficker for her was dead long before Arno put a bullet in her."

Poe drooling more bile-infused phlegm made a feeble try at wiping his lips with the hand of his injured arm. He moaned distressingly and dropped the arm. "It was you up in that window shot me?"

Spinks with only a fuzzy recollection of the seconds or minutes before he'd heard three gunshots and looked down at Arno's smoking Colt extended in his hand out the open attic window said, "Finding you here with three bullet holes in you makes me pretty sure I did."

Poe whispered pathetically, "We had a good talk that day at my place way I remember it. About feelings, attitudes, shit like that we had in common?"

"Most of what I remember from that day, besides those young ladies I should have seen at the time were silently begging for my help, is you bragging about luring a bunch of clueless ducks to your pond each year to serve as shotgun fodder for you and your closest friends."

Poe reached for the drool again, this time with the hand on his uninjured arm. He made an awkward swipe at it and held what he'd come up with in the palm of his hand in front of his face, seemingly puzzling on it. He dropped the hand mumbling, "Why ain't you a ghost, man?" He looked up at Spinks. "I emptied the safe in this house with what you emptied from it I'd be a thousand miles gone from this zip code."

"I didn't empty any safe."

"You didn't what were you doing running from the cops with the only person from this house walked out of it alive that night?"

"An Angel jumped in my truck saying she was being chased by demons," said Spinks. He pictured a cluster of jumbled thoughts in his head as a creature slowly emerging out of darkened woods. "She'd been hiding in the woods close to two days after she'd hidden in the attic of this house paralyzed with fear while listening helplessly through the floorboards to your employees slaughter to death her sister, brother-in-law, and eight-year-old nephew."

Poe drooled more blood and said, "Sometimes I wish I'd

made a different career choice."

Spinks said, "I don't doubt you do now."

Poe made a sound a mortally wounded animal might make watching the hunter who'd failed to quite kill it walking at it levering a fresh shell into his rifle. "The business I'm in corrodes a man's soul. I didn't start out this way."

"I doubt Hitler started out how he ended up either. You two can commiserate in hell not long from now over the bad choices you both made."

"Those three went off the rails." Poe burped up more fluid and involuntarily farted, his bodily functions evidently now on autopilot. "Their job was to kill that rat bastard Gans and get back the diamonds I'd given him to turn into cash after I learned he'd made a deal to turn them over to the feds and hang me for a half-dozen upstate jewelry store robberies. Only when they get here Gans is tied to a chair and gives them some story about an armed man in a mask breaking in not two hours earlier and forcing him to give up the diamonds and while Gracie and Arno—this is all second hand from the three bumbling assholes I sent here on a simple job mind you—are working on Gans to come up with a better story the mother and kid arrive home from the county fair an hour earlier than they were supposed to account of the rain and, well, you know, what Arno told me, once those two had seen their faces…"

Spinks put the Colt between the eyes of the ghostly face peering up at him through the mist. "How is it me and an emotionally disturbed teenage girl so traumatized by what she witnessed that night she thinks bats can talk and can't remember her own name were targeted for stealing your fucking diamonds?"

"Gans said the robber knew coming in there were diamonds in that safe and the girl, after showing up as a resident of this house we didn't know about, was the only one alive we could figure could have told him there were. And the next time anyone lays eyes on her after she's seen running out of this house she's climbing into some dude's truck tries to drive away from the cops with her on Black Cat Hollow Road."

Spinks pressed harder on the Colt's barrel. "Did the sheriff of this county give you that information?"

"Christ, man! Ease off will you?"

Sprinks pushed harder on the barrel. "Or was it his deputy? Weren't no one but them two on that road when we went in that stream!"

"Our police scanner picked it up on their shortwave. I didn't know it was your truck and you the dude was in it until you shot me just now!"

Spinks pulled the Colt from Poe's forehead struggling to make his disconnected thoughts fit together like loose wires into the correct outlets on a circuit board. "How'd you know Gans had given you up?"

"A weak link in the chain like Gans gets pinched and out of the slam the same day it makes me suspicious. Especially when I don't hear about it from him and when the source I do hear about it from tells me that an FBI agent was at the meeting with Gans's lawyer and the DA that gave him the early walk. All of it reaching me a day after Gans had me get him all the weight I had on hand, from six months of jobs, promising me he could wash it all at a cut rate with a new contact he'd made."

"Your source tell you the feds were working with local law enforcement to bring you down?"

"Dude's a city cop in Manhattan—where Gans got pinched. He doesn't know from shit about the investigation up here."

Spinks looked off at the early morning sky, the color of wet slate starting to dry. He tried to remember his life of twelve hours ago and in his mind saw only the sun hat he'd believed for four years to be hiding Rebecca's face. The black veil lifted up to reveal, not Rebecca's face, but Angel's face. Seconds later Angel's face dissolved into Gracie's face and Gracie's face dissolved into Iris's face as Rebecca's voice like a verbal soft breeze blowing through Spinks' mind whispered, "I loved you most for loving all of me and only wished you'd been strong enough to make me love myself."

He heard a groan beneath him and looked down into the grass at a skull-sized block of chalk with ugly slash marks in it for eyes, nose and a mouth. How a demon looks on the way out, thought Spinks. He said down at it, "We met in the psych ward, just two mixed up kids. She was more mixed up than me. I was mostly angry at my parents for dying and leaving me alone. Loving her cured me of most of that."

Poe said, "Take me to the hospital, man."

Spinks said, "How long was it after the murders—an hour? two?—you got the idea to drive here with one of your crew in this SUV and torch the place hoping to make it look like the butchered family inside had died in the fire?"

A groan and weak fart all that came out of Poe.

"An Angel was watching you—in that same window I shot you out of. Two demons stepping out of a car with orange running lights came at her down this drive. And then—heat, hotter than she'd ever felt before."

Spinks straightened up.

Poe said, "I can't feel parts of myself anymore, man! It's like I'm getting switched off a piece at a time! I ain't going to make it you don't get me to a doctor soon."

Spinks said, "The diamond dealer describe to your crew the masked robber he claimed stole your diamonds?"

The chalk block moved painstakingly up and down beneath him. "Big, husky—a weightlifter type—is what he said."

Spinks took in a deep breath, let it out slowly and said, "Can you still see me? Or are you too close to dead?"

The chalk block moved up and down again and Poe whispered, "I see you, man. Your shape I mean. In the mist. I don't believe I ever did see your face."

"Seeing only my shadow ought to tell you you and your crew of demons waiting in hell for you were fucking idiots ever believing me and that girl stole your diamonds."

Spinks turned his back to Poe.

"Don't leave me here dying slow, man, fearing what's coming. I'd sooner you finish me now let me get on with it!"

Spinks pushed the Colt into his belt. He walked at Arno's Explorer deaf to human noises in the night past the sound of his own feet impacting the dew damp grass.

# 31

A lighter shade of black in the sky over the spectral trees lining Pinecone Road alerted Spinks to the knowledge, once and for all, that the darkness enveloping him wasn't eternal.

He wasn't in an alternate universe wrapped in timeless blackness. He wasn't in a dream.

He was in the world at night.

A night that was creeping steadily toward its end.

Stars receding from his vision like vehicles driving away from him on a desert highway forewarned of morning light.

Light that would land on him amid the horror of this dark world he had stumbled or been led into.

What felt to him like an eternity following a lifetime since he'd stopped his Durango for Angel Olivet stepping out of the woods in front of him occurred only hours ago. Of the people he'd encountered since then all had died violent deaths or vanished into the ether. Only he, Jack Spinks, was left to explain the night's carnage to the horde of law enforcement sure to descend with the daylight onto the hollow. Jack Spinks, convicted drug dealer with a history of psychiatric problems going back to his teenage years, driving an SUV registered to a man he'd gutted to death before using the man's pistol to put three bullets into another man he'd left to die outside the charred remains of a house a married couple and their eight-year-old son were murdered in. Jack Spinks, government-trained killer, who following the murder/suicide of his wife and daughter had spiraled into depression, substance abuse and fits of violent rage. Jack Spinks whose blood and DNA investigators would find on the gutted man's corpse, on the body of a young woman with a bullet in her heart concealed under bluestem grass not far from it and on the remains of a sheriff's deputy with his head bisected by a hatchet lying a few miles away atop an exposed hilltop.

Spinks' hands shook on the Explorer's steering wheel.

He had no idea where he was headed—or where he should be headed.

He needed a plan, a strategy, to save himself, but lacked the focus to form one.

Should he turn himself into a police agency, any police agency in the state not headed up by the sheriff of this county, and hope to be put in the hands of a sympathetic—or, anyway, objective—group of interrogators?

Or should he turn the Explorer north and drive as fast as he could for the Canadian border before a police bulletin with his name and likeness on it was circulating in every police department east of the Mississippi River?

He turned right onto the highway where it intersected with Pinecone Road. A couple miles on, feeling magnetically drawn that way, he turned right again, back onto Black Cat Hollow Road. A mile up the road he realized why he was driving back toward where his nightmare had begun an indeterminate number of hours ago.

He wasn't going to turn himself in.

He wasn't going to light out for the Canadian border.

He wasn't going to do either of those things. Not yet.

Not before he was satisfied to in extremis he couldn't accomplish the good thing he'd set out to do when he'd half-pulled and half-helped Angel Olivet into the cab of his Durango. He pictured her lying frightened and disoriented in that dark attic filling with smoke, drawing what little courage she had from a horde of bats squeaking down at her from the rafters as she whispered up at them.

Was she as real in the world as she was in his mind?

The question crept like morning fog into his consciousness.

Then he remembered the physical weight of her and her small voice interjecting harrowing, disjointed thoughts into the night as he carried her through the woods and the thought struck him that he'd been living the last four years of his life in anticipation of a chance to save her from dying a second time—

The Explorer's headlights touched as lightly as a painter's brush a large, boxy shape half-hidden in the trees as he neared the spot in the woods Angel Olivet hours earlier had stepped out of in front of the Durango's headlights like an image stepping out of a dream into the world as a flesh and blood person.

He jerked the Explorer to a stop.

He backed it up and aimed its headlights into the woods several feet off the road at—a black sedan shades blacker even than the night.

Spinks had seen enough unmarked police cruisers—even ridden in the back seat of a couple of them—to know one when he saw one.

The cruiser's entire driver side was caved in and left front tire flat assuring him it couldn't have been moved more than the short distance it had evidently been pushed up the road into a thick stand of Jack pines across from where Spinks and Angel Olivet in the Durango had careened off it several hours earlier.

He stepped into the woods toward the damaged vehicle he had, in the aftermath of his bloody encounter with Arno and Gracie down by the stream, walked blindly past on his way up the road to Arno's Explorer and would have driven past now absent the Durango's headlights subtly pointing him to it sitting as inelegantly as some long abandoned junker under the pines.

He recalled the two human figures who had stepped out of the cruiser that to Spinks and Angel Olivet, peering toward it from the Durango's cab, had appeared as two glowing white eyes between a set of smaller bright orange eyes.

The thick figure—a "weightlifter type" is how Sebastian Poe described the hulking masked robber of his stolen diamonds—of the sheriff's deputy Carl Ames.

The tall, rangy figure of Deputy Ames' boss—and criminal partner?—Sheriff Grey Poncet.

Spinks flashed back with a shiver to the sight of Deputy Ames' body in the woods above the woman's cabin with a shirt knotted around its head to keep the head from coming apart more than the hatchet Spinks had thrown into it had already caused it to.

And to Grey Poncet electing to leave the body there for animals to have at.

Poncet with his impenetrable eyes.

Poncet who had vanished like a ghost from the piece of night he'd been occupying with Spinks.

Spinks remembered, as if from the remnants of a dream, lowering his eyes from the trees to see the tall lawman as vanished from the spot Spinks had been holding a gun on him in as the visions of Spinks' wife and daughter Spinks had been fixated on were from the treetops he had been envisioning them in.

He experienced his memory as a field of long fallow earth being turned over by a dull-bladed plow and his perceptions and hallucinations two varieties of fertilizer intended never to be combined in the same soil being mixed into it.

He yanked on the cruiser's driver door and found it locked.

He tried the other three doors and found them locked as well.

He picked up a rock from the shoulder and smashed it against the front passenger window until he had enough of the shatterproof glass out to reach inside and open the door. He slid into the passenger seat. The two-way radio in the console was as dark and silent as a grave. He opened the glove compartment. Only a few official-looking police papers and a ticket book inside. He felt under the front seats, then climbed behind the wire cage in back and felt beneath and between the rear seats. Nothing.

He popped the trunk, stepped out of the car, opened the trunk and found in it only a spare tire, jack and a couple shotguns.

He got down on his back on the forest floor and, holding his flashlight in one hand, slithered beneath the car. He shined his light up and down both sides of the undercarriage. Nothing appeared to be there that shouldn't be. He slid out from under the car and stood. He opened the car's other three doors and looked closely at each one. The front passenger door panel appeared slightly looser than the driver door panel. Spinks with a little effort was able to wedge his fingers behind the loosened panel. He tugged and the panel's cloth cover came off. A small leather bag was taped to the inside wall of the panel. Spinks removed the bag, unzipped it and looked inside.

He zipped the bag closed again. It was too big to fit in a pocket so he pushed it down the front of his shirt and firmly tucked in the shirt.

He closed the cruiser's doors and walked back to the Explorer.

He took Arno's Colt from off the seat, shoved it in his pants waist and walked across the road and carefully down the embankment toward the stream.

# 32

In the storm's wake a steady drizzle as monotonous as the hum of cicadas on a warm summer night further soaked the saturated ground.

"Callender? Goddamn it talk to me, Callender! Bobo?"

Spinks in the relative quiet strained to hear a voice from the black opening in the earth his throat was raw from yelling into and couldn't.

Not even while on his knees, inclined up to his waist in the opening.

He tried several times to find Callender with his flashlight but the beam had grown too weak to penetrate to the bottom of the black channel containing him.

He suddenly wondered if his light couldn't find a bottom because there was no bottom.

The darkness went on and on to infinity.

In his exhaustion he pictured Callender dropping through an endless wormhole that under the rain's relentless assault had opened up in the earth beneath him.

He tried not to close his eyes but did anyway and saw in the dark space closing them had opened a monstrous creature, with a glowing empty eye socket taking up most of its face, snatching Callender out of his free-fall and pulling him into a hellish eternity in the earth's core housing, among its horde of human victims, Rebecca and Iris.

The rescue team emerged out of the rainy mist frosting the predawn darkness badly shaken after having been nearly washed away by flash floods that had delayed them several hours in the mountain passages.

A platoon medic, an ammunitions specialist with civilian EMT training, a corporal adept at climbing to high places owing to her stateside job as an arborist and a nineteen-year-old private first class and former high school gymnast with a small but muscular stature who'd been in country less than two weeks when given the assignment of going into the narrow hole after Callender, they peered by the light of a hand-held spotlight into the kariz.

The five soldiers let out a collective gasp.

The top of a combat helmet that looked to have been stomped on until it had been entirely buried in a solid floor of black dirt all they saw.

"Poor bastard was buried alive," breathed the medic.

The former gymnast started to cry.

Spinks dropped to his stomach and, inclining his upper body into the dimly lit hole, deduced that Callender below his helmet was not planted in dirt. He was submerged in water his face was either resting inches above or floating face down in. Spinks hollered at Callender to move his head if he could hear him. Callender didn't move his head. Spinks kept hollering to him until the medic and ammunitions specialist afraid he would drop down on top of Callender grabbed him by his feet and forcefully pulled him out of the hole. Spinks rolled over onto his back and said up at them, "Get me the rescue harness."

"The kid's supposed to go in after him," said the medic.

Spinks looked at the former gymnast shaking from head to toe over the dark fissure scarcely wider than he was he'd been earmarked without being consulted to go down. The few dead people he'd seen in the States had likely all been nicely made up and dressed in flower-adorned coffins. The injured ones neatly bandaged in sterile hospital beds. Spinks told the boy to go sit down on the giant tree the lightning had felled earlier and draw in his mind happy pictures of himself and the people he loved most together in a place thousands of miles from these woods and this war.

The harness was attached at one end to a hundred-foot rope.

The rope's other end was secured to a large tree not far from the opening. Spinks stepped into the harness, pulled it up over his shoulders and secured the belt attaching him to the rope around his waist and chest. He stepped to the near edge of the hole and nodded to the ammunitions specialist and arborist corporal who were gripping the rope between him and the tree it was secured to.

He took a step back and dropped into the hole.

# 33

A tall figure walked out of the trees across the stream from Spinks stepping out of the brush at the bottom of the embankment.

The figure peered at Spinks through the fracturing darkness over the rushing water.

"All's well that ends well, Jack."

"What are you thinking has ended?"

"A hellish night." Poncet turned his face up at the treetops. "Almost."

"Could be an even worse hell in the morning for some of us."

Poncet lowered his gaze from the sky back to Spinks. The warbling water gave his voice a far-off feel though his words were as clear to Spinks as if they were being spoken directly into his ear. "I'm rarely wrong in my prognostications, Jack. Look of that sky says we're heading into a gorgeous day."

He took a step closer to the stream. He raised his right hand from down by his hip revealing to Spinks the hand was holding a rifle. "Came upon this downstream. Made me feel safer, and just better about the world in general, that the man holding it was dead." He moved his eyes in the direction of Spinks' drowned truck. "Even more so when I uncovered beneath some bluestem grass not far away the body of a young woman Carl and I had been pursuing through these woods in connection with an arson fire on Pinecone Road. A young woman who for sure had a hand in the murder of a female therapist kind enough to open her cabin door to her and an insurance salesman she'd charmed into believing a version of her that didn't exist."

Spinks pictured his mind as a twig spinning endless circles in a swirling pool of current in the flowing water separating him from Poncet.

"I tried to tell you, Jack."

"You tried to tell me what?"

"Was nothing good in that young woman's future. Only a lot of real bad shit in her past you or no one else could do anything about."

Spinks looked up at the gray face in the fading moon and back at Poncet's face in three-quarters darkness and didn't see much difference between the two. Both of them using constantly changing light and angles to remain largely hidden. "I never laid eyes on the young woman I buried under that bluestem grass before I pulled her out of this stream after she tried to shoot me! I didn't hear her say more than a dozen words and then only when Arno allowed her to. Was him who put the bullet in her heart, but Sebastian Poe killed her first—years ago."

Poncet nodded. "A lot of sad stories in the world, Jack. None sadder than those of the unfortunate young women Sebastian Poe over the years has snared in his web and put to work for him."

Spinks said, "The young woman who jumped into my truck on this road didn't work for Sebastian Poe. She wasn't involved in anyone's murder. She was just a scared out of her mind kid with serious emotional problems and a sad story of her own."

"A sure way for a man to go crazy, Jack, is to make every sad story he hears into the one sad story he can't stop hearing."

Spinks stepped closer to the stream. Water colliding with a jutting boulder near his feet jumped up and hit him in the face like spray from an aerosol can. He swiped at his eyes straining to find Poncet through the fine mist. "Was a girl named Angel—not that dead girl Gracie downstream—I carried through these woods."

Poncet appeared to Spinks to let out a long exhale at the moon.

"Must be awful crowded in your mind with all the people living in it, Jack."

"She isn't living in my mind! She was living in her sister and brother-in-law's house on Pinecone Road when Sebastian Poe set fire to it after Gracie and the other two psychopaths on his payroll killed everyone else was in the house! She's the dark-haired girl witnesses told you they saw running from it!"

Poncet moved his shoulders up and down in what Spinks took for a shrug.

"There's a lot of dead people out in these woods, Jack. And there's you and me."

"What?"

"We're the only live ones in them I know of."

"A scared young woman who got out of a psychiatric hospital just last week—the same hospital I met my wife in twenty years ago—is in them and unaccounted for. She was in the attic of Gans' house when Sebastian Poe set it on fire. Was her—Angel Olivet—you two were chasing through these woods!"

Poncet made a slight head movement that, as replicated by his distorted shadow on the bank fronting him, suggested a large resting animal alerted to approaching footfalls.

"Wasn't for your deputy robbing those diamonds from her brother-in-law she wouldn't have had to run. Poe's people wouldn't have murdered his entire family after finding the diamonds gone. And Poe wouldn't have set the house on fire."

"That's an interesting theory, Jack. I wonder how you came up with it?"

Spinks stepped to the near end of a fallen tree spanning the raging water between them. "I convinced Poe to unburden his soul to me."

"I'm guessing doing so didn't save his life."

"He was breathing when I left him. I doubt he is now. A thick-set man in a mask stole Gans' diamonds. A weightlifter type."

"Sounds like Carl all right. I never did entirely trust the man. And he had a terrible gambling addiction that had him in some financial trouble makes me think you've raised a sound theory,

Jack. Problem is, you've killed about everyone would need to be interrogated to prove it."

"I'm not interested in what anyone dead would have had to say on it. You don't get to the truth talking to murderers, thieves and liars."

Poncet made the same indistinct head movement he'd made earlier. He stepped to where the tree over the water landed on his side of the bank. "The truth is what you and I decide it will be facing each across this stream."

Spinks took a few careful steps onto the tree. "The truth is the truth. Nothing you or I decide can change it." He reached down his shirt and pulled out the leather sack he'd unearthed from the cruiser's door panel. "A whole family lost their lives over your deputy's theft of these. You tell me you weren't in on it with him I'll hand these to the state troopers when I turn myself into them and let them know where I found them."

Poncet raised Arno's Panther toward Spinks standing on the tree at midstream. "A gang of murderous pimps and robbers stole those diamonds from businesses already made whole over their losses. Wouldn't be but a few insurance companies hurt if they never showed up again. Carl and I didn't anticipate in a million years anyone would get hurt by us taking them. Never mind killed."

Spinks emptied out of the bag around half the diamonds—they were larger and heavier than he'd expected—into his hand. "Finally, the truth."

"I'm no demon, Jack. I'll live with that family getting killed the rest of my life."

Spinks held the loose diamonds out over the water. "Don't you feel better coming clean with yourself over it though?"

Poncet raised the Panther so that it was aimed at Spinks' chest. "Put them back in the bag, Jack. And toss them here."

"Then what?"

"Go back to your life. Spend it searching for the girl you invented if you want. Only not in these woods. You were never in them tonight. Your truck was stolen early this evening while you were up the hollow with your farmer clients. The people who stole it and crashed it into that stream and went on a murderous spree in this hollow killed Carl while he was helping me kill them."

Spinks looked down into the stream and saw the faces of two young women he'd pulled out of it and, though his eyes told him they were two very different young women, his mind's eye told him they were the same young woman twisted by life in two very different ways. He closed his hand on the loose diamonds. He walked across the log at the far shore. "If you were telling me the truth about not being a demon you'll make sure a good part of what you get for these will go to helping your dead deputy's family." He reached the far shore. "If you are a demon I guess you'll shoot me and keep the whole handful yourself and the ones in the bag too." He looked up at Poncet and the tall man took one hand off the Panther he was aiming at Spinks and held the hand out, palm-side up, at Spinks. Spinks carefully placed the dozen odd diamonds he was holding into it.

Poncet, watching Spinks close the bag on the rest of the diamonds, kept his hand out at Spinks and the Panther pointed at him, his masked eyes revealing to Spinks no more than they ever had about the man behind them. "After claiming to me not to care for money past what you need to live on, Jack"—Poncet closed his hand on the loose diamonds and shoved them in his front pants pocket—"you've renewed my belief in the universal greed of mankind."

Spinks pushing the bag holding the remaining diamonds back down the front of his shirt said, "I wasn't responsible for anyone but me when I told you that. Now I am."

He walked past Poncet, into the thick trees. He said over his shoulder, "Be best for us both you wait a few hours before calling reinforcements into these woods."

He heard only the rushing water behind him.

# 34

Spinks' shouted instructions amid the storm's cacophony had, against all odds, seemingly found Callender who, despite his injuries, had managed to summon enough oxygen from his partially collapsed lungs to inflate Spinks' dropped trousers into a rudimentary flotation device.

His head and neck rested face down on the swollen pants floating atop the water the rest of him was entirely immersed in. Spinks, dangling in the air space above him, couldn't tell if Callender's eyes were open or closed at the impermeable wet blackness immediately confronting them.

Nothing he could see in the restricted glow of his flashlight assured him Callender was even aware that someone had entered the hole with him.

Other than a gentle swaying in rhythm with the water containing it, he saw no movement at all from the submerged body or the head attached to it.

He touched the point of his boot lightly to the top of Callender's head.

Callender didn't respond, verbally or physically, to the touch.

Spinks, against a sudden panicky feeling rooted in a long-buried nightmare he'd waken to night after night at his grandparent's small mountain-enclosed house in the wake of his parents fatal car crash, asked Callender, in a voice quiet enough to not startle him but loud enough that he'd be sure to hear it in the event he was conscious, was he ready to return to the earth's surface?

Callender in response to the question made no reply or movement.

The mountains in Spinks' recurring nightmare were tidal

waves looming over him in an endless ocean he was alone and adrift in.

He said down at Callender in a slightly louder voice, inflected with the deeply ingrained sense of dread his flashback to his childhood nightmare had recalled in him, that if Callender could hear Spinks' voice to move any part of his body.

No willful movement was evident from Callender, above or below the water.

"What's his status?" a voice shouted into the shaft.

Spinks understood this as a request to know would he be bringing to the surface a severely injured man or a corpse.

"His head's above water!" Spinks hollered.

"He's alive then?"

"Undetermined! I can't get a response from him!"

"Can you drop down next to him and see if he's breathing?"

"Not without pushing him up against a side of the hole and if he's not dead now that's likely to put him a lot closer to being!"

Silence from above.

Spinks hollered up into it, "Give me another two feet of rope!"

He put a leg into the watery space to either side of Callender's shoulders in the narrow opening his body was nearly filling and, using the slack the crew provided him with, slid down so that his crotch was just above the top of Callender's head, his legs inches from touching the walls to either side of it. He leaned forward as far as he could and reached with one hand into the air in front of Callender's face. He placed the hand directly in front of Callender's nose. An irregular series of weak puffs of air touched his hand. Spinks felt a combination of elation, fear and dread of the sort a miner must feel trapped by a cave-in under a mountain of shifting dirt and stone. He hollered up the shaft to the assembled soldiers that Callender was alive but that getting him in his condition into the rescue harness in those tight quarters was no dice. He'd need to carry Callender the sixty feet up the shaft holding him under his arms.

The four member rescue crew, even with the aid of a hand pulley, was over an hour getting the injured man and his liberator out of the earth, their strained grunts and curses floating down to Spinks gripping the one-hundred-eighty pound Callender under the armpits, fighting to not let his arms give out, expending every ounce of his energy, every fiber of his muscle in a struggle to save a life that in his unconscious mind had become a struggle to save three lives.

# 35

Angel was a waif.

Lost and alone in a world she couldn't remember who she was in.

Even if she could remember her name she had no family to return to.

She had no mother. No father. Both were deceased or had abandoned her.

The only person who'd cared for her enough to take legal responsibility for her was her murdered sister.

The only home she knew outside of a psychiatric hospital was a pile of ashes.

She would need someone to take care of her going forward.

To feed her, clothe her, pay for her medications and mental health needs.

Make sure she got a proper education, including college if she was suited to it.

Teach her how to drive, hunt, fish, see through bad and manipulative people, ride a horse, tell wild mushrooms from toadstools in the woods.

These thoughts became certainties to Spinks hiking in the grey pre-dawn light up the stream bank he had hiked down hours earlier to his drowned Durango. In the dying darkness, birthing shards of first light, towering trees creaked and groaned in the way of arthritic old men in their waking movements. Sporadic chirps, whistles, rustling issued from unseen sources in the dense canopy. A woodpecker's metronic pecking like a giant clock ticking toward the end or commencement of something. The renewed optimism of countless forest creatures at the start of a new day as palpable as the temperate mist dampening Spinks' cheeks as he moved through it.

"Take her for a long walk in your woods."

A demand, not a suggestion, from Rebecca.

Made on an afternoon, on a day like any other, in the final week of Spinks' leave before he'd shipped out for Afghanistan the second time.

Not the woods. Or our woods. *Your* woods.

Not a walk. A *long* walk.

Spinks thinking back countless times on that day had wondered if in phrasing her request Rebecca even then had been pointedly excluding herself from her husband's and daughter's lives. If her seemingly out of the blue request that Spinks take Iris on a long walk in the woods without her had been a veiled warning to him that she'd developed an aversion so strong to her family she could no longer stand being around them?

Or had she been motivated not out of hate for Spinks and Iris, but out of a love so strong for them she'd been trying—consciously or unconsciously—in banishing them to the woods that ringed their rural house like protective wrapping around a glass figurine to get them as far away as she could from the darkness in her she sensed was about to take control of her?

He couldn't remember now if after that day she'd ever gone with Spinks and Iris again into what the family had referred to as their *magic forest.*

Magic to the three of them from the time Iris had been a couple months old and Spinks and Rebecca, on their long walks together, had taken turns carrying her in a belly pack on deer trails through thick virgin stands of elm, oak, maple, cedar and pine trees packing a picnic basket and towels to dry off with from their frequent skinny dips in the stream running through the forest.

Every door out of their house an entrance into it.

A few short steps and they were in a world of intrigue, wonder, magic.

Nearly every morning that Spinks was home, before it was even full light, in winter, spring, summer and fall, the three of them ventured together if only for a few minutes into their magic forest.

A family walking together but never alone.

Through a wooded city full of hidden creatures seeing them without being seen by them.

Eavesdropping from the thickly foliated trees on their conversations.

Iris's idea that the three of them talk loudly when saying nice or complimentary things about the forest's inhabitants and in hushed whispers through their cupped hands when discussing subjects—like the low quality of a particular bird's singing or how poorly constructed a fallen nest they'd found on the ground was—that might needlessly hurt the feelings of one or more of them.

To clap their hands and throw pinecones in the air to show their overall appreciation of the birds singing, chirping and whistling she was certain began only when the three of them entered the woods and ended when they left them.

To make chattering sounds back to the chattering squirrels because even if Iris, Rebecca, and Spinks spoke squirrel poorly the squirrels would appreciate them trying to speak to them in their own language and feel the love they were conveying for them in the effort.

People were taken from the world to make room for other people to come into it.

Or they were taken from the world and came back into it over and over again as the same people in forms only people who'd known them intimately in an earlier form would recognize them in.

One had to look and listen closely to recognize a person they'd known and loved in another form.

One had to have a piece of the missing person permanently in his heart.

# 36

Callender's weight sapped Spinks in ways he became aware of only when he was free of it.

The strain of dangling him by his armpits over certain death for well over an hour caused in Spinks' hands and fingers a near paralyzing pain that radiated in pulsating waves to his neck, back, chest and abdomen and rendered his arms nearly numb.

They felt like strings of jelly appended to his sides as he peered up exhausted from his back on the damp ground into the greasy, fractured light the mist was making of the early morning sun for evidence of a presence loftier than mere human beings.

He saw only an illusion of stars the bright light was manufacturing in his brain.

He wondered if all his efforts to save Callender's life had been less out of a concern for Callender than they had been his desperate attempt to purchase from a God that didn't exist goodwill toward his wife and daughter he had more and more over the course of that turbulent night come to fear were in dire need of it.

The rescue crew was directed to carry Callender by stretcher to a recreation field halfway back to the village. A spot flat and open enough in the mountainous terrain for a med-vac helicopter to land in once the weather had sufficiently cleared for the bird to safely get in the air.

Callender's blood pressure was dangerously low and his breathing erratic. He was shivering, his lips and extremities tinted blue. His eyes opened while he was being secured to a weight-stabilizing stretcher, but didn't seem to register much beyond pain. The medic put an IV drip in his arm and injected him with morphine. He lapsed back into unconsciousness as the crew carefully cut off what of his wet clothing they could and draped him in a wool gown and blanket. The medic splinted compound fractures in both his lower legs.

They heard the chopper well before they saw it emerge like a giant insect out of the puffy, dry clouds filling the gaps between the mountains.

Callender, as if roused by the sound, opened his lips and whispered a word the arborist corporal standing closest to him didn't make out. Not sure he wasn't mumbling in his sleep she laid a hand lightly on his shoulder to let him know someone was listening and put her ear next to his mouth.

She straightened up and waved Spinks over to the stretcher.

"Your name I think," she whispered to him.

Spinks looked down at Callender and wondered if his head had always been as large in proportion to the rest of him as it appeared to Spinks to be now. His eyes were closed though he seemed to know Spinks was standing over him. He reached a hand up from the stretcher and put it in Spinks' hand and Spinks realized Callender's hands, like his head, were a better fit for a larger man overall. Spinks leaned in next to him and heard him whisper, "Good bud."

Spinks whispered back to him. "You're going home, Callender. You'll be with your wife and sons before you know it."

Dampness like groundwater bubbling up from an underground stream seeped out from around Callender's closed eyes. His lips worked silently a few seconds before they got out the words, "I'm so sorry."

"Any one of us could have stepped into that hole," whispered Spinks surmising Callender in his drugged state to be apologizing for being the unlucky one of the four of them who had stepped into it and made an unpleasant night for the others.

He looked down at Callender's head rolling slowly side to side and more water seeping from his closed eyes and understood Callender hadn't been apologizing for stepping into the hole or apologizing at all and had heard every word that Spinks had said down into that well of blackness Callender had been silently channeling God in. He applied what pressure he could muster to Spinks' hand and whispered, "None of us on earth are equipped to understand His ways."

Spinks had a sudden urge to grab and shake Callender by the shoulders and force him to reveal to him what God had revealed to Callender at the center of the earth about His intentions toward Spinks' wife and daughter. A moment later a wave of shame washed over him. He recalled that he was holding the hand of a man consumed by his own pain who, if he lived at all, would likely do so in a greatly reduced way while forever asking of the emptiness his faith told him God occupied why had He put that hole under his foot. And he said, "You're going to be fine, Callender. I didn't pull you out of that hole for nothing!"

Callender tried to squeeze his hand harder—a newborn baby grabbing his finger would have done a better job of it—and said so softly Spinks had to listen to the simple phrase reverberate in his memory before he was certain he heard it right, "Thank you."

Spinks looked down at their clasped hands slick with sweat. Tears leaking from Callender's closed eyes like oil from a frayed gasket. Each breath like a bedsheet being unevenly torn. The incoming chopper playing a reveille to a new chapter in an altered world. Spinks said, "You'd have done the same for me."

Callender coughed, a sound like a backfire five blocks away. Anemic beats of his heart in Spinks' hand like a fish gasping for air on a riverbank. "The devil stole me in the night, Spinks. And you stole me back from him."

Spinks from a sudden constriction in his chest could hardly breathe. "Feels like nothing will ever be the same after it," he whispered.

Callender through another cough said weakly, "The sun will still rise and set. Nights will still be dark. God will still be up there doing what He can."

Spinks watching the incoming helicopter hovering just

above the ground like a book's uncertain ending in an engaged reader's mind mouthed so quietly he wondered later how anyone outside his own head could have heard him: "I'm afraid of what's coming."

A tremor starting low in Callender's abdomen traveled up through his body like a ripple from a large fish swimming just below a pond's surface and exited through his mouth in a tortured groan. The water seeping from his eyes magically dampened Spinks' cheeks. He said, "Don't let anything in this life turn your soul black, Spinks. Everything we go through here is just a test."

Spinks when he was able to call home later that afternoon was given the news he had been afraid would be coming ever since he'd screamed aloud, amid that tree-rattling storm, his long buried fears and unacknowledged truths about the woman he loved to Callender and/or God at the center of the earth.

Rebecca and Iris had crashed onto the ocean shore rocks not fifteen minutes after Rebecca had hit send on her final email to him.

# 37

His flashlight grew weaker, sporadically flickered. Then died completely.

Spinks took it as a sign that he didn't need a light.

He put the flashlight in his pocket and trusted his memory and instincts, as much as his eyes, to guide him through terrain fuzzily familiar to him. In the emerging grey dawn landmarks he'd not been consciously aware of in the heart of darkness appeared now like aroused memories from a recaptured dream; a defeated-looking beech tree, reaching not for the sky's light but bowing like a sycophantic house butler at a ninety-degree angle to the ground; boulders evenly spaced around a bald patch of earth like fossilized teepees around a buried fire pit; a perfectly intact skeleton of a coon-sized animal resting in a grassy swale as if its former inhabitant had chosen the spot to peacefully lay down and die in; an underground spring, speaking in the peeps and croaks of its amphibious inhabitants, bubbling up into marshy soil like oil from a buried reservoir.

A stream bifurcated into dual waterfalls by a giant rock at the top of a hundred-foot cliff towering above him.

The cliff he'd stopped a step short of plunging over hours earlier, before gazing out from its top at a pinprick of light upstream near where he'd just walked from, a light that when he'd reached its source had affirmed to him that he was wide awake at a black time in the world and not unconscious in a vivid nightmare.

His muscle memory led him up a brushy incline left of the cliff to a plateau dense with virgin hardwoods. He pictured as he walked through them the towering trees—oak, maple, beech, elm, ash—warily eyeing him while in mind of a ghostly male figure with a strikingly similar physique to his who, in the darkest part of the night, had walked stealthily along the same route through them with a dead, or deathly still, small woman or girl in his arms.

A vague movement ahead preceded the emergence out of a patch of mist he was walking into a mature black bear, ambling along on all fours, its face to the ground as if it were on the lookout for an object it had dropped along the route earlier or potholes to avoid stepping in.

The bear stopped walking a number of seconds after Spinks did.

With an irritated sort of groan it grudgingly raised its eyes to Spinks.

Its attitude toward him told Spinks he was of little interest to the bear other than that he was in its way.

Spinks carefully sidestepped a few yards off the roughly trodden trail he and the bear had met on. The bear, its mind clearly on matters of greater concern to it than a human hiker briefly delaying it on its way to wherever it was on its way to, lowered its head again and ambled past Spinks without a sideways glance. Spinks watching the animal disappear into a stand of birch trees was reminded of what little resonance his—or any living organism's—concerns, joys, heartaches, voice had in a world so vastly populated and laxly overseen. He thought of the woman Angel Olivet had called The Bear lying with her throat cut and head bashed in on her cabin floor. He pictured her death resonating outward like ripples from a pebble dropped into a pond to negatively affect other lives. She'd had a poet's warm soul so likely had had many close friends and family. And a therapist's caring heart her clients no doubt would be damaged by the loss of. She wouldn't, Spinks was certain, have willingly let three psychopathic killers take Angel. As afraid of Angel as she might have been she had to have seen in her eyes what Spinks had seen in them. She had died trying to save her. Or she had died after Angel had saved herself.

Rebecca stepped out from between two trees in front of him.

Without the black sun hat and veil over her face.

Spinks for the first time in four years let himself look at her.

"I'm sorry I didn't protect our daughter by seeing how sick you were," he whispered, the words out of his mouth before he could suppress them.

Rebecca shook her head as if out of all the things he could have said to her, he'd said the wrong thing. She said, "Do you remember where we met?"

Spinks nodded. His eyes filled with tears. "You were the most beautiful sick girl I ever laid eyes on."

"And you?"

"I wasn't sick. I was angry mostly. And depressed."

Rebecca shook her head in the disapproving way she had earlier. "Love is a sickness too," she said.

Spinks just looked at her, as beautiful now as she had been when she was alive.

"From the moment we met you were too sick with love for me, to see how sick I was."

Spinks watched her gracefully turn away from him and bound into the trees. As elegant a deer as he had ever seen. A doe with perfect coloring and what he imagined to be a twinkle in its eye. Probably mothering a fawn back in the brush.

# 38

Spinks had no idea how Callender had tracked down his mailing address. In a letter he received at his home a year or so after Callender was shipped home with his injuries Callender had written that he'd recovered from his misstep overseas in every way that he was going to. He would never regain the use of his legs, but claimed not to miss them as much as he'd feared he would in his otherwise blessed life, in which he and his Five Course Meal By Candlelight were anxiously awaiting the birth of their second child. A girl this time who, after praying on it, they'd decided, out of their love for and gratitude to Spinks for saving Callender's life and in honor of his lost little angel, to name Iris. He prayed every day for Spinks' well-being and hoped Spinks could feel the love he was sending out to him and would write back to him and let him know how he was doing. Spinks didn't write him back and threw in a drawer without reading them the many letters Callender had sent him after that. Not from dislike of or anger at Callender. Not out of envy of his blessed life and loving family. Not because it pained Spinks too much remembering that while he had been doing everything he could to keep Callender alive his own two angels had been dying. Simply from shame. Shame at having been too weak to heed and follow the advice Callender, newly yanked from the bowels of the earth and not sure if he would live or die, had given him—his good bud—in his final words to him.

# 39

Unmasked from the night, the cabin appeared to Spinks just as desolate and haphazardly placed among the pines as when he'd followed Angel's eyes down this same hillside to the structure's ghostly outline in the moonlight.

He made it for a dilettante builder's dream slapped together in a forest of saplings and abandoned decades ago as the result of some long-forgotten tragedy. Decades during which the sapling forest had grown into a forest of mature trees that had three-quarters swallowed the cabin like a carnivorous plant engulfing a trapped insect.

The building's pitted, moss-encrusted log walls, highlighted in the emerging light like the wrinkles in a crone's unmade-up face in the morning sun through her bedroom window, standing in even sharper contrast to the picture Spinks had retained of the personalized home they enclosed.

Squirrels performing high-wire acts in the drooping branches shrouding the roof thick with pine needles blue jays and sparrows foraged for edible things in.

A fox, coyote or small dog sniffing the ground near a downed rotted trunk a pileated woodpecker loudly mined for insects.

Spinks warily watching from above uncertain if he was in the closing scene of one horror movie or in the obligatory placid opening scene to a second one.

He walked down the hill, sending the sniffing animal—a silver fox—scurrying into the woods and lowering the volume of the nearest birds.

The dawn's light, like an artist's fine brush applying lighted highlights to a painting of a midnight scene, showing him all that he'd missed standing here in the dead of night yelling toward a rifle-toting bear-shaped shadow in the cabin doorway.

A roughhewn podium constructed of axe-chopped logs he gloomily pictured the former therapist/poet reciting her poetry aloud from to an audience of concealed but mostly appreciative animals.

A knee-high wall of various shaped rocks around three large upright stones in the ground marking, surmised Spinks, the graves of dead former forest dwellers the woman Angel had known as The Bear had grown especially close to.

A thick length of rope dangling from a tree limb high in the canopy Spinks pictured the muscular weightlifter pulling herself hand over hand up to the top of each morning to stay fit.

A life rich with interests, fueled by curiosity.

A desolate feeling in Spinks recalling how he had led the demons to her door. And left her alone with Angel to face them.

The blood he and Poncet had followed through the woods to Slade's gutted body was moist still and more plentiful near the cabin doorway than he recalled. Though possibly the darkness he'd been looking down at it in had masked all of it but for the drops of it his flashlight had found.

A shed snakeskin on the ground to one side of the doorway. So neatly laid out a human hand might have placed it there. The V-shaped bands and tail's dark coloration said a timber rattlesnake had wriggled out of it. A rattler three to four feet long and thick as a fist. Spinks speculated the snake lived under the log the silver fox had been routing in. Or under the cabin. Or that the woman had found its discarded skin hiking in the woods and carried it back here with the intention of adding it to her collection of interesting artifacts.

Had he and Poncet closed the cabin door when they left?

Spinks didn't remember if they had or not.

It was closed now. And latched.

Spinks unlatched and opened the door.

The creaking sound it made reverberated in his memory like a dead loved one's voice unexpectedly heard on a telephone answering machine.

He stepped into the cabin with the sensation he was stepping into a mausoleum the ghost of its murdered inhabitant was intently watching him from.

He looked across the room at the crow, perched so still above the fireplace it might have been the stuffed corpse of the bird named Midnight Spinks remembered Angel holding in her hand and Angel had remembered complimenting with a flap of its wings the dead woman's poetry. The bird's unblinking black eyes followed Spinks into the room without seeming to move. Spinks had the unsettling sensation in the crow's fixed gaze of being secretly tracked from a great distance through the scope of a high-powered rifle. He had an urge to make a gesture toward the bird to see if it would react and was stopped by a sudden fear that it wouldn't. The crow, with those eyes, had seen what no other living creature—man or animal—had seen. The horror. Inflicted by demons on the woman who'd loved and cared for it, while Spinks had been out in the woods chasing false demons. The crow knew what had happened to the emotionally disturbed young woman Spinks had carried through the woods to this cabin.

The crow knew if that young woman was the young woman who had tortured and killed the poet/therapist lying dead in the next room.

The crow knew if the young woman Spinks had picked up on Black Cat Hollow Road and believed he'd recognized his daughter's eyes looking at him out of was buried three miles downstream under armfuls of bluestem grass Spinks had laid over her after Arno had shot her through the heart while Spinks was gutting him with the knife the young woman had slit the poet/therapist's throat with.

The crow knew if Spinks was more than moderately mentally unstable and sporadically explosive from years of depression and alcohol and drug abuse.

The crow knew if Spinks was from all the damage he had done to himself full on delusional.

Spinks had agitated on all the possibilities and eliminated all of them but for the one that made perfect sense.

He walked at the crow hoping that what he longed to be true, the crow knew to be true.

It made no movement—not even a flutter of its wings—in its frozen posture on its perch as Spinks stopped walking directly in front of and facing it.

He opened his eyes wide at it, exposing his inner world to the bird. All the secrets, anger, anxieties, delusions, suspicions, fears, regrets that had led him on a tangled, uncharted path to this tiny, remote spot he found himself standing in, naked of everything but hope. The bird's laser-like eyes took it all in without betraying they were anything other than glass eyes implanted in a taxidermy crow.

Spinks, certain the bird was alive, refused to let it pretend to him it wasn't. He opened his eyes as wide as they would go, wanting the crow to see under all the negative thoughts and emotions he'd been wrapped in for four plus years, the hope he was growing like a new skin. The optimism. The beauty.

The love.

The crow's eyes moved to the right. Only slightly, but enough.

Spinks visually followed them through the open bedroom doorway.

To the woman's sheet-draped body lying where he and Poncet had found it in a pool of blood against the far wall. To the bloodied weight disc. To the upturned desk. To the upturned chair.

He heard a fluttering of wings and turned back around at the main room.

The crow was in flight toward the front door.

It flew out the door on an upward trajectory and vanished into the trees.

Spinks surmised the crow, having made up its mind to trust him, was relieved to be free of the dire responsibility its dead owner had left it with.

He turned back to the bedroom doorway.

He began softly talking to her as he walked through the doorway, into the room.

"Hello, Angel. It's Jack Spinks. The man who stopped for you out on the hollow road and brought you here through the woods."

He didn't want to frighten her more than she already was so spoke only loud enough for her to hopefully recognize his voice, even if she couldn't at first make out in the small space enclosing her every word he was saying.

"I've come back to tell you it's safe to come out now. All the demons are back down in hell. I promise."

He picked up the overturned desk chair and placed it beneath the hidden door in the ceiling.

"I'm going to step up on a chair down here and unlatch the door and open it so that you can come down when you're ready. Don't be frightened by the sound."

He stood up on the chair and found the hidden bolt and pulled it out of its latch. He pushed the door open a few inches. Five or six bats flew out of the opening. "I'm going to open the door now, Angel. Stand back so that it doesn't hit you when it comes down."

He pushed the door all the way open and heard it bang down softly on the floor above. "You can come down now, Angel. There's no one alive anymore who wants to hurt you. I promise."

Several more bats flew out of the attic. Spinks watched them winging about the room, banging blindly into the walls. He looked back up into the black opening suggesting an unlighted tunnel leading away from the world.

"I'll come to you then, Angel—don't be afraid." He put his arms up onto the attic floor and started pulling himself up into the attic. "I'll help you down. Then I'll bring you home."

# Book Club Discussion Questions

1. Jack Spinks is a man filled with contradictions—a man clearly of good intentions, yet also capable of violence. Given the circumstances they occurred under to you believe the violent acts Spinks committed in the novel were justified? Why or why not?

2. Spinks is compelled to save the girl he encountered on the road partially out of a feeling of guilt/frustration that he didn't/couldn't save the lives of Rebecca and Iris. Given all we learn about Rebecca and Spinks and their relationship did you find those feelings at all merited? Why or why not?

3. Sheriff Grey Poncet is one of many characters in the story hard to get a handle on. Did you feel at the end of the book Poncet was basically a moral or immoral man?

4. There is a surreal quality to parts of the novel and Spinks at times experiences flashbacks and visions. How much of what occurs did you believe at the end of the novel occurred in fact and how much in Spinks' mind?

5. What part does nature/atmosphere—the woods, trees, streams, the darkness, the shadows, the birds and animals seen and barely seen—play in the novel?

## PRAISE FOR *A RECKONING UP BLACK CAT HOLLOW*

"This tense, gut-wrenching, and ruminative novel is highly entertaining from start to finish."

—*Booklist*

"A blistering tale of the human condition filtered through a rural lens and sealed with the kind of gut punch that only Jones can deliver. A novel both thought provoking and smart, yet brutally tense and paced faster than a bullet. For everyone that didn't already know, Matthew F. Jones is the true heir apparent to the kingdom of Cormac McCarthy. Yeah, he's that fucking good."

—Brian Panowich, author of *Bull Mountain* and *Nothing But The Bones*

"*A Reckoning Up Black Cat Hollow* is as fast-paced and unrelenting as any thriller you will find, but what makes Jones's book so compelling is its psychological, at times metaphysical, journey into one man's tormented soul. Reading the novel is like entering a clear mountain stream. You take a few steps and suddenly plunge into depths you'd not imagined. Matt Jones is an immensely talented writer, and this harrowing novel deserves a wide and appreciative audience."

—Ron Rash, author of *Serena* and *The World Made Straight*

"A psychological thriller cut on the steepest grade with more switchbacks than a mountain haul road. *A Reckoning Up Black Cat Hollow* roars downhill with the brakes on fire. Jones sets a masterful pace."

—David Joy, author of *Those We Thought We Knew* and *When These Mountains Burn*